SABLE'S JOURNEY

DEL REY JEAN

DEDICATION

God, Serenity, and the unnamed muse for Gabe. Special thanks to Janelle for dealing with all my crazed rants about this and helping me organize my overactive thoughts.

CHAPTER 1

She couldn't tell which was worse: the screams of the innocents dying or the cackling of the demons that were slaughtering them.

Every sound of anguish or horror reverberated up each disk in her spine, dragging claws through her mind until she thought the blood dripping down would choke her. The gleeful shrieks when a cry was cut short into gurgling silence added a scarlet tally mark to her heart.

One more person she couldn't protect.

One more death for which she was responsible.

An electric jolt of panic speared through her chest and for the breath of a single moment, it felt as though it was foreign. She inhaled slowly, forcing the air down over a stone settled on her collarbone and willing her lungs to inflate. Long ago, inside of her torment as a young child, she'd befriended fear and had only grown closer to it since then; she had no reason to lose her composure to it now. She raised her arm, which held a simplistic pale brown recurve bow. As she curled her fingers around the string and pinched the nocked arrow, she examined the cloaked figure commanding the chaos. Her mind took the gaping wound of her drawing arm into its calculations with little effort, telling her to aim just to the left of her target on account of the pulsating ache in her bicep.

She pulled in another long breath, allowing the oxygen to push her icy walls into place and block out the wailing mayhem surrounding her.

The moment she began the pull, her aching back protested loudly, begging her to remember her struggle just to reach that place inside the demon horde, but she locked her jaw. Her muscles complied and settled her arm into a familiar position, even as lightning skittered across her spine. The creatures had put up a good fight when she made her way through, hunting for the figure she aimed at now. Her bicep screamed, frothing red to the dry leaves crunching beneath her feet.

The arrow followed her exhale as her body relished its release and eased each aching muscle back to rest.

Two houses down, the source of the madness fell from his rooftop with a sickening thud, puffing up a cloud of dirt.

Like a glass shattering, the chaos halted. Silence echoed down the streets. The apparitions faded into black dust that floated through a gentle breeze. Charred homes stood fragile in the aftermath of the unnatural flames, disappearing as if ashamed of the destruction they had caused. Even the black clouds above ran squeamish from the murders below as the woman fought bile down from her throat. She pulled up her royal-blue hood, casting her face into shadow just in time for the awed gazes to spot the weapon clutched in her shaking hand.

Ducking her head, she clenched her fists at her sides, blood pooling through the sleeve under her armor and dripping off her knuckles.

She managed two steps before someone called out.

"Stranger!"

A puff of warm air pulled down her heavy, defeated sigh.

"Please," the weak voice begged, "let us tend to your

wounds and give you goods for your travels. You saved us. Do not leave us in your debt."

It was a sensible request. In these times, it was dangerous to be indebted to a hero; true heroes did not exist anymore. If someone had power, they wielded it, whether for good or evil decided entirely by the direction of the wind.

She did not want to linger in that place though, where darkness was receding from tainted buildings. It agitated her blood, and the stench of death curdled her stomach.

She frowned, her gaze wandering down the street. The body her arrow had pierced had disintegrated into dust while the people crowded around it. She grew weary with their confusion. This was the third humanoid creature to die easily at her hand, yet they have wielded the power to destroy with similar ease.

The dust was new though. If she weren't so tired, she might have noticed a brush of wind leaving that pile and swaying toward the east. She might have recognized the shape of a small grey serpent flying away.

The girl stepped forward, intent on ignoring the invite in its entirety.

Another voice stopped her. One she knew well, and which spoke inside her mind.

~Accept their offer. You are not yet meant to move on. Allow yourself to rest and remember to remain ever observant.

"Yes, my lord," she replied under her breath.

Reaching behind her, she slipped her bow over the red leather-bound handle of a sword strapped across her back.

"I will stay," she said, though her tongue seemed to quiver.

Murmurs of thanks and subtle rejoicing surrounded her as she turned to face the one who had addressed her. The people were crowded into the street, standing away from the elder, who was smiling at her. Children danced in their easily regained safety, while in contrast, the somber adults appraised her with suspicion despite their invitation. The old woman seemed like the only one with pure, unabashed appreciation. Her sunken grey eyes said she had seen many things.

"What do we call you, stranger?" the elder's voice rasped through a strained breath.

The girl's frown deepened beneath her shadows, wondering if her name was safe in this place she'd been commanded to remain. In response, laughter whispered through her mind.

~*Would I ask you to remain where I could not protect you?*

My lord, forgive my reminder, she replied deep within her secret heart, *but you have had me stay in places that have tried and at times nearly destroyed me. I have stayed in snake pits, in prisons, and at the hands of unstable kings only in the last three years alone.*

~*You do not yet understand, my child, but it is alright. Tell me then, how did you survive those hardships?*

Her eyes drifted down out of respect. *You have armed me with wisdom and gifts that I command only because you allow them to obey. I am your servant and your child; therefore, your gifts lead me to victory, not I them.*

~*Do you trust me?*

Yes.

Though the elder did not hear any of this, she was wise and waited with patience as her town's hero deliberated.

Finally, the girl pulled away her hood to reveal coal-black curls gathered about her shoulders, her long bangs pulled to each side in small braids that knotted behind her head. It left her face clear of obstruction, aside from a few stray locks framing her large, round eyes. They were a fierce amber, flecked with black-and-yellow threads like the disturbed coals of a forge just after a sword had been plucked from its heat. They held the weary stare of one who had seen more than someone her age should have. She was as old and wise as the woman before her.

"You can call me Sable."

It came out with more strength than the quivering fists at her sides would have suggested. The elder did not react to that name as she turned to lead her away, but it did not stop those within earshot from muttering.

That name was associated with legend. Sable had been the child mistress to a madman who had slaughtered his way through a hundred cities far to the west, or so said one version of the story. The bottom line was that she was not supposed to be real. Those were nothing but stories to frighten children at night and to sing about in taverns late into the evening. Sable was a myth. However, her eyes of fire, a witch's gaze of too much wisdom, revealed the unsettling truth.

A shudder passed through the crowd as they came alive with the rumors pouring out, perverting her past in every possible light. It was far too late to try correcting any of them. She listened instead, the stone on her chest growing heavier with each word dropped from ignorant lips. True memories reared their ugly heads as she walked, correcting in her mind each piece of the lies that mutated the real horror.

". . . stolen from her bed."

Wrong.

"No, no, that's not what I was told."

Oh, really?

"A witch sold her off."

Parents, actually, but who would ever suspect such a thing was possible?

"No, you dolt, she was a princess."

Sable choked on a harsh laugh. *Hardly.*

"No, a slave!"

Close, but think worse. A concubine. Too young.

Like it mattered anymore.

Sable shut her eyes tight and pulled in a long, slow breath, forcing her hand not to try easing the pressure of the stone that threatened to shatter its mantle.

They glared at her as she passed, talking louder as if jabbing her with their ignorance.

"She was always with him, that's for damn sure."

He freed me, and I was far too young to survive on my own. What did you expect me to do?

"I heard she would even laugh sometimes when he was slaughtering 'em."

I wouldn't put it past me, but I don't remember that.

One voice, quiet and modest, stood out with a question everyone else seemed to miss: "Why would she save us then?"

At another moment, she would have laughed. *Yes, why indeed?*

"Where is the demon?"

Long, long gone . . ..

~~~
~~~

Inside and away from the grumblings of the terrified town, Sable allowed herself to ease the tension in her fists. She was handed a cup of tea, which she accepted but did not drink. Instead, she watched out the window to her left while shadows worked through the sunset to bring some semblance of order back to their town. She was in one of the few homes untouched by the horrors faced down by others, because it was on the other side of a small stream dividing the town.

Her host had welcomed her with little suspicion, though the subtle glances or twitches if Sable moved too fast did not go unnoticed. She introduced herself as the town's overseer, appointed by the townsfolk themselves. Her name was Varylah.

"Forgive my prying, ma'am," the elder started, dragging Sable's attention back to her wrinkled face, "but what brought you to our village? I don't mean to sound ungrateful, but it's strange how you arrived so soon after our nightmare began."

The corners of Sable's lips curled into a small smile. "My master tells me when to travel, when to stay in a place or leave it, and when to make camp. He knew you would need me, and I understood my purpose when I saw the rising smoke. I acted accordingly."

Silence replied loudly in her ears. She tilted her head back, her large eyes connecting with her host and daring her to speak the fear in her thoughts.

"May I ask . . . who is this master of yours?"

Sable's smile grew. "You are afraid of the stories. You wonder if I am the child in them and if my master will destroy your town, if I saved you only to lead you to destruction, correct?"

Varylah nodded. Sable could appreciate that level of honesty. She hoped her softened gaze would be read with sincerity.

"The stories are true. I am that Sable," she admitted, raising her hand to prevent Varylah from panicking. "He is not with me; I assure you. The stories do not tell how it ended, but we parted ways many years ago. He is imprisoned, and I do not seek to witness any more destruction."

Varylah pondered this for a moment before continuing

with the obvious question. "Then who is this 'master' who brought you to our aid?"

Sable did not answer right away, wondering how to put him into words.

"He is not known anymore by his creations," she began slowly and quietly. "We have forgotten and replaced him with ignorance. He is one who is above even the deities who are well known and worshipped. Mine is the creator of all things, the lover of all lives, and the father of this world."

Varylah gave the exact same reaction Sable had become accustomed to; darkening of the eyes, sharp intake of insulted breath, and even raised her hand to her mouth as if she needed to wipe away the insult of Sable's words before she could speak. The gods of their world were known by many on intimate, personal terms. Almost any person could say they had met their chosen god. This worked against Sable at every possible turn when the conversation topic rose.

A smile crept across the old woman's lips. "Do you mean to claim that you have found a creator other than Light and Darkness who made all things and gave us life?"

"I mean to say that I serve the only creator that has or ever will exist."

The way Varylah's eyes sank into their sockets gave her glare an extra kick, which would have shaken any other warrior to their core. It merely spurred the fire in Sable's gaze, though she turned back to watch the shadows again instead of burning the woman. Her grin was the only evidence of the flickering flame within.

"You don't have to give me the speech. It's nothing I haven't already heard, nor is it original," Sable said with steady boldness. "I don't expect you to believe me. I will be gone by the light of the morning anyways, so it will not make any difference if we argue."

She turned her glowing forges back to Varylah, who was watching her with newfound suspicion. "One of us is wrong," Sable continued, "or we could both be wrong. We do not need to fight over it, because the truth needs no defender. It remains true whether you call it so or not. Facts do not care about feelings or opinions."

The old woman's face was like stone. "I want you to leave."

Sable yawned, if only to mock her host. She retrieved her weapons from the table and put down the untouched tea. Not another word was exchanged as she made her leave, neither did she make eye contact.

He came to her again when the night air cooled her cheeks.

~*You could have handled that better.* Though he chastised her, his tone was gentle, even amused.

I cannot abide useless people with no intention of finding the truth when presented with new possibilities, she explained, understanding that he already knew this.

~*And how do you expect them to face such a possibility when they have been taught differently their entire life? You must be patient, my daughter.*

"Did I fail you just now?" she asked out loud, her voice trembling.

~*No, you did not. I only want for you to learn from this moment. That is all.*

She made her way into the cluster of trees near the village, aware that her instructions to remain still held fast. Mechanical and weary, Sable built a small encampment. She placed her weapons and her quiver to the side of the little fire she had made. Loosening the straps at her sides, she slipped off her chest piece, flinching when the metal front clanged on the stone that she placed it against.

The process of removing the guards on her forearm and bicep was slowed by the chilled fingers on her drawing arm. Her wound and the ache in her muscles seemed to give the joints of her fingers trouble with curling and pulling. She breathed a hard exhale when it was finally done.

She placed her thick cloak on the ground where she would lay and sat with her knees drawn up to her chest, curving her arms around her legs. Shuddering, she pulled her long sleeves, so they came down her palms, as if that would do any better at bringing warmth to her tender muscles.

The fire's light seemed stronger than its warmth, but she didn't mind: she welcomed the night's chill into her aching body. She tried to ignore the weight of the stone at the base of her throat. She didn't do it well, but she tried.

Even with a path of righteousness, she was ostracized by her own people. The reason had shifted, but the result remained the same. She was growing tired of the human race she'd vowed to protect.

~*But you are the only one who can lead them right now, child. You will not always be alone.*

She released a heavy sigh. This was not the first time he'd reminded her of that.

Are you going to tell me about these beings that I'm fighting yet, or am I still going into battle blind?

~*You will understand soon. Rest for now.*

As if she could sleep. Her blood was agitated, and her mind was spiraling. How many times had she walked this circle? She was aware of the pattern in her foes but couldn't focus past the deaths on her hands. Evil or not, she did not enjoy ending lives. Too many had already died under her watchful eye when she was young.

Technically, she was supposed to be searching for her old teacher, the one who had taught her to wield her sword and shoot a bow after the chapter with her dear Kazious had ended. They'd left each other on violent terms, but just as she couldn't leave the murderer to his evil heart, she couldn't leave the other to her blind hatred either.

She had been torn between fixing the woman who had taken her in for a decade and preparing for the man who had saved her life when she was a child. Both needed her master, yet neither could be saved just yet. The one who had gone missing had been her priority all this time. What else could she focus on with Kazious imprisoned by immortal creatures and her master not yet willing to subvert their power for her?

Somehow, the search had led her to this pattern of death and nightmares she'd been interrupting at each town she approached. She still wasn't sure if this was a journey all to itself with a purpose void of her loved ones or if it somehow played into finding a way to them.

Letting out a frustrated grunt, she stood and slipped her belt on again with its dagger attached as she ventured farther into the trees. Movement could settle her thoughts, even if only somewhat.

Now, where was she? Trying to understand the pattern. Right.

How many had she killed in the last year alone? Four of them? All with strange powers and armies of monsters that appeared out of thin air and then disappeared the moment the master's heart stopped beating. What did they have to do with her teacher, the woman marred by Sable's own hand in their last confrontation?

Her mind flashed with golden eyes widened in shock, a pale hand raised to the gaping wound torn down her face and shoulder. Chocolate curls matted with the gore they fell upon as she scrambled to stand.

The stench of mold from wet stones took over the memory, dumping her right back in the that god forsaken well. . ..

Her dearest friend, her teacher, had not been entirely honest, a fact she'd discovered when the woman had lashed out with a power from which Sable had no hope of defending herself. Knocking her out cold. Waking up. *I'm going to die down here.*

She closed her eyes and shook the images out from her mind, ignoring the fact that her fingertips began to sting with the remembrance of scraping them against wet stones. *Focus.* The past could not help her with this mystery. A breath shook her trembling lips. Was any memory in her mind not soaked in blood?

The humanoids didn't bleed though. This new brand of magic spilled too much scarlet to the earth, yet the body it held would only disintegrate upon death. *Return to those thoughts.* They were not so red.

Sable was familiar with much of the lore and the many inhuman races in that world. Yet each of the men she'd shot an arrow through had been anomalies. Even the summoned demonic entities these beings controlled did not resemble or act like any demon she'd ever known.

The string was leading to a source, but on her own, she could not hope to understand.

She neared the yellow glow of her camp once again, allowing her exhaustion to creak inside her bones. All this death was like a heavy blanket across her shoulders.

Thick tendrils invaded her mind, curling around it like a spider's legs and combing for information. Bile rose in her throat as she recognized the touch of a psychic hand. Of all the things in this world of mages and monsters, the violation of the mind was one she loathed most of all.

Someone was coming, and they were dipping inside her

mind as they neared.

CHAPTER 2

"Wow... You're all grown up," a deep, thundering voice stated as she reentered her camp.

Sable grimaced as she turned to face the tall familiar man. He had been a friend once. Gabe Arenreeth, the great legend himself. Out of instinct, her muscles tensed, ready to fight, not that she'd have any hope of defending herself. In the back of her mind, she wondered *at what point did I start to fear him*?

He leaned against a tree, arms crossed over his chest as he grinned at her. His wild lion's mane of thick black hair was speckled with twigs. No change there.

Despite his towering height, he had a rather small but toned build, like a bamboo tree. He had just enough muscle over his bones to be defined with strength but not enough to make an adversary think twice before throwing a punch.

Her breath caught for a moment as the last day she'd seen him repeated itself in her mind. Swirls of pain shifted inside her guts, his sudden appearance shoving glass into her bowels. It had been a warm summer night with the moon casting their gathering in a pool of light. He had worn that smile back then too when he called down the Tazera Illusionists to lock away her demented companion. When he'd betrayed her. Her hands trembled as they pulsed with her child self, who pounded fists against stones until they bled.

He had left her too afterwards. First there were two unstable immortals in her young life; each more than capable of destroying her with little to no effort. Both showing their own strange form of kinship despite her being infinitely weaker. And then she was alone, as easy as a gasp.

His amused mismatched eyes held a maniacal edge to them which she had grown accustomed to back then. Now it served instead as a reminder of his betrayal. One shifted its shades of blue depending on the time of day or the level of mischief behind it. At the moment, it was like staring at a glacier in the naked glow of a full moon. The other was a stark contrast: dark brown like the tea that Sable had denied back in town.

She glared at him, opening her mouth to demand why he'd suddenly shown up again after so long.

His chuckle stopped her as he quipped, "so, where's that tormented one you followed so faithfully all those years ago, hmm?"

Of course, he would poke at the wound. He was the entire reason Kazious was gone in the first place. But Gabe was nothing if not cruel. Her heart squeezed exactly how he wanted it. She watched his lips quirk up to the right when his power told him of the sting.

"What are you doing here?" she asked instead, careful to lock away her master's gentle command from before: *You are not yet meant to move on.*

What was Gabe's role in her remaining there? She knew better than to call it a coincidence; her master did not work in such things.

"I was coming back to record the progress of a game, but it appears to have run its course without me," he admitted, a threat behind his words.

She scoffed. "You toy with innocent lives. I wasn't going to sit by and watch while people were slaughtered. I'm especially glad to know my actions halted one of the famous ploys of the Immortal Trickster."

His unofficial title drew another chuckle from his lips, and he stepped toward her. Her hand twitched to the dagger at her hip, which she noted how he pretended he hadn't seen. No one had ever gotten away with threatening him.

Or so said the stories.

Yes, just like Sable, he was supposed to be a myth, a great puppeteer with incredible psychic powers who could manipulate a mind or snap it into pieces as easily as breathing. Not that he needed that power to do such things. His intellect alone gave him insight into the clockwork of a mind, and he'd spent his long life studying the many jagged pieces of those who had been shattered.

Sometimes those studies were dubbed "games," because he would set pieces rolling with his lips and stand back to watch them "play." He could turn almost any creature into a stringed puppet like it was nothing. With the use of few words spoken to fewer individuals, he had manipulated entire ages to his desires.

Not even Sable could guess the purpose of his long-crafted study, but she could see where his hands had twisted aspects of her own life. How could he resist a human girl who watched with a heart of stone as her fellow humans were slaughtered by the thousands?

As she thought back on those dark days, blood began to stain her vision. In a way, Gabe could claim that he had saved her. Her life traveling with the madman, Kazious, would have destroyed her soul someday. Logically she understood that, but was it so horrid for her to want Kazious saved too, not just locked away to rot?

Gabe took another step forward, pulling her back to the present as his eyes narrowed. "This isn't the first time one of my games has been cheated and cut short. I'm sure you, of all people, can understand when I say that I *hate* losing control."

She locked her jaw, hearing the test within his voice. He was reminding her that a monster was locked inside his mind with much more destructive capabilities than her old companion. Her heart skipped a beat. *He wouldn't dare. He loathed that demon.*

It had been over a decade since they'd last been together, though, and she couldn't let herself forget that. Could he have found a strange alliance with the beast inside? The god of chaos trapped within him. *The Calamity,* she corrected in her mind.

"It's not my fault if you can't choose your pawns wisely anymore," she retorted, proud of the nonchalance in her tone, even if her hands were shaking.

Her attitude seemed to surprise him, and he arched an eyebrow in response. Then he grinned. The threat, the tension, the flames inside his eyes, all soothed and wiped away with that movement of his mouth. He was in front of her by then, and as she expressed surprise at the shift in his emotions, he reached out to her as if to clap her on the shoulder like they were still friends.

Instinct sang from within though. Her skin skittered, sending her two steps to the side as she yanked her blade from its sheath and poised for attack. It took her a long moment to realize what she was doing, not to mention the threat to her life for daring to raise a blade against the legend. She felt the beat of her heart in her throat.

She pulled in short, shallow breaths and commanded her nerves to settle. Gabe was not looking at her, which gave her a measure of comfort. Instead, he was transfixed on the place where she'd stood. Understanding pulled his lips down hard. His hand curled into a fist, falling back to his side. If his power had not revealed that part of her past long ago as a child, then this did with certainty.

"I see," he mumbled, hanging his head as he confirmed her suspicions. "There's still so much that I don't know about you. I . . . I apologize. I am normally more considerate of personal space."

He brought his fist up before his face, opening it to stare at his palm as if it were foreign to his eyes. How strange to hear an apology from him. Gabe was not the sort to understand when he did something wrong. Not until he analyzed the response to the action and concluded that he'd made the other individual uncomfortable somehow. Then again, perhaps that was exactly what he had done in that moment.

"Since when does a person's discomfort bother you?" she couldn't stop the question.

He flicked his eyes up at her with clear surprise. "Certain things people should be able to handle and eventually heal from. Others will haunt us for the duration of our lives no matter what we do." He glanced away from her, a sad smile forming on his lips. "That kind of pain I loathe for anyone, human or immortal."

Sable didn't respond, allowing the silence to swell between them. She never considered that Gabe had compassion for anyone, especially humans. Even when she considered him a friend, she knew better than to think she mattered to him.

"So, what will you do now that I cut your game short?" she pressed, causing him to refocus his darkened eyes on her.

Gabe frowned, perhaps considering whether he should be honest with her. Then he shrugged.

"I don't know yet."

The man she'd met as a child had his next ten steps plotted out, having already predicted the previous nine of anyone with whom he was interacting. His intellect alone was enough to drive that precision. It was unstoppable when his psychic power was added to the mix.

She refused to believe his uncertainty.

~And what was it that I taught you to do when I bring you into someone's path? Look into him, not judging him for what you assume him to be.

The chastisement caught her by surprise for a long, startled moment. Sable pulled in a deep breath, obeying her master without another second of hesitation. She closed her eyes and pictured a hand reaching down into her chest. A pale blue light fluttered there, glowing out of the cracks inside her heart. She brushed the gift with care, gently caressing its sleeping form.

It shuddered.

She didn't see the movement inside her mind; that was only her imagination helping to command the gift. No, she *felt* it in her physical form. A warmth spilling out from her beating heart, rising as if stretching from slumber. It waited, patient and fluttering like a cluster of butterflies behind her ribs. *Let's look into our friend,* she suggested.

Let's find out how we can help him.

The warmth bloomed until it was just short of burning, yet it was without pain. Then it took off, excited by the word "help." It raced into the fires of her gaze, which she lifted to catch Gabe's mismatched eyes. *We're searching,* it whispered.

Not for their surface amusement, which seemed ever present, nor the obvious twinkle of mischief that came when he noticed her strange demeanor. No, once they located the doorway, they dived into the depths of his soul. Her gift acted as the anchor that drew her deep into a place thick with black oil and a child's hallowed screams.

She couldn't breathe through the thick ooze in his soul that pulled at her like quicksand. Her skin itched as she wandered through the mess, unseen claws slicing into her from within the oil. The pain seemed real, but she locked her jaw from crying out. *It isn't real, it can't touch me.* She chastised herself.

She followed the sounds of the boy crying out, yanking one foot at a time from the muck while the other sank.

"Where are you?" she called into the darkness.

As if to answer her, blue light shone up ahead. It cleared away the swirling smoke she hadn't realized was surrounding her, and there he was, clutching a bruised, torn heart that thumped slowly in his quivering hands.

"It hurts," he whined.

"What hurts?" Sable asked as she neared the ledge.

The oil had risen behind him, climbing an invisible wall. It pulsed and slithered, contorting until she realized it was not oil but a serpent. As it bent over the boy and lunged, its hiss vibrated through the goop around her until she was launched back into the world, where she stood on shaking legs. The color in her cheeks had rushed away.

Gabe stared at her in shock. She didn't need to be psychic to know his curious gift had shown him what she'd just seen.

He was so lost.

Deep inside, all he had was hopeless black ink that was suffocating him beneath all his humor and games. A stark realization struck her so hard that she was breathless. *The damned studies. . ..* They were no more than a powerless tool to obsessively try to fix what was destroyed within him.

She thought back to being a child and finding out about the legend of the trickster. She'd already been well acquainted with him for months, but she had never known who he was outside the time he spent with her until the circulating rumors described the man she knew.

"Am I on strings, Gabe?" she had asked.

And he had replied with a riddle, as was his custom. *"Everyone is on strings. Even me. I'm wrapped up inside all the marionettes that I build. I am knotted up in a mess of strings. And you have been strung into it too. Long before we met. We are all puppets. Every last one of us."*

The memory stung in her eyes, but she pushed it away. At the time, she had not understood what he was saying. But she did now. He was without purpose, at the mercy of his own darkness, and all he knew was pain. He needed his games. They kept him from going mad. They gave him a false sense of hope that he could smother the snake coiled around his soul. Without them, he had nothing but an endless darkness stretching into eternity.

Sable knew the feeling all too well. She couldn't imagine the horror of life extending forever with such a burden. At least she could have grown old and died eventually. It would have ended someday.

She was no longer that girl though, the one who had been left staring at the outside of prison walls, her heart shattered at her feet, unable to face life on her own at the ripe old age of thirteen. Sable had a purpose now: to free others from their shackles. She took a deep breath.

"Gabe, considering that I ruined your game, would you join me?" she paused to take in the surprise on his face, "I'm trying to find my old teacher, and I'm tracking strange, magical beings that I have never seen before. I wouldn't mind the company or the help in these odd matters. Especially from someone slightly stronger than me."

"Slightly?" his voice shook, even as he tried his hand at sarcasm. He appeared shaken still from earlier events.

"Please? I'm sure a brand-new discovery is more than enough to replace whatever silly plot I may have stumbled upon."

He didn't consider her statement for long before allowing himself to grin again. "Only if I get to be the deranged one in the duo this time," he replied, reminding her again of her imprisoned companion.

She forced a smile and nodded. This was about to become a long and difficult road for him with the strength of that angry serpent inside his soul. She just hoped she would have the patience and strength to lead him to liberty from it.

~*This will be one of the hardest hearts for you to lead back to freedom. It will prepare you for the one that you love most.*

Sable let out a long breath. She was ready to save Gabe Arenreeth.

CHAPTER 3

They sat on opposite sides of the crackling fire. Sable was praying with her eyes closed and her face turned to the sky. Seeking direction, that was what she'd explained to him.

Gabe watched her in silence, poking absently at the flames with a long stick. He did not inquire about her vision of his innards or question the bizarre actions of the present moment. Instead, he studied her. What else could he do?

He hadn't seen her since her childhood, when she'd been attached to the side of a monster. Part of him found surprise blooming in his chest to realize that she had grown into such a young warrior. Granted, he had been certain that her "friend" would kill her someday, so he'd never bothered to consider her future. And when he did consider it, he'd been frightened enough by what he imagined that he did something she hated him for. Not that he regretted it. He'd do it again in a heartbeat. The day that her dear friend, Kazious was taken by the illusionists, Gabe had taken his leave of her as well. He had to. It was all for her, but she would never understand that.

Sable had always been strange though. She'd been almost mute, with an intense and analytical stare that would put a normal man on edge. Now she was much more unsettling with the flaming swords inside her eyes . . . and the faith. Believing in a god was not difficult in their world of oddities, but the fact that Sable was submitted to one was a sight he had ever considered possible. No one had ever told Sable what to do. Not even Kazious.

Who was this being who had tied her to his wrist? Gabe would have loved to meet the spirit who could convince the girl of stone to obey its orders. He wouldn't mind destroying it either.

"Why are you staring at me?" Sable demanded when she opened her eyes.

Gabe shrugged. "Curiosity."

She glared at him with obvious suspicion that he understood. For Gabe, curiosity was not always a good thing. He caught that thought, letting a gentle smile curl the corners of his mouth.

"Can I be honest with you?" he asked.

"Go ahead. Though I know honesty is not your strong suit."

He looked down at the dancing flames. They reflected in the blackness of his dark eye, piercing its blue mate with shades of gold across the ocean. "I wasn't sure you would ever leave that place. I had thought for certain I would come back someday, and you would still be there. Starved and rotten. I never imagined that you would leave him, no matter the years or the consequences to your life," he admitted with genuine concern.

Sable avoided his gaze as his words took her back there with him. His gift let him see the memory play out again in her mind. *She could have sworn that night had grown as cold as ice when the silence settled in after the horror. A broken girl far too young for her ability to staunch her tears. She'd just watched, stunned and confused. When those stone gates locked, and she felt the rumble of their finality crack the egg on her collarbone, the dam had finally shattered. She'd wailed and pounded the walls with her weak fists, crying out, sobbing . . . suffocating.*

She would not press her hand to the wound now though. The only evidence of the shattered pieces still remaining was that the bottom of her vibrant eyes sparkled with a brush of liquid.

"I didn't want to leave. Had things gone differently, I would likely be long dead by now," she admitted in a quivering whisper.

"What changed your mind?"

"I made a desperate prayer, and it was answered."

Gabe realized from her lack of ability to look him in the eye that she expected him to laugh or ridicule her. And maybe on another night, he would have. He hadn't seen her in over a decade, though, and this grown woman was far different from the young girl he had thought he'd saved all those years ago. She was stronger and the fire was more stable inside her. She was also much harder. Gabe could sense the way her bones were like lead with the weight of her sorrows.

So, who was this entity that had answered her prayers and guided her into this life she led now? Who turned the broken child into a warrior of marble? Who could he blame for distorting the conclusion to the one good deed he'd ever done in his life?

Gabe's brows furrowed, and he leaned back, inhaling a long breath as he thought about where he wanted this conversation to go.

"What was the prayer?" he inquired after some time.

She raised her eyes to the stars as she recited it from memory. "If you are all-powerful, you can change even the darkest of souls and save this madman from his own damnation. I would forfeit my own life if it would pay for his salvation; just take it. If only you will free him of the very evil that has taken him from me."

She would never forget the words or the ugly way in which she'd wailed them to the heavens. At that time, she'd believed with every shred of her heart that her life would end the moment that she finished the prayer. And she had been more than ready to sacrifice it.

Gabe smirked at her, all the seriousness from a moment

ago wiped away. His heart clenched, but he pushed that away as he released a chuckle.

"Well, of course, when you offer your soul, *something* will answer. That is guaranteed." He leaned forward, clasping his hands and dropping his voice to a tumbling whisper that mocked her. "How can you be certain this 'master' isn't someone with powers like mine? How do you even know that Kazious is still alive? That prison isn't known for hospitality, you realize."

"It's a mixture between intuition and faith," she replied without hesitation.

Gabe's lips pulled into a wide, toothy grin that held no actual mirth. His chuckle earned a frown from her as a flame began to build inside his gut.

"Come now, Sable," he began, his voice twisting with a maniacal edge. "Do you know how I admired you when you were so very young, far too intelligent for your age? You were fascinating. I loved you back then. Now you're sitting here and talking about faith? Even while the life of the one man you ever cared for hangs in the balance, my little stone witch? My Clo-Caillea."

She narrowed her eyes at the old nickname.

"Faith is for the easily manipulated," he continued before she could respond, stepping around the fire to tower over her. He didn't want to scare her, but he couldn't stop the desperate terror climbing up into his veins as his tone reached a booming roar. "The people who must enslave themselves, because they have no strength to stand on their own two legs. You *of all people* can do better than faith, you fool!"

Sable did not turn away when his face drew to within inches from hers. She did not flinch when he grabbed her arms in bruising holds. Her strange amber eyes regarded him with pity, enraging and terrifying him further. He shook her violently, at a loss for the words to bring back her senses, yet her only response remained a deep, calm frown.

She must have seen terror galloping behind his anger, because her guarded face softened just enough to punch him. *She understood.* He was not angry with her for becoming weak and foolish; he was frightened by the strength she carried, which had been absent when he'd known her as the stone witch. To put it simply, he was confused.

A long, tense moment passed where he breathed raggedly in her face, battling the fire inside him that wanted to wrap his large hands around her pale neck and force the cold, logical child to come back out. *Or so help me, I'll destroy this version of you.* The violence let his mind snap back into focus in another second as he recoiled from the intrusive thought. *You haven't seen her in thirteen years. Don't ruin this now!*

He loosened his grip, though his hands did not fall away. He breathed out heavily, searching her face for the answer to a question he was not ready to ask.

Sable spoke into the silence, tracing its shape with gentle ferocity. "Tell me, Gabe, what stopped you from choking me the way that you wanted to? Is it out of respect for the stone witch you once knew, or are you afraid, not knowing the extent of the power my faith allows me to access?"

His mouth dropped open, but he couldn't answer. *How the hell did she even know?*

She leaned closer to him until their noses brushed at the tips. "By your calculations, who here is truly weak, or is fear *not* one of your methods of manipulation?"

He yanked his hands off her as if they burned, stepping back until his legs hit the log he'd sat on before. Her unwavering gaze held his, though she did not mirror his rage or scorn. She regarded him with understanding and a shred of sadness. The pity had disappeared from her face.

He hated her in that moment.

"Damn you," he muttered as he sat down with a heavy thud.

She chuckled, smiling gently. "Come now, are you giving up that easily?" she asked, earning a halfhearted glare. "Let that incredible mind of yours find the truth. Otherwise, you'll always have doubts, and you can't trust someone you doubt to come into battle at your side."

He let the humor of the moment take over, a smirk gracing the edge of his lips. "You are a strange, little woman. Do you know that?"

Sable let out a hearty laugh. Her smile illuminated her eyes in a way that caught him off guard. "You haven't seen anything yet," she whispered.

He realized within that statement that the glow was not just an effect of her beautiful smile. An actual light was dancing beneath the gentle slope of her cheeks. He squinted, leaning toward her from across the fire.

Yep. It was alive.

"What the hell is that?" he shouted, pointing an accusatory finger at her. "You didn't have that before. What the hell have you done?"

Sable glared at him. "Settle down. What are you talking about?"

He stood up, gesturing toward her. "Your face! It's glowing! Humans don't glow, and I *know* you didn't do that when you were a kid. What the f—"

"Gabe, it's him," she interjected, her anger falling into a look of boredom. "He calls it the Spirit of Truth or the Holy Spirit. It's an advocate for my father, who dwells within us all and awakens by our love for him. You have it too, but its dormant."

He scoffed, plopping back down with a grin that wiped all the confusion and misplaced anger away again. "That sounds like possession to me."

"As if you can talk," she replied, compelling him into abrupt silence.

The silence eased around them like a calming blanket. He refused to pursue the topic, turning away from her and staring into the fire. Gabe's brow furrowed in thought.

"I was unaware this quest involved battles," he mused, chuckling. "In fact, I didn't even know you *could* fight."

She smirked and Gabe caught her mind whispering, *yeah right.*

"How do you think your puppet was destroyed?" she prompted. "I doubt my witticisms would do much damage." Her smile faded as she turned away from him. "Perhaps if you had been around after I lost Kazious, you would have known that I took up the sword and the bow."

She studied the fire, a sad smile taking her lips. The flames stirred up memories of those years, and Gabe followed them down deep inside her shaken core with the sharp edges of their darkness threatening to tear at his gift.

It had not been easy to learn on her own how to wield the small arsenal she now traveled with, and her master had been so new to her that she had a hard time trusting his guidance. Survival alone was hard enough and at times almost impossible, let alone training with sticks until she finally obeyed his commands.

He had led her to a woman who took her in as a student with no hesitation. Her weapons had been gifts from the strange new friend. The woman had gone by the name Rose, and for a decade, they trained together as Sable grew stronger as a warrior. Rose was an honorable woman who kept her word and valued the girl like a younger sister. She taught Sable so much more than fighting. She taught her to honor her weapons, her instincts, and the people that she saved *and* fought. She had also taught Sable how to survive in the wilderness.

They had traveled together across the land, and while Sable's relationship with her master grew, so did her relationship with her teacher. Rose was more than willing to accept Sable's faith as long as the girl could understand her teacher would not join it. The two mentors complemented her life, giving her an illusion of peace and finally understanding slightly what family was supposed to feel like. What being loved felt like.

But when Sable's gift to discern the shape of the soul had awakened, everything fell to pieces. She wasn't trying to hurt her teacher and friend. She had only wanted to help. How was she to know that the beautiful golden-eyed woman loved her vendetta like a husband? How was she supposed to know that Rose would flip a switch in her mind the moment Sable tried to teach her of the peace she had learned along those years with her master? She didn't know. She only wanted to help.

Instead, they battled. Or rather: Rose had lunged, Sable had defended, and then . . . with blood spraying from her teacher's face and shoulder, she'd been taught one final lesson: it was dangerous to push peace where hatred was worshipped.

That had served as her understanding as to why Kazious was still imprisoned even after her prayers were answered. Of course, she had a lot of time to ponder such things during the four days she'd been trapped at the bottom of the dry well, where Rose had dumped her unconscious body.

Gabe had to cut in for fear he would be wrecked by the

guilt of what he'd left her to suffer with. His deep storm cloud of a voice worked to bring her back as he explained, "believe it or not, Sable, I did worry about your wellbeing after it happened. I mean it. I cared about you, but you were so young. I—" He broke off, sighing in frustration and running his hand through his wild hair.

He chewed his lip as he fought for the right way to explain, fully aware of the fact that nothing would ever make up for what he did. Saving her from Kazious was one thing; abandoning her as a child was another.

"I wasn't going to make history repeat itself though," he finally said. "You had spent so long with that cracked man. I don't know what happened to bring you to him in the first place, but you were so broken, and you needed healing. I couldn't bring myself to replace one unstable mind with another. You had a chance to regain some kind of normalcy to your life. I couldn't take that from you."

He grew quiet again, closing his eyes and hanging his head.

The weight of her intense stare would have been amusing if not for the disbelief swirling around inside her mind. Sable never would have thought in a thousand years that Gabe could have feelings like that. She had always assumed that people were just pawns for his study purposes. Even as a lost young teen, when she'd wished he would come back to her one last time, she never thought he truly cared for her. He couldn't blame her for thinking any of it, though. She didn't speak any of those thoughts aloud, but he doubted she didn't feel the press of his power shuttering against them.

Letting out a strained chuckle, she sarcastically mumbled, "yeah, it really turned out normal."

Gabe glanced up at her, seeing a flash of himself through her gaze, his blue eye luminous in the moonlight, like a clear lake. He grinned, though it was somewhat forced.

"Yeah, I guess I should have known better." After a pause, he continued. "You never did tell me what this journey was though. What exactly did I get myself into?"

Sable smiled, mischief glinting in her eyes. "All I know is that I started this journey to find my teacher, and now I've killed four 'pseudo-immortals,' as I've dubbed them. I don't know if they connect to her or just took precedence over her, but thus far, my master hasn't revealed much. They destroy entire towns and cities with ease, controlling strange phantoms and unnatural fire."

"Oh . . . sounds like fun." He didn't seem to agree with his own words. His brow furrowed again. "Was that what my guy was?"

She chewed her lip for a moment and then nodded. "I wasn't sure if you were the orchestrator of his existence when you showed up, but I believe he simply caught your eye after he was away from his maker."

Gabe quirked a corner of his lip. "I like not being a suspect of things I am incapable of."

She chuckled at his statement, but he didn't miss the glow of fear in the quiet forge of her eyes.

CHAPTER 4

Morning light warmed Sable's face as she woke, opening one orange eye to check her surroundings. Her arm was tucked into the gap between her jaw and shoulder, her dagger resting on the ground below her hand.

Easy access, just in case.

The fire was only smoking black coals, and on the other side was a thick log. Gabe was nowhere in sight.

She eased herself up, cringing at the tension in her abused muscles and frowning as she glanced around her small camp. Why she'd expected still to see the trickster somewhere, she wouldn't admit to knowing. He'd left. Again.

"No surprise there," Sable muttered.

She denied the way the stone egg thrummed upon its mantle. He would not be honored with such pain. Not after all that time she'd gone without him, she wasn't about to be that weeping teen left behind again. She was better than that.

She brought herself to her knees, her hands clasped at her chest as she turned her chin toward the heavens, directing her attention and effort towards what truly mattered. White clouds crawled slowly across the blue sky as her lips moved in an almost inaudible prayer.

"Thank you, my lord, for another morning on which I am able to open my eyes, and my heart remains strong. Please, bless me with your armor over my own. The strong belt of truth around my waist, the breastplate of righteousness in place, and the helmet of salvation upon my head. Prepare my feet with the gospel of peace as I wield the shield of faith that halts the flaming arrows of the adversary, and the sword of the spirit, which is your word. I am yours to command. My trust falls on you alone to sustain my travel as I do your work. I love you, Father."

She took in a long, quivering breath and then stood to collect her gear. As she turned for the discarded parts, she halted.

He was leaning against a tree, arms crossed over his chest just like the previous night, brows drawn together. His lips were pulled down, but he did not appear upset. Instead, Gabe seemed . . . disturbed.

"I thought you'd left," Sable said, pulling her chest piece over her head.

"Does he ever answer you?"

She smiled as she tightened the strings that held the metal and leather together. "Not at all. He hardly responds to my morning prayers. When it's needed though, he speaks to me as clearly as you do. I have conversations with him almost every day. And yet, some days he remains silent."

By the time she finished speaking, she was tightening the guards for her weaker arm. Her hand worked with smooth precision, which made her weakness all the clearer when she moved to attach the pieces for her strong arm.

The hand in charge shook just enough for Gabe to notice, though it was the difficulty she had with curling her fingers around the leather straps that caused him to raise an eyebrow. He didn't say anything about her struggle, though his observance didn't go unnoticed by her.

"How do you know he is what you think he is?" he prompted.

Her smile widened as she attached her sword across her back, slipping her bow over the scabbard. She fastened her dagger and quiver onto her hips before she replied.

"Because it is only when his spirit pours into me that I know peace and can breathe clearly. The stone on my chest is removed." She pressed her gloved hand against that place, turning away from Gabe's narrowing eyes. "It hurts to be this way, you know," she admitted with quivering lips.

He didn't have to ask what she meant. His nickname was enough to show his understanding of her form of survival. He'd told her when she was a child that the first time he met her, he'd felt the marble encasing her bones as if it were his own. That was why she was named the Stone Witch, because she'd locked her heart away deep inside the rocks so she wouldn't suffer anymore with its infected wounds. What she referenced wasn't a literal egg sitting on her chest, but rather it had become the physical reaction to her subjective emotions that her mind couldn't handle. It was similar to the way a panic attack could feel like a physical ailment in one's heart even though it was entirely contained inside their mind.

Gabe pushed himself off the tree, approaching the woman who had turned her sparkling eyes toward the sky again. Whether he meant to comfort her, she wasn't sure, but she felt him enclosing on her and locked her jaw. *Don't touch me*, the quiver in her muscles almost begged.

"We should get going," she mumbled, turning to him again and lighting a warning flame inside her eyes.

They left the trees in silence, returning to the town to follow the road toward her next destination. Sable raised her hood as they wandered the wide main street. The town had been built around one of three grand highways that crossed the region.

Eyes bore into the pair as soon as they were spotted, and Sable wondered if the elder had told them about their conversation. Whispers chorused, agitating Sable's nerves. She clenched her fists, digging her nails into her palms.

You would all be dead if I hadn't come, yet today I am still hated.

The stone egg began to hum and grow, creaking her bones like a shelf not built for the weight it bore. Then an ethereal hand settled across it, soothing its song.

~ *Wait. Observe . . ..*

She came to an immediate halt. Gabe just about ran into her, but he sidestepped at the last moment and stood still, watching her with amused confusion.

In the silence, she scanned the houses surrounding her, noting that all eyes turned away as soon as she began her observations.

The village was in repair; children were even helping to bring wood, tools, and nails to the adults rebuilding their terrorized homes. The horrors of the previous day had sunken in their eyes and haunted the hands that tore away the smoke-stained pieces of their devastated hovels.

A gentle wind lifted her curls from her shoulders.

She heard the whisper of splintering wood to her right and faced its source. Mere steps away stood a decrepit doorway into one of the blackened shacks. It was giving way under the easy push of the breeze. One more scratch came from the darkness inside, and Sable realized why she'd been warned.

She had a split second to act.

Give me the strength, my lord, Sable prayed, throwing herself into the crumbling home.

She secured her long arms around the waist of a short, elderly woman who had been shuffling outside with a bag of belongings. Sable shifted around as she surged forward, trying to shove the woman into a safer place and in doing so, put herself further inside the home.

The building groaned, and before she could take one more step, it gave in. Shattered wood and heavy iron nails rained down on the two. Her knees quivered under the weight of the rubble, and it was all she could do to protect the elder's smaller frame from the brunt of it. A fire ignited in her shoulder, screaming that the leather had been punctured, but she refused to cry out.

Her arms were emptied so fast in that terrible moment that she almost yelped.

Her eyes shot up, and she tried to lunge from beneath

the rubble, failing miserably as her back protested under the weight. She briefly caught sight of one laughing ice-blue eye assuring her to remain calm from outside. Gabe had an arm around the hyperventilating old woman, who appeared more frightened than hurt.

The clattering pieces stopped falling on her, but replacing the noise was a solid weight pressing down on her, overwhelming her until she fell to her knees, where lightning bolts rushed up her legs into her hips. She dug her fingers into the dirt, locking her jaw as black spots blotted out pieces of her vision. More lightning struck, scattering pieces of rubble across her back while nails bit into her.

~ *There was an easier way.* He chuckled behind her eyes, spilling warm syrup into her bloodstream and soothing her screaming wounds.

As if to prove his point, the rubble shifted, and she was free. Long, spidery fingers appeared in her vision, offering aid.

Her smoldering eyes traveled up to Gabe's smiling face, but her heart squeezed at the thought of trusting in his support just yet. She looked to his other hand, raised above him as he hoisted the wreckage. He wasn't touching any of it though. A twisting grey ball hovered over his palm. Little cyclones twirled out of it like tiny arms, holding up the ruins of the home.

Sable shifted her gaze back to the ground, lifting herself to her knees and pressing her bruised palms against her legs. They protested the pressure, and she hissed.

"You're certainly more reckless than I would have expected, you know. Stronger than I gave you credit for too," he remarked around his boyish grin, which rounded out his jaw and made him look much younger.

"That strength is not my own," Sable said, rising to her feet and pulling the pain away from her expression with ease.

The limp was not as easy to ignore. When her left leg buckled, Gabe reached out to steady her, but her forges lit back up and halted his second attempt to help.

As she walked away, he frowned at her. He made a motion with the hand still under the rubble, pulling a breeze past Sable that whipped her curls across her face.

She turned back just in time to see the wind throw the remains of the building into a heap away from the immortal. The air grew still. She turned away again.

Gabe trailed behind her, eyeing the crimson that streamed down her back from the holes in her armor. He didn't miss the way she was limping either.

"I wonder how many places you can bleed from before you collapse?" His words indicated amusement, but the tone was a warning.

She couldn't respond to him though, because her master returned to her mind in the next moment.

~Get out. Get out now.

It was a simple and distinct order that made her heart race.

"Stop them! Don't let them leave," a weak, airy voice called from somewhere to their left.

Sable closed her eyes. *Why can't you people just be grateful you're alive*? she thought as she continued her slow pace.

No one moved against her, seeming confused and startled. Gabe had come up beside her though, like a guard. It almost made her laugh.

"She's a witch!" It was the other elder, Varylah.

You have no idea. She was sick of being called that.

"A blasphemer consorting with demons. Don't think we will be fooled by any good deeds, devil woman! You've shown your true colors to me!" she continued to scream about their conversation the night before, nearing hysteria.

Sable clenched her fists at her sides, her aching wounds joining with the erratic rhythm of the woman's wailing.

Beside her, Gabe whistled as if he were surprised. "You really are crazy, you know?" he whispered. "Trying to tell an old hag her entire belief system is a lie? Not very smooth."

"Shut up," she hissed.

Footsteps thundered toward them from all directions. The shock must have worn off. She sighed heavily and braced herself for the ache of sprinting with the billowing throbs in her knees.

"Yeah, no. You promised me a study and adventure, not a witch hunt. Here we go," Gabe muttered far too close to her ear.

He scooped her into his arms, shocking every nerve

ending in her body. Her pain was drowned out by a more primal instinct as her insides thrashed, demanding she be released. She pushed against him, her skin igniting wherever it made contact with him. *Don't touch me*!

"Hey, settle down," he reprimanded from above in a soothing rumble. "It'll be safe soon, and I'll let you go. Just hang on."

Sable's eyes snapped open, a spark of terror in her chest at what that indicated. *It isn't safe right now.*

"Gabe, don't hurt anyone," she begged.

He scoffed. "Look around you. I don't need to hurt anyone. You forget that I wield illusions like magic." He smiled down at her.

She glanced about as they neared the edge of town, confused at first before shock came through with understanding.

The crowd had been drawn to a halt. Each individual stunned by whatever Gabe was projecting from his mind. Some were trembling, others stood transfixed and frozen, mouths hanging open. Others had fallen to their knees and pressed their foreheads to the backs of their hands. A sign of prayer.

"What are they seeing, Gabe?" she asked under her breath.

"You tried to tell the ol' lady that your god was the true creator instead of Light and Darkness, correct?"

She nodded slowly.

"Well, whoever truly created everything has power over the angels. That's the basic assumption everyone can agree on."

"You made them see you as an angel," she stated.

"Halo and all," he replied, grinning again like a schoolboy.

She turned away from him. "You're deceiving them."

"Would you prefer they tie you to a stake and burn you alive?"

Sable didn't answer.

~It's alright, my child. Have patience and know forgiveness. This lost child will teach you these things as you help him. Settle your nerves.

Sable sighed at the sound of her master's voice. Those were the very things she lacked more than any others, although understanding was coming around at a slow pace through empathy.

She realized this was going to be just as rough for her as she expected it to be for Gabe.

Great.

CHAPTER 5

"So, where are we headed, oh cryptic one?" Gabe asked after they'd traveled about an hour out of town.

He had let her down soon after they made their escape from the crowd, but only after Sable began to struggle and fidget with her flaming nerves. She'd taken great care to keep a considerable distance between them after that, focusing her thoughts on the path ahead instead of the feeling of iron shackles at her wrists that allowed hands too large to have free roam of her young flesh.

"I don't plan that far ahead. If I'm told to move, I move whether I know the destination or not."

"Ah, so we're most likely lost," he concluded, not sounding at all worried.

"No, I have a map inside my head," she replied. "Plus, I'm sure you've passed through here at least once in your extensive travels, old man."

He laughed. "Alright then. So, where are we?"

Sable didn't respond right away. Instead she turned around so she was walking backwards while she raised her arm and pointed to the horizon on their right.

"Have you heard of the Caladhvik Forest?" she asked, smiling slightly.

"Nope. I'm twelve thousand years old, and I have never ever heard of the forest that is *impenetrable* to literally everyone. Not at all."

She snorted, shaking her head. "It's in that direction just over the hills. We're pretty much on its doorstep. This road runs parallel to it eventually."

"Please, tell me we're not going there."

"Don't tell me you're afraid. What could *you* possibly have to worry about? I'm the human here."

Gabe glared at her. "Just because I haven't figured out *what* kills me doesn't mean I can't *be* killed."

She smiled. "Alright fine, I *won't* tell you where we're going."

He roared with laughter. "You're insane. Why are we going there?"

Sable frowned, stopping in her tracks and fixing her gaze to him.

"Uh oh. We're serious." He straightened up, crossing his arms and narrowing his eyes. "Why are we serious?"

Her master answered Gabe's question with a flash of color behind her eyes. "There's a city deep inside. That's where the next attack will happen." Her lips trembled as she spoke. Her eyes were no longer seeing Gabe but the carnage. It was as clear as if she were there. Even the smell of burning flesh was real and choking her. "They aren't screaming. No one is reacting to the fires engulfing them. They're just standing there. It's like a trance. The city is under a spell, and they're all going to die, unable to fight for their lives."

Her knees quivered, and she clenched her fists. The images withdrew, leaving her mind empty and her heart heavy.

Gabe didn't say anything and she safely assumed his gift had touched the vision too. No sarcastic quips to make then.

Sable regained her composure after a few long breaths. Then she continued to explain, her master answering Gabe's questions with deliberate detail. "You know about the guardian of the forest, right? Well, we're going to continue as far down this road as we can before we're driven off. And then we'll go straight for the forest. I don't know how we get in, but we'll be directly steered towards the gates."

She had not been shown that part in a vision but rather instructed as the sound of the guardian's roar rattled inside her mind. It reverberated across her collarbone, choking her for the space of three hard breaths.

~*Fear not, child. You have not been given the spirit of fear but of love, power, and a sound mind. I am with you.*

She tightened her fists at her sides, setting her jaw. *I trust in your will. Let it be done accordingly. Protect us on this journey, and give me the strength to wield my weapons in your mighty name. Amen.*

Behind her, Gabe's eyes turned analytical. He had not missed the exchange, and it intrigued him. This relationship between the girl and their unseen party member fascinated him. Her blind faith and resolve almost impressing if it didn't also have him convinced that she had a death wish. The resolve alone didn't surprise him, though; the stone witch never did know how to fear anything. It somewhat relieved him to still recognize some part of the child he'd known back then.

In the silence as they continued, a smile crept up Gabe's face. He *did* recognize this area.

To their left was a drop-off that followed the road until it reached the gates of a kingdom that was a solid week's ride ahead of them. At the base of the cliff was a raging river inhabited by a deadly breed of fish. He had learned that from experience.

He had come that way during the Old War. The road had been choked by the army marching toward the kingdom he had just left. He could have killed them all where they stood. After all, he knew the queen with whom they were at war. Technically, he should have been on her side. But he did his best not to interfere with wars. It made his long life easier to manage. Let the humans and immortals fight. What did it matter to him? Aside from proving that *no one was really immortal.* Everyone could die. Except for him. So far.

But boy, did those fish try.

Gabe jerked back to the present when he noticed Sable become tense. Her shoulders had grown tight, rising toward her ears as she clenched her fists. Her breathing was heavy yet slow, controlled and preparing.

A shack came into view to the left of the highway. He frowned at it. That hadn't been there before.

A moment later, his arm was stinging. He didn't look down at the arrow piercing him but released an irritated sigh.

"Sable, would you mind *not* taking the lead when we're getting shot at?" he muttered, grabbing her arm and yanking her back until she thudded against his chest.

Two more projectiles flew past him. Sable would have caught each with her face. He turned, so his back faced the incoming third wave.

Sable pulled away from him and bolted off the road.

"Oh, yes, this is the part where we run headlong into a beasty rather than killing the wretches *shooting at us*!"

"Oh shut up, old man!"

Gabe rolled his eyes. "Right. Orders from the top. Can't argue with that. Even if it *is* suicide."

Pain sparked through Gabe's shoulder, irritating him further as he pushed to keep himself between his unbearably vulnerable companion and their pursuers.

Sable yanked her bow free from where it hung and grabbed an arrow. She inhaled a long breath and halted.

Gabe sidestepped again just before he tripped over her and then watched as she aimed with her flaming eyes. She yanked back the string and cried out at the same time. Gabe realized her back was reminding her that a building had just fallen on her a few hours earlier. She released the arrow in the following moment, but Gabe was more interested in the blood spilling to the grass beneath their feet than whether she hit her mark.

"*Don't* do that again," he snarled, grabbing her arm before she could nock another arrow.

She glared at him, but it just caused him to tighten his grip. He raised his free hand toward their oncoming attackers. He recognized even without his psychic gift the exact moment when she remembered who Gabe the legend was.

His hand glowed with a crimson light as black smoke rose off his skin, dripping ink down his fingertips. It was like oil lit by glowing blood, and for a moment, his mind flashed with images of Sable trudging through thick, boiling oil and a child was crying in the distance.

Three metal snakes, each as thick as his fist, tore through his palm. Her eyes followed them, her jaw loose with shock as they flew across the field.

The thieves stood no chance. Each fell with a solid spike embedded in his chest. Sable had to turn away, facing her friend with closed eyes as a baby Gabe at the back of her mind cried out, *It hurts!*

Gabe drew his shadows back into his palm, leaving the bodies with gaping holes through them. The once-innocent grass was stained with so much dripping gore that it could no longer sway in the wind.

The breeze lifted Sable's hair across her face and brushed her cheek with a gentle hand. She did not shed a tear for the dead. She swallowed her bile.

"Let's get moving," was all she managed to say. Her jaw was quivering when she turned from him and began to walk again.

Gabe watched her, stunned by the shift in her. Hadn't he saved them? Was it the deceased or the magic? It couldn't be death. Of all the people in this world, she was the one who would be the least affected by it. It had to be the magic, which confused him further.

The child had seen so much death without flinching, yet his power could curl her stomach? He stared at the palm of his hand, now clear of its smoke and ink. It seemed normal, if not a little rough with callouses.

He had almost forgotten about the core of his being; he was an abomination.

Gabe was a god's creation gone wrong. He shouldn't have lived. He raised his fingers to brush the scar at the side of his neck in the curve where it met his shoulder. The mark of the royal beast.

Right then. He squared his shoulders and followed the woman. *Thank you for the reminder, Sable.*

Oh, how wrong he was.

He wasn't ready to see how broken his stone witch was.

~I will make you both whole if you allow me to.

Sable did not show that she'd heard her master. For the first time, she found the pain in her chest too distracting to allow his peace to settle with his presence. How odd. After all, who would ever think to choose agony over peace?

The two journeyed in silence, each lost in their own thoughts.

Gabe cursed his powers as Sable cursed her gentle heart. Neither understood the hurt of the other, though they both seemed to understand they'd affected each other.

Sable found herself wondering if the immortal thought her weak for growing sick at the sight of death.

All they had to do was reach out.

~Why would you condemn yourself for something that makes you good?

She could have laughed, but she didn't. Instead, she glanced back at Gabe. His mismatched eyes were hard and narrow.

Do you miss the child who built a mantle out of guilt over those three years? she wondered, a piece of her heart hoping his gift was listening. *Do you miss the little girl who ensured her older self would break if she ever turned her heart back on?*

He frowned as he turned his gaze away from her. Perhaps that alone was her answer.

She never had the chance to see the clarity that sparked inside his eyes. The roar of the beast snapped the fog from their hearts.

"So, do you know anything about this creature?" Gabe inquired as they came to a halt.

"It really likes its trees," she replied.

He gave her an incredulous look, only to see a smile on her lips as she hung her bow on her back. Yeah, she had a death wish.

He faced the creature barreling toward them. At that distance, it could have been easy to mistake it for a horse. Grey smoke trailed to either side, spilling from its nostrils as it galloped. Around each ankle was a tuft of black fur, the rest of its coat glowing deep purple up its strong legs. It was bigger than the bandit's shack.

Gabe's lips curled into a maniacal grin. "Well, isn't this

guy adorable!" He shouted, opening his arms as if to hug the creature.

Sable gaped at her companion, watching him take huge steps to meet the beast that would trample him with little concern. She tightened her fists, remaining still as the wind rushed past her. "What do you think you're doing?"

Gabe ignored her, holding out his hand as if offering to let the creature smell his scent. That was when she realized his hand was smoking again. He had control over the same power that was spilling from the guardian.

"He's going to manipulate it," she whispered.

She lifted her eyes to the sky, pressing her hand to her chest. *Can I allow this? Is this okay? It doesn't seem right, my lord.*

~ Where does his power come from, child?

That was not what she expected to hear. She didn't know the answer.

Don't our gifts all come from you?

~My gifts do not destroy what is good, nor are they unclean. Where does his power come from then?

I admit I do not know, my lord. She turned her gaze back to Gabe, frowning.

~Find his source. Differentiate between what I gave him at his creation and what he has gained from elsewhere. This is how you will save him. Trust in the powers that are clean.

Yes, my lord.

She wondered if her master already knew what he was asking her to discover. She wouldn't put it past him.

Gabe smiled as he pressed his face against his horse's forehead. It could have fit two extra heads on either side of his, which made the moment seem bizarre.

A low horn sounded from the tree line, lasting a full minute. The creature pulled its head from Gabe's affection and turned up to the sky, howling like a wolf.

The horn blew again, closer now, and Sable saw another figure approaching. Gabe stepped back beside her, raising his fists. His black smoke still swirled as he readied for an attack.

"Who are you?" came a query from the atmosphere itself all around them, the voice thundering into Sable's bones. "What manner of demon can fool my servant and meet no harm? Answer me!"

"Demon?" Gabe repeated with scorn. "I'm no bloody demon, you blind old fool."

Sable acted on instinct, grabbing his wrist as his smoke pulsed red. The power hissed, diving for her fingers and drawing blood from a hundred tiny pinpricks that bit into her skin. She refused to cry out as she yanked on her friend.

"We have no idea what we're facing, Gabe! Settle down."

She released him once he responded with a hard glare. By then her hand was numb and covered in blood.

"I will know who deceived the creature into complacency. You should be long dead, and I should have only been here to clean up the mess. How do you still live?"

The words floated around them in the air, loud enough to be felt within Sable's quivering muscles yet it had no discernable source. Gabe's lips were pulled back into a sneering grin at what it had said.

The figure approaching them was a mere man. He was shorter than Gabe's six feet but perhaps taller than Sable, and he was dressed in shabby, threadbare layers of tunics and cloaks. Even his head was covered with cloth, so only his mud-brown eyes were visible, along with a short span of dark skin across the bridge of his nose.

"She wasn't deceived," Gabe countered, quieter and much more sinister in his rumbling thunderclap voice. "She simply knows that we are similar and it appears your precious pet was weary of being alone in its kind."

The muddy gaze fell on Gabe's showcased hand as he moved his fingers through the smoke.

"It's hard to kill something that takes on a likeness of yourself, especially when you thought you were all alone."

A trace of laughter swirled about them. "And yet you stand there claiming to be no demon, expecting that I will believe you. Tch."

The figure stopped. They were just out of arm's reach.

"You don't even know what you wield, do you?" his words whispered through the air, yet they were ferocious somehow.

Silence was Gabe's answer.

"Exterminate," the muffled voice murmured behind many layers of cloth.

Sable's chest bucked as if a fist had grabbed her heart and yanked, jolting her forward. Light spilled from beneath the stranger's clothing.

"No!"

She pushed Gabe aside, opening her arms just in time for the lights to form into one focused beam that struck her in the stomach.

CHAPTER 6

Gabe stood frozen in horror, his arms outstretched for her as if he could have saved her, his slack jaw catching flies.

The light faded reluctantly, as if it were ashamed of its use. Sable stood unharmed with her fists clenched at each side, her orange eyes rolling magma. She had saved him. An immortal by all accounts thus far had been saved by a human stepping into the line of fire *without even flinching*. He never would have expected the girl would do such a thing for anyone—especially him. After what he'd done over a decade earlier, the moment felt like one of his illusions. Impossible.

People didn't risk their lives for people like Gabe.

"What sorcery is this?" the stranger exclaimed, flexing his hands at his sides as if he would attack with his fists next.

"You cannot harm one who belongs to the creator of the very light you would weaponize," Sable declared, stepping toward her attacker.

A tense moment passed as he narrowed his eyes at her. Then the guardian's demeanor changed. He seemed to hear truth in her words, because he brought his hand over his heart, releasing his tension. He tilted his head forward and took two steps back, removing the threat he had made.

"I apologize, m'lady," he said. "You come here for the holy city then, I presume."

Sable nodded.

"I am weary to admit you will not be able to enter on your own, despite who sent you. You will need a blessed symbol to prove to the gate that you are sent by God or Calamity. It does not open for just anyone."

Sable's eyes widened, and she smiled softly, erasing all hostility from a moment ago. "I'm surprised you know to call the imposters by that title. Is it not enough that you could do me no harm? That is not a symbol to tell you what you need to know?"

He shook his head, casting his eyes down like she was a queen he shouldn't look upon. "No, I do not open the gate. I only guard it. It decides if you are worthy to enter by sensing the power of the one who sent you. At times even a strong curse has been admitted. That is why I am here: to try to sort the good from the evil."

His eyes shifted to Gabe, and she watched a flash of threat enter his muddy gaze.

"Am *I* not blessed?" Sable countered, yanking his attention back to her.

He chuckled quietly, his eyes telling her that he was smiling under the cloth. "You are more than that. You are alive and holy. It must be something that is without conscious thought but still holds the blessing of God or Calamity."

Agitation rose in her blood, and she crossed her arms. "My father is not confined to symbols."

"Then the gate will remain closed to you, m'lady. I suggest you depart from this place now before you force my hand."

He bowed his head one last time before turning, holding

his hand out to the creature waiting beside him. They began to walk away from her, but Sable bolted forward to grab him.

"Hang on!"

Her dreadful mistake registered when the beast turned its massive head, appraising her with a disinterested stare like she was a fly to swat away. Its mouth opened, and grey smoke rolled out to engulf the two strange beings in a cloud that swirled and darkened until it was made of inky night. They could no longer be seen within it.

She had no warning. Time seemed to slow to a crawl, but it did nothing to help her realize her danger.

No sound, not even a whistle as it sailed through the air told her the spike was flying until it was too late. A dull pressure built up in her arm just below her shoulder, but it lasted a mere moment before it turned into searing pain. She didn't cry out as the magical black spike pierced her, sinking in until it tore through the other side. Something cold dripped into her torn muscles, spreading down until the chill almost paralyzed her trembling arm. It all happened in an instant, and she had no control over the white terror that spread up from her spine. The power was consuming her. Her shaking orange eyes, dim with shock, turned down to the smooth obsidian embedded just above her armpit. She'd had no way of knowing it was coming, and now it was poisoning her.

"Sable!"

Gabe's arms wrapped around her waist as he pulled her to the ground, crawling over her. The ice flowed into her back, following each vertebra. Dazed and far away, she watched more black spikes fly over them, trailing oily clouds that dripped the night itself onto Gabe's pale skin while he moved to shelter her beneath him.

She focused above his shoulder on the single thread of blue sky glowing through the overpowering magic.

"Father, save me," she begged, her chin trembling.

Gabe scrambled to cover her with his arms, so she wouldn't get any of the tainted raindrops on her. He stared at her as she prayed.

"Bind the ice. The darkness and its evil," she continued, much to his dismay.

"Are you freaking serious right now?"

"The blood of your son was shed to free me from evil," she continued, "and I declared that freedom as mine, my lord."

He could swear he heard tears catch in her throat.

She's not even sure he'll answer her! A thread of raw rage snapped at the immortal's spine.

Gabe's back began to sting as the rain ate through his clothes. Sable began to cough, signifying to him that the chill coming from her wound had reached her esophagus. He was intimately familiar with this kind of magic; she was going to die soon.

"I will not be overcome." She continued, her voice so small, it almost didn't match the words. "Bind it and rebuke it in your mighty glory!"

Ice and blood raced down Gabe's arms and spine. His skin began to peel back under the bite of the chilled poison raining down on them. He turned his attention to the black oil threatening them. It roared like a storm, showering deadly magic. He had to do something before it was too late. His body would heal, but he couldn't say the same for his torn-up companion.

He opened his mind, reaching around the two of them with the psychic arms of a giant, sheathing them in a clear dome that pattered with the rain. It was stained obsidian within seconds, but nothing came through, and Gabe allowed himself a calming breath. The girl's silence shot a thread of panic into his heart, but he wasn't done removing the threat.

"Come to me," he whispered to the wind, his voice rumbling into Sable's throat.

In his mind, he pictured a swirling cyclone tearing about their barrier and picking up the smoke, capturing it within. He could not see if the wind was following his commands, but the pull in his chest was enough to confirm obedience.

His skin began to glow, pulsing red light from beneath. Outside through the darkness, he saw a tower of flames rise. Its crackling was only audible once much of the storm was eaten up within its heat.

Slowly and with great care, he tilted the barrier over with his mind. It rolled off them like a bowl being overturned, and then he released it altogether.

One more relieved breath passed through his lips.

"Alright, let's see that wound," Gabe said, turning back to the girl he assumed would be in shock.

Instead, she was staring up at him, frowning, her eyes clear of their fog from moments earlier.

"Off," she ordered.

Gabe stood, stumbling over confusion as he analyzed her scowl.

The spike had faded from reality, leaving a gaping red hole like a gouged eye glaring at him. It dribbled slow, angry crimson, much to his dismay. When that kind of magic mixed with human blood, it would turn a shade of purple as the victim froze to death from the inside. Yet he gaped at the beautiful shade of red that she seemed to be ignoring. No surprise there.

"How did you stop the poison," he inquired, breathless.

Sable's eyes narrowed to slits. "How did you know it was poisoned?"

His gaze hardened at the sharpness of her voice, the blue becoming clear ice, the brown almost synonymous with an abyss. "I'm old enough to be familiar with dark magic. Don't you *dare* start acting like I'm here to hurt you too," he warned with a low, rumbling growl.

She leaned up into his challenge, eating him alive with the fires in her eyes. "I can't help but notice that what you did to those thieves looked nearly identical to what just tried to kill us!"

He stepped forward into her space, a darkness coming over him as he pointed a finger in her face. "You of all people should know there's a difference between a power's source and the way it's used. Don't go accusing me of something I haven't done!"

She scoffed at his response. "Haven't you spent this entire time trying to tell me about the dangers of being manipulated by a lying 'source'?"

Silence greeted her, earning a satisfied smile as she glanced back up. Gabe's expression was guarded. She could see the gears working behind his eyes though, which was reassuring. He was stubborn, but he was far from naïve.

She let out a sigh, closing her eyes and turning away. She held her hand on the wound in her shoulder, pressing against it. White electric threads of pain sparked up into her head.

"I'm fine, Gabe," she muttered. "My father has authority over all things. I am his child, and that gives me the authority to remove what does not belong in his creation."

"We should still bandage it," he said, stepping closer. "And I really hate it when you speak gibberish. That's my thing."

Her lips quirked into the ghost of a smile. "You only think it's gibberish, because it's hard for you to admit it could be real. You hate hope."

The silence returned. She enjoyed being able to strike the trickster speechless so often. It meant she was hitting nerves that needed to be bled out.

"Let's go," she said, shrugging off the hand he was about to place on her good shoulder. "We need to find something blessed by my father, and I haven't the faintest clue what to look for."

She did not see the way he clenched his jaw in frustration or the anguish clawing his eyes from his throat. Her lack of trust in him dug into an old wound that had torn open the day that he had saved a beautiful little girl from a monster in angel's clothes. All she knew was the hesitation in his strained tone when he responded with his usual sarcasm. "Why not just ask your dad then and see if he'll make this easy on us?"

Sable laughed. "That was my plan."

The immortal shook his head in disbelief, allowing himself to laugh with her. "You're insane."

He had hoped she would have found peace by now. It seemed all he'd managed to do was free her from a madman and hand her off to a phantom.

CHAPTER 7

They returned to the road a few miles down from where the bandits had attacked, avoiding the topic of the misunderstood aftermath to violent death. Silence embraced them like a mediating friend that begged the two to drop their barriers. Not that either would ever listen. But it tried.

Sable didn't pray for guidance like she said she would. Instead, she was tormented by the chill that clung to her after the attack. It haunted her, clawed at her. An abrupt reminder of how easily she could die on this journey. How weak she was. The magic would have killed her if her father had not responded to her prayer. She'd even considered crying out for Gabe's help instead, which further strangled her heart.

Gabe had betrayed her. Her master had made her whole

again. Yet, it was the immortal she had almost turned to before the one who had never let her down in the thirteen years he'd guided her. She closed her eyes, hugging herself.

"So, there was this one time I traveled this road in the middle of a war," Gabe piped up from behind her.

The jolt of his rumbling voice seemed to shake something out of the egg, and she snapped her gaze to him. He was smiling at her. Aloof and unaware of her guilt.

He continued his story as she turned back to the path, his voice grating against her fried nerves. "You've probably already noticed, but this road doesn't give a man many places to detour if he can't stay on it. Either he's forced to face the giant horse demon thing and her obnoxious pal, or they go down a cliff."

"Is there a point to this tale?" she hissed.

"Filling silence," he answered without skipping a beat. "Anyways, I was coming this way once during that war a couple hundred years ago when this young lady queen basically had the entire world decide to hate her, because her peaceful juju stopped working. It was complicated, and I probably didn't help any with involving the goddess that was protecting Light for a while."

Sable rolled her eyes, growing agitated as her egg began to sing.

"An army was on their way to kill her once and for all—or so they thought. But they had no clue about the kind of tricks she had up her sleeve. She was sort of awesome."

He sounded like a kid who had consumed too much sugar. How he could go from quiet and solemn to this was still lost on Sable, who was trying to *stay* solemn.

"I didn't feel like slaughtering a bunch of people that day though," he continued, "So, when I saw them coming, I took a chance with the fish at the bottom of the cliff. Not that I knew there were fish before I jumped, mind you."

She let out a little growl, her fists clenching at her sides. "Gabe, they aren't just fish. They're flesh-eating monsters."

He let out a laugh that climbed up her spine and caused her to clench her jaw. "You think I didn't figure that out when they started gnawing on me?" he asked. "By the time I got out, I barely had any skin left. Took two weeks and a stinky potion Edge concocted to heal from it."

At that moment, her only thought was that whoever this

Edge guy was should have let Gabe suffer longer.

"Could you just shut up for a bit, please?" She snapped. "I *prefer* silence."

His obedience allowed her to let out a long, slow breath. Her agitated nerves were jittery at best, and she couldn't take much more of his thunderclap voice rolling over them.

"Sable?" he prompted, not missing the way her shoulders rose with tension.

"What?" she asked, a knife in the word.

"Are you afraid of me?"

She stopped and lifted her face to the darkening sky. Angry grey clouds were coming their way. Another storm. She exhaled as if all her energy had been pulled out of her.

"It's not about fearing you," she said, her voice shaking as she watched the heavens crawl. "I'm still human. No matter the power my faith lends me from my father, I still fear death and pain. I'm still tormented by each brush with the end. I need to remain cautious, Gabe. But on top of that, I fear *for* you."

He stepped up beside her, watching her soak in the moonlight. He studied the slope of her throat, travelling up her square jaw, across the curve of her cheekbone, and finally reaching the dull shade that had come over her eyes.

"What do you mean?" he asked, his voice almost inaudible.

Sable chuckled. "We both know how easy it is to be misled in this world. You're staying with me, because you're worried your Clo-Caillea is being fed lies, aren't you? Is it really that hard to believe I could be worried the same is happening to you?"

He threw back his head and belted out a laugh that jolted Sable's sensitive nerves. "My stone witch would likely laugh at me if such a thing happened—if she reacted at all." The shape of those words looked like sadness dancing off his tongue, even as he tried to hide it with humor. He looked up to watch the approaching storm. "I guess I should be grateful that you could find the energy to worry for me."

Sable grasped his arm and drew his attention back to her glowing eyes. "Understand this, Gabe. I am selective. I am not heartless, nor was I ever. I can be angry with you over our past and hesitate to ask for your help, but you are still a dear old friend, and I do care for you."

"Then tell me why you still jump when I touch you," he demanded, raising his hand to her cheek.

She turned away before he could reach her. Her eyes fell to the ground, and a breath shuddered out of her lips. At her sides, her fists were clenched.

Gabe looked at her with a pointed glare, stepping closer, daring her nerves to do it again. Her eyes ignited at his advance, and a lopsided smile snuck across his mouth. "See? Why can't I come near you without being greeted by either fear or fire?"

"And why is it imperative for you to come close?" she countered, crossing her arms.

He advanced again, standing close enough that he had to look down at her. She stood her ground, but her fingers tightened against her arms.

"You can't trust someone you fear to come into battle at your side."

His calm tone surprised her. She recognized her own words, now spoken against her. Defiant and enraged, she did not respond. Instead, she turned away, and they resumed their journey.

Not another word was spoken as Gabe trailed far behind her. His eyes sparked with a battle deep inside. The twilight spilled into his blue eye, illuminating it like a magical spring that twisted with worry. Its neighbor reflected the light of the stars above.

He hated being on the outside of that wall. Once, they had been friends, and she had no reason to deny any question he could come up with. She would admit her fears and pains without hesitation. Not because she trusted him. That would have been a sign that the world was coming to an end. She just had no reason to hide back then.

But she was no longer a child. Something had broken inside that had not been there before. The woman he traveled with now would not know trust in any living creature and would never allow herself to be seen as weak. Gabe chuckled to himself. Weak. She was anything but. However, if she didn't slow down, her wounds would bleed her dry, and then whose responsibility would it be to ensure she was alright? He picked up his pace, catching up to her.

"Sable, you need rest," he said once he reached her side.

"If we make camp on the side of this road, not only will

we get rained on, we will more than likely wake up with knives to our throats. You should know better than anyone this is the most dangerous road in the region."

He tried to ignore the way her monotonous tone tugged at his chest.

"Do you honestly think I would allow anyone to disturb us?" he asked. "I'm also slightly stronger than a thunderstorm, if you're worried about getting wet."

She stopped walking, turning her dull eyes to him. "Gabe, I will not rely on your powers to do *anything* for us until I know where they come from. Understood?"

He clenched his fists and glowered as she resumed walking.

~*The nearest town is another two-day's walk, and you are mortal,* her master reminded her.

Gabe's gift let him hear the words as well, pulling him into the squeezing heart of his companion as Sable closed her eyes and replied, *I don't want to insult you if he is using something that comes from evil, Father.*

The trickster didn't quite know how to feel about those words, but something inside him dropped from his chest to his toes. Her master's laughter tickled inside the hollowed out hole that had just opened up, despite the fact that he was speaking to her.

~*Your care is noble, and I love you for it. Let this moment increase your wisdom: you can take authority and pray for the atmosphere around you to only be that of righteousness. That way you will ensure that which is of me will be free, my child.*

When she looked up again, her gaze connected with the hard, studious stare of Gabe as he silently awaited her response. Her frown told him she suspected his eavesdropping, though she did not say anything about it.

"Fine, we'll make camp. But I don't want to see any red lights, black smoke, or sludge," she warned.

"Those are called illusions, Sable," he muttered, rolling his eyes.

He sighed, irritated, but he still obliged. His plan was nothing more than re-creating the psychic barrier he'd protected her with earlier, though creating a shack would have been much nicer.

"Hey, you know," he began, a wide grin on his lips as

the power came around them, "the best part about this is that we don't have to worry about a fire. I can make the dome generate heat."

His humor fell when she lowered herself to the ground, ignoring him. Her stiff muscles made the descent slow and clunky. She had to lower to her knees before she could slump into a seated position. He didn't miss the agony washing over her face, though she tried to smother it. Her eyes were glossed over, the flames faded into coals settling after the forge had been left to cool.

With mechanical fingers, she undid the hooks and belts holding the thick leather padding over her arms, sliding her wounded arm free of its protective confinement. Beneath the guards, the long sleeves of her vibrant blue shirt were tainted by the red soaking into it, turning it a deep midnight purple. As she worked her good arm free, Gabe saw her hand shake. Her fingers couldn't even bend around the first loop.

"We need to look at those wounds," he declared, standing over her.

She was so sluggish, his speed didn't even phase her. "I can bandage them myself," she snapped.

Gabe frowned, reaching for her scarlet arm anyway. He did so with care, allowing her to register his advance before he touched her. She let him hold her wrist, but she turned her face away. Her ministrations froze.

An ugly sadness registered on his face, but she didn't see it, although she heard it strangle his words. "Please, tell me what you're so afraid of, Sagentar Clo." He slipped another ancient word into her growing range of nicknames.

"What did you call me this time?" She whispered, unwilling to respond to the question.

"Guarded stone," Gabe replied.

She scoffed, shaking her head as a volatile smile came over her lips and her chin quivered. "I wish that were true," she admitted, turning to meet his mismatched eyes.

He looked down at her as if she were a precious gift that he'd broken after receiving. It caused the egg on her collarbone to shudder, scratching into the surface and threatening to crack open.

Pulling in a long, painful breath, Sable finally relented. "Do you remember the first time that you actually let me meet you? The day you named me the stone witch?" she prompted, her voice so soft it was almost missed.

He nodded, wondering where she was going with this. She faded from him though, her sad smile seeming lost as her gaze drew far away. Gabe held his breath.

"Why did you do that? What was it about me that told you that I belonged to those particular words?"

Gabe drew back at the inquiry, wondering with narrowed eyes if this was a trap. Would she use his answer to shut down this moment, or was her question genuine?

"That was what I saw," he explained after a pause. "You were a child, but you were not. You had the age, the body, sometimes even the naivety of one, but there was more. You were haunted and old. In your mind, I saw no dreams or fantasies, just a bleak understanding that you should never have known. And you were so cold. Ancient and intelligent beyond your years, you were like unforgiving ice. That was only the witch part though."

He removed his hand, reaching over her for her good arm. She didn't stop him. He kept his touch careful and slow as he undid the guards.

Gabe leaned back when he finished, giving her space. The silence had a strange comfort to it. He sat there appraising the woman with her blood-soaked sweater and her arm guards scattered around her. The metal across her chest seemed dull in the moonlight, unable to shine with all the grooves and scars it had taken to protect her. With her black curls spilling down like a river of coal and her jaw locked as she stared at the ground, he could see nothing of the child who loathed him for saving her life time and time again. She had grown into a fierce warrior, but it wasn't the armor that proved it. It was her willingness to face the aches she had spent her entire life trying to bury.

"I know about the stone egg you locked your feelings into when you were young," he admitted, answering a question she had asked herself as a child.

They dived into her memory together as his gift urged him along when she thought back, turning her eyes to the sky and remembering his arms around her the first day she met him. He'd saved her from thieves who had thought to sell her into slavery all over again once they realized she had no other worth to them. Her back had been held flush against his chest as she fought and squirmed in his grip, his harmless, ringing laughter already easing some of the rage even as she snapped at him.

"Don't touch me! He will destroy you!"

They both knew that her dear Kazious hadn't even begun to miss her yet, and Gabe had grinned at her statement. "I'd like to see him try."

That was the day she met the boy with a voice like storm clouds rumbling in a black sky. It soothed the egg incubating in her chest, the one she'd stuffed her emotions into when the shame and the fear had overwhelmed her younger self. The one that had grown with each hurt locked away until it threatened to suffocate her or crush her collarbone.

And yet, back in the present, Sable smiled, reaching up to pull at the laces for her next piece of armor, working with one awkward hand and one strong hand. "Do you know that the egg has been broken, and it's leaking out things that I still can't face?" she whispered.

Gabe frowned, shaking his head. She laughed. It was genuine and surprised.

"When exactly did you decide to stop exploring the depths of my mind?" she inquired, lifting the metal and leather over her head and laying it beside her.

"I tried my best to not pry from the moment we met. Some things my ability will just seek out without my direct commands though. I have always respected the boundaries of your mind." His voice became solemn and almost hurt.

She hummed in response, seeming to accept his answer. "So . . . You knew about Kazious, and you knew about the stone. Do you know how I came to have that burden and find my place at his side?"

Gabe shook his head, though he immediately played back the events of the night before when they were in the woods. Remembered the way she had dodged out of his reach when he meant to touch her shoulder. He'd sensed the way that her skin skittered, as if the reaction were his own.

His lips pulled into a tight line, and he dropped his gaze as she untied her cloak. She gave him time to think, her movements becoming mechanical as her throat closed off.

She started to reach for the hem of her sweater before

Gabe's hand rested on hers.

"What are you doing?" he asked, somewhat breathless.

She frowned, narrowing her eyes into flaming slits. "Likely not what you're thinking," Sable replied through her teeth. She seemed to become aware of herself though, seeing the misunderstanding. Her gaze dropped. "I'm going to let you help me with these wounds, alright? And I'll explain . . . everything."

Gabe's face lit up with a childish grin that sparked a new light into his mismatched eyes.

"You're going to trust me," he concluded, careful strings of hope fluttering behind the words.

She understood though, of course she would. She was the only person who'd ever been able to read him like an open book: The Immortal Trickster was not one who experienced trust from others in a genuine fashion.

"Yes, Gabe. I trust you," she said with a little smile as her sweater come off, revealing skin the color of moonlight and far too many scars. "I was a slave," she admitted.

CHAPTER 8

No sound escaped Gabe's lips. He frowned, drawing down his hollowed cheeks and highlighting the prominent bone structure of his face. His eyes darkened with a burning rage, and his fists remained clenched at his sides.

The wound on the front of Sable's shoulder was sticky with scarlet as it released blood in a steady stream down her arm. Another scabbed wound on the curve of her bicep cracked open in the deepest parts, adding to the blood that coated her delicate skin.

Her chest was covered by a cloth wrap, but she still raised her good arm to guard the area from Gabe, though his gaze was drawn elsewhere. Scattered across her ribcage and belly was a story written in pale innocent threads or thick, ugly, bloated cords. Some he recognized as souvenirs from numerous battles: a stab wound over her hip, arrows dug from her ribs, glancing blows from a blade deflected. Too many had a darker origin. They swayed up and around her abdomen like dancing snakes that bulged from her skin in shades of pink and lavender. Ropes of a foul memory that she would never be able to forget glared at him as if it was his fault they existed.

He turned away, denying the salt and liquid that appeared at his eyes. His thoughts bashed on his skull. *Stupid, stupid fool! You thought it was Kazious that she had to be protected from? You never saved her.* He could have laughed at the irony if it didn't make him so sick.

"Gabe," she said, "I still need your help."

Right, he reminded himself, turning back. She'd pulled out a cloth and was wiping away the red stain on her arm. Gabe moved to her side, avoiding the recognition of further silver white lines being revealed. He recognized letters carved into the curve of her hip, glaring at him from the pale indentations in her flesh. He locked his jaw, focusing on cleaning her wounds.

"My parents had the town convinced they'd been tricked by demons and lost their real child," she began, her tone as thin as mist. "I still only have guesses and speculations of what could have been so abhorrent about me as an infant that drove them to such measures."

The effort it took to keep his mouth shut already had his full attention. She handed him a rolled-up bandage, and he padded the open wound, locking his jaw as he worked. She continued in strained monotone, lost so far inside her history that his rough hands didn't make her flinch, even when he jostled her wounds.

"Eventually, they found a satisfactory way to get rid of their 'demon child,' so they wouldn't have to feel guilty or judged. Our mayor had a hunger for flesh. He used to call women and their children to the council chambers when the men were in the field. I solved that problem . . . sort of."

As soon as he tied off the bandage, Gabe dropped his hands from her as if her skin was fire. He flexed them a few times, curling his fingers until his nails bit into him and then releasing. His jaw followed suit. Clench. Release.

"Sometimes, I wondered if the others were left with so many scars. Did he sign his name on them, or was it just me, because I was a 'special treat'? I never spoke. I don't think my mother ever heard my voice unless I cried as an infant. I didn't fight back. I was just . . . there. A presence. A doll. Even before they gave me away. That was why it was so appealing to him. He didn't have to feel guilty, because I didn't cry."

She tilted her head, sounding far away and strange. Gabe heard a door in the back of her mind creaking open just a crack, then his gift watched as she was flooded with images that blinded her. Silent screams echoed in her ears as those hands came. The stone egg resting on her collarbone grew cold as the memories pulled at her. It stole away any reaction she might have shown, growing heavier with her misery until it once again threatened to shatter bone. Not that Sable would complain.

~*Come back*, her father whispered, the words coated with his love and jarring the man working on her wounds. ~*You are not your past; you were freed from it. Give this ache to me, and come back to this night.*

"Sable?"

Clarity returned like a mirror shattering overhead. She slammed the door shut, locked it, and cleared her throat.

Gabe was pressing some kind of ointment into the scab on her bicep, but he'd stilled in his ministrations to watch her. At that angle, she noticed the strange shape of a burn on his neck, which had been hidden from her until then. It was a circle nestled into the crook that curved into his shoulder. Inside, it had an arc on the top and the bottom with a small pill-shaped oval between. It was the shade of lilac, pale blue in some places. The scar tissue bulged as if it would be sensitive to touch. He turned back to his task, hiding the evidence of his torments from her once again.

"It's okay if it hurts, you know," he said as he massaged the skin around her wound. "Anyways, this should stop the scab from pulling apart the next time you draw your bow."

It took her a full thirty seconds to realize what he was talking about. She frowned at her bandages and the grey cream on her wound. His first statement had nothing to do with any physical ailment.

"I think my back is wounded," she mumbled. When Gabe moved to check, she appeared to wake from a daze and raised her hands. "Wait, no. Don't look. It's alright."

His blue eye flashed in the moonlight with easy recognition. He let out a heavy sigh. "It's worse back there, isn't it?"

Sable turned her face away, the first hint of crushing shame reaching her quiet orange eyes.

"I'll just look at the fresh wounds. I won't ask about or acknowledge the rest. Alright?"

She hung her head, allowing it. Gabe moved behind her, crouching down and biting back the gasp that grabbed at his throat.

It was all bulging ropes of scarring. They crisscrossed each other in layers across her shoulder blades. Some had been torn open by those overlapping them. He gulped down something that tasted like murder.

The purple painting covering them only highlighted the silver cords. Bruises blossomed like spilled ink, blotting over the back of her ribs with edges of midnight blue. In three places she had shallow wounds from when her armor had been pierced, but they had scabbed over and stopped bleeding. The red on her back had dried into the bruises, flakes already falling on their own.

"I don't suppose that 'master' of yours has healing capabilities," Gabe said with a sneer. He reached out but halted before touching her skin. "I'm going to touch you, okay?"

Sable nodded. Her gaze was far off, hard as steel and singing in terror. She didn't flinch when her aching muscles struggled to cry out under Gabe's rough, calloused palms. His fingertips worked over her back in slow, deliberate prodding. White fire raced through her at the irritated bruises, though she showed no signs of such pain.

"You probably tore a few muscles over your ribs, but the bruising should fade quickly. These wounds back here may not leave scars if they're taken care of properly. Unless, of course, someone could heal it supernaturally," he mused aloud.

She heard the grin in his voice, but his humor didn't register. Her silence wiped the look from his face, and he dropped his hands to his sides. She didn't know what he was talking about.

Shaking his head, he returned her bloody sweater to her. "If your master is who he claims to be, healing is something he should be able to do for you."

The haze in her eyes shuddered awake as she accepted the piece of clothing and slipped it on, freezing with tension when it was halfway down. She snapped her head around to look at him, fire raging in her eyes.

"How would you know that?" she whispered.

This time, the amused look had a malicious tilt in the side. "I wanted him to be real once too."

She clenched her jaw, narrowing her eyes. A long, slow exhale forced itself through her nose while she weighed the sincerity of that sentence.

"Horse crap," she declared finally. "You wouldn't give up control of your fate if your life depended on it!"

For a moment, she watched something dangerous cross his face, but the shadow faded. He gave her a studious expression, analyzing each curve of her face. Finally, he shrugged, his boyish smile returning as if he had been caught by an adult saying a dirty joke.

"I like that I actually have to try if I want to fool you," he declared with excitement.

"Or you could refrain from thinking I'll put up with your games altogether," she growled.

"Ah, but we're all part of a game, or did you forget that?"

Sable's frown deepened. She couldn't forget even if she wanted to. Her mind wandered back to the words he had used to answer her question years earlier. Before she'd learned about the legend of Gabe, she'd simply known him as a powerful stranger named Gabe who was bizarre, poetic, and gentle to an almost odd degree. She'd finally discovered his title as the Immortal Trickster after six months of being visited when she was away from Kazious. It had shifted something in their time together when she'd asked, "Am I on strings, Gabe?" She wasn't sure he had ever looked at her the same way since.

We're all puppets. Every last one of us.

Sable smiled sadly. "I think that was the most honest thing I ever heard you say. Yet even then, you were just talking in riddles."

His dark eye glinted with a mischievous spark. "Was I?"

The question struck her like a punch. *Maybe he does know a thing or two about the truth.*

Laughter tickled her mind, and she welcomed her

master's presence.

~*You mustn't forget he has lived a long time, child. He knows more than you realize.*

Sable felt her master's amusement like it was her own, and she smirked at the man before her. She had to remember he was not the twenty-year-old that he appeared to be. He was over twelve thousand years old. It was unlikely that she was the first person to reveal her master to him.

"Since we're on the topic of grand Daddy-O, have you figured out where this object is that's going to get us through that forest?" Gabe asked, the enthusiasm in his voice sounding silly with its deep rumble.

She shook her head. "I haven't actually asked."

He huffed a laugh, regarding her as if she had grown a second head. "The way you talk about consulting the voice in your head sounds a lot more normal to you than I ever would have expected."

She shot him a glare, but it held tamed flames. She closed her eyes, ignoring him. "Well, Father," she began, earning muffled chuckles, "where do we go now? How do we find our way to enter the gates and protect that town hidden within?"

Her father's laughter joined with Gabe's, and a moment later, her eyes popped open.

"You know where it is," she whispered.

He shrugged. "I must have missed the memo."

Sable frowned. "He didn't mean it like that, you putz. You know the person who has what we need."

He sniggered. "Well, he's going to have to be more specific. I'm an old man, Sable. I know a lot of people and have a fuzzy memory on top of that!"

He winked, earning an eye roll, though Sable smiled. She proceeded with the hints being fed into her mind. "The one who cares for you but constantly fights with you. A friend." She snorted. "Funny, I never knew you had those."

"I have only one, and not only does he not fight me unless I am not myself, he doesn't bother to worry over my wellbeing."

"Not the arch demon," she said, much to Gabe's obvious shock as his eyes asked her, *how would you know that*? "He's . . . he's an angel. But he's under the wrong title."

"Wrong title," Gabe echoed, knitting his eyebrows together.

"He doesn't believe he's the same as his brothers, because his blood is tainted."

A smile pulled back Gabe's lips. "You're talking about Abdaziel Lazyre. The first Mearizinaught, also known as a divine half-breed; as in: part demon." He leaned back on his hands and nodded in her direction, "guess who his daddy is?"

She frowned. "Do I need to care?"

"Probably. Abdaziel is the bastard child of Lucifer himself."

Her lack of reaction stole his humor away, and he settled into a somewhat serious demeanor. He raised his hand and counted off points as he spoke. "Okay, first, Zade is not a friend. That guy would rather swallow his own tongue than be civil with me. Second, how in the hell did *he* manage to get *your* master's symbol?"

Sable shook her head, her eyes bored and partly closed. "I'm not the one to ask, and neither do I care. Where can we find him?"

"Oh, that's easy. Just leave me within five feet of an easy-to-break mind, and he'll come swooping in like the hero he is to save the damsel in distress from my oh so evil tactics." He grinned.

"Don't mock," she grumbled. "Sometimes your tactics *are* evil. How *else* can we find him?"

Gabe heaved a sigh, hanging his head as he thought. She half expected him to say something about her ruining his fun, but he didn't. She waited as patiently as she could through her oncoming exhaustion. The blood loss and travels and possibly the building falling on her seemed to all catch up to her in that moment like a thick syrup was taking over the blood in her veins. Sable realized why her master had told her to rest. Her bones were growing heavy, and her eyes were stinging.

Her eyelids were half closed before Gabe glanced up. He frowned at the sight of her. If she were in her right mind, she might have noticed the reluctant clarity in his gaze, or the way it was chased away by something almost like shame.

"I know where he is," he said, his voice solemn as the

thunderclap reverberated through her chest. “But he doesn’t like strangers knowing how to reach him.”

He wouldn’t meet her eyes.

“What will we do then?” she asked, even as the syrup solidified into lead and demanded she lie down.

Gabe let out an irritated sigh. “Don’t worry. It seems I can kill two birds with one stone this time.”

Her heart skipped. What did that mean?

But it was too late. She couldn’t keep her eyes open anymore, and blackness stole her away. The only thing she recognized was Gabe’s warm breath against her cheek.

“Don’t be afraid,” he whispered into her ear.

Her stone egg choked off her ability to breathe. Arms wrapped around her, lifting her up beside a drum so soft it almost comforted her galloping terror. With the last of her sluggish will, she threw her thoughts out and begged, *Father, help me!*

His presence came over her, snapping into place in response to her desperate prayer, but he did not wake her. Instead, he settled over her like a blanket, and even though tears streamed down her cheeks, peace swelled within.

Sable slept.

CHAPTER 9

He sits across from me, his thin lips pulled down into a hard frown. A glowing white ribbon is wound across his eyes, tied behind his head, his long silver hair pulled back by a leather cord. He has his arms on the table between us, his hands clasped together. His nails are like glass, shiny and clear. A memory flashes, briefly reminding me of how lethal they are.

Kazious seems a stranger to me at this moment.

I wish to reach out to him, but the movement is denied by my body. The limb didn't move from my side. My throat seizes with terror, choking me as I clench my jaw until I see colors behind my eyes.

"Where have you gone?" my dear friend asks, an edge of irritation in his voice.

My mouth drops open to answer, but no words will

come. Where have I gone? How Can I tell him what I have done: that I reached out for help from the one being whom he's dedicated his entire existence to loathing? How many times can I remember him telling me that he will make the angels and their creator weep from the heavens?

I have no words for the betrayal that I have committed to save his life.

The way his frown pulls back into a hard line and his jaw clenches tells me that he already knows the answer. I have forgotten that he has the same gift as my deranged companion.

"So then, even you - with your intimate understanding of abandonment - would leave your savior and friend."

Tears sting the corners of my eyes, but I can't utter a defense despite the words squirming like worms in my chest. The initial horror at my immobility has been drowned under the weight of his disapproving frown.

"I made a mistake in my judgement back then," he states in a level tone. "It appears that even with your experiences and your wisdom, you are still no better than the rats that I saved you from." His words crack open my ribs with measured blows. He shakes his head slowly, leaning over the table. "I should have killed you that day," he mutters, as if speaking to himself.

The utterance pulls the floor out from beneath my feet. My heart falls into a blackened chasm. My entire journey has been reliant upon finding a way to release the very hatred that is blinding him as he speaks.

He cracks his knuckles and I feel their pop inside my heart. "That can be rectified with ease though."

I close my eyes when he lunges, too tired to care about my defense.

His hands clench around my throat with bruising force, squeezing until fire races across it and down into my collarbone. Warm fluid drips down my cheeks, but I do not raise my hands to claw at his. He lifts me out of my seat. My throat throbs and my arms remain limp at my sides. I think something has collapsed in my throat. I can't breathe. The air stills in my lungs, diving away from the violence. I cough.

As my mind begins to fade, it draws up that moment when I was a child and had first met the blind man. The hands stealing away my life now had been dripping in scarlet that day when he'd commanded me to place my chains into them. The strength that is taking its careful time choking the life from me had disintegrated the linked metal into dust with a simple gesture. I'd walked out of that place with my tiny hand clasped inside the red stain of his larger one.

~If you are unwilling to fight the evil within him, you will never save him.

"I-I'm so sorry," I choke, not quite sure for whom the apology is meant.

~~~

An ugly sound tore through the room when her eyes flashed open, and she bolted upright. The remains of the fire in her throat still licked at her skin, even as the pressure of the powerful hand fell away, replaced by her own frantic hand feeling for a phantom. The sting in her throat confirmed the sound had been her own scream, cut short by the blockage where the stone egg had grown to close it off. Her heart pounded, each beat aching in her chest.

"Sable, you're okay now," the voice of rolling thunder coaxed as he placed a hand on her shoulder.

Reality snapped into focus. "Get your hand off me," she hissed, "before I chop it off!"

He obeyed, pulling away and standing up from the bed. Gabe took three steps back, his expression tight with worry. His brown eye glowed almost gold as flickering light illuminated that side of his frowning face.

"You were having a nightmare," he explained.

Sable turned away as a fresh tear slipped down her cheek.

"Kazious tried to kill me," she whispered.

Gabe's eyes widened, and his mouth fell open. He didn't make a sound though. It was as if his response had tumbled to the floor instead. The silence pounded in her ears while Sable struggled to regain her composure.

He gulped, regaining his voice. "Do you think it was a real attack from his mind gift, or just a dream?"

She shook her head, wrapping her arms around her body. It wouldn't make any sense for the prison to allow his gifts to reach beyond its walls. She shivered and closed her
~~~

eyes. Pulling in a long breath, she counted down inside her mind. *Let it go . . . three . . . two . . . one . . ..*

When her eyes opened, the fire was alive again.

"What did you do to me, Gabe?" her voice was like stone. "You orchestrated that somehow. The way I passed out, I mean."

He sighed heavily in resignation. Then he pointed to her arm. She glanced down and realized her gear was gone, as was her sweater. Instead, she was dressed in a short-sleeved tunic and a pair of slacks, which let her see the softened scab on her arm. The grey ointment had been wiped away.

"I didn't know if the side effects were what I assumed they would be until it started to affect you. All I wanted to do was help; that's it," he explained, his words quickened in a way that seemed unlike him.

"You can start making sense now," she said, glowering.

"I made that ointment to help with healing. It was mostly for me, since I heal almost as slowly as humans do," he began, wringing his hands. Yet another indication of uncharacteristic anxiety. "I could only guess at how it would affect someone weaker than me. At least my suspicions were correct, and all it did was make you take the rest you sorely needed."

He shrugged, looking down at the floor in perfect misery. As if he was actually worried about her. She would have scoffed, but he was still talking.

"I put it on you to help with that wound's healing, since your archery was keeping it open, but I also hoped it would let you rest. The plan was to get you to sleep for a few hours. That was it. But then you wanted to see Abdaziel, and if you didn't want him bashing in my skull upon arrival, you couldn't know how to get here. Hence what I said before you passed out: Two birds, one stone. The ointment put you to sleep, and I brought you to where your master instructed."

Sable crossed her arms over her chest, a sinister smile on her lips. "So, out of the kindness of your heart, you drugged me and took me to a stranger's home, from which I have no ability to find my way back?"

He narrowed his eyes at her, the blue orb a chilled glacier, his jaw set, teeth clenched. "I brought you exactly where you wanted to be."

"You could have told me! This is why no one trusts you, Gabe. You wouldn't know transparency even if it bit you," she snapped, throwing her arms out in anger.

Gabe didn't respond, and maybe it was the silence that made her realize the shape of those words. Her eyes went wide, the flames dimming. He swallowed a hard breath, looking away from her toward the door.

"Gabe, wait—"

He raised his hand, silencing her. "You're right."

"What?"

"You're better off without me around screwing everything up."

Lost for words, she watched him leave. His eyes were dull, fogged with something that could have been a memory. Or many.

~He is misguided, child, but you were in no danger. I was with you, as always.

Sable bowed her head to the chastisement and breathed in a slow, calming breath. How could she fix the new wound she'd punched into him?

She heard the thud of a door slamming, and her throat constricted. He'd left the house. The house of the stranger who would *bash in the immortal trickster's skull* for making a mistake.

More thudding told her someone was approaching the room. She stood up, her heart rising into her throat as she readied herself. Where was her armor? Where were her weapons? Would any of that even matter against the divine creature?

An angel with tainted blood. The bastard child of Lucifer himself.

When he came to the doorway and saw Sable raising her fists like she'd fight him with her bare hands, a gentle smile graced his lips. He didn't enter the room, and he even raised his hands to show he was unarmed.

"I guess you're Abdaziel," she stated, squaring her jaw.

He nodded slowly, his burgundy bangs falling across his dark midnight blue eyes. His long, curly hair tumbled like a thick red river over his shoulders and down his back. It pulled color into his pale skin, dusting his cheeks like blush and giving them warmth.

No, she realized. He was glowing. Lights swirled like

fluid beneath his skin, as if his blood were filled with tiny dancing candle flames.

His features weren't as sharp as Gabe's, giving him the soft, smooth slope of a gentleman's face. He had a roundness to the top of his cheeks, so when he smiled, he appeared just short of drunk. A jolly man's cheek. He was shorter than Gabe, close to her own height, yet his stature seemed huge somehow.

As if inspired by curiosity, her gift stuttered half-awake inside to let her see the waves of power bending in the air, rolling out of him in time with the rhythm of a heartbeat. She fought down the surge of instinctive jitters.

"Don't be afraid," he whispered, whether to her gift or her fists, she was unsure.

Did he share the same mind gift as Gabe? She could only guess.

His words seemed directed to the egg inside more than to Sable, and they floated across to her on a warm wind that pressed gentle hands to her collarbone, soothing the tension. Her heart still skipped a beat.

"Don't talk," she gasped.

He ignored her instruction, tucking his hands behind his back and glancing out of the room. "He won't hold it against you; I wouldn't worry. Gabe doesn't hold grudges. If he did, he'd never have anyone to wrap up into his little games."

Sable narrowed her eyes as the egg shrank with the calming touch of his voice. *I don't know what this power is*, she prayed silently, *but if it's not of his angelic side, remove its effects from me.*

"I don't think 'little' is the right word for his games when they involve the possible harm of innocent people," she said aloud.

Abdaziel nodded, smiling in satisfaction. "I had a suspicion about you when he arrived here."

The wind curled into her chest again. She let out a long, heavy breath and then finally allowed it to ease into her muscles. *Fine.* She raised an eyebrow at his statement, bidding him to continue.

"He doesn't normally care about the effects of his antics. With you . . . he was actually worried about how you would feel. He kept muttering about how you were going to kill him when you finally woke." He chuckled, his smile widening. "I would love to see that."

"No, you wouldn't," she deadpanned. "You don't hate him. You just have no patience for him. That little façade is insulting to my intelligence though."

She half expected him to snap at her. Instead, his smile became full and glorious. The light from within bloomed until it looked like the sun itself was shining from his bones.

"I do hope you will succeed where I was not strong enough," he said earnestly.

Sable shook her head. "I'm not here for Gabe's sake nor for your approval. You have something of my father's, and I need to retrieve it before more innocent lives are lost."

His demeanor settled back into the gentle jolly man, his light fading to a subtle glow. He even pulled back those powerful waves, tucking them away somewhere. She could almost mistake him for a human if not for the cloud of peace lurking behind his lips.

"Well, come then, we have much to discuss," he said, turning out of the room with his eyes half closed, as if bored suddenly.

So, is this what angels are like? She mused while she followed him out.

~Only those who are confused, my dear. He needs your help too.

"Of course he does," she muttered.

CHAPTER 10

She followed him out into a short hallway. It was void of decoration save for one lopsided painting just before they reached the next room. It was of a girl with thick, curly wisps of blood-colored hair and pale, glowing skin. Her grey storm cloud eyes were flaked with shards of gold, the edges pulled down by the frown on her pouting lips. It was as if she were moments from weeping or had come to the painter just after breaking down.

Her sadness clung to Sable as they entered the shack's main room. It was divided on one side by a sheet hanging off crude hooks nailed to the ceiling. The visible side had a stone fireplace with an iron grating over it for cooking, positioned just a few steps from the front door. Between that and the sheet stood a small black dining table with grey steaming mugs already waiting upon it.

Sable remained standing when her host took a seat at the end of the table that sat in front of the window next to the door. Sunlight pooled across his shoulders, making his curls glow like warm blood.

"Was she your daughter?" she inquired.

He gave her a confused look, prompting her to point back toward the hall. "That painting. She looks like you, I thought . . .." Her voice trailed off as his face fell.

He remained subtle about it, but his set jaw caused something dark to flash behind his eyes, and he looked away. "She was someone I was meant to protect. Creators forgive me."

She asked no further questions. Silence surrounded them as Sable stood wringing her hands and fiddling with her fingers. She avoided the misery in his gaze, looking into the coals of the faded fire beside her instead.

"Tell me about your father," Abdaziel prompted, causing her to jump. He gestured toward the chair across from him when she glanced up. "Come sit. Let's see if I can help you while we wait for Gabe's return."

She didn't start right away but rather fell into her secret heart to pray again. *How do I do this?* she asked. *How do I get the answers that I need? I don't even know him.*

No response came as the seconds ticked by into a quiet minute. Abdaziel was patient though, watching as she allowed herself to be seated at the table. She stared into her tea, frowning.

"Do you know much about Calamities?" she began, choosing her words with care.

The man tilted his head to the side, shooting her an inquisitive smile. "Disastrous events? I have seen many in my long lifetime. Does a particular one stand out to meet your needs?"

She chewed her lip, narrowing her eyes. His tone was off, as if he were mocking her. It was subtle though, easily misinterpreted.

Does he know what they are? she prompted, caution wrapping a fist around her throat. She couldn't afford to be as blunt with him as she had been with the elder the other day.

Silence came to her mind, and she closed her eyes for the space of a short breath. She couldn't afford to wait either. She took the lack of response as a sign of trust, so she followed her gut.

"A race of creatures by that name has masqueraded as something they are not. The Calamities have deceived many for thousands of years," she explained.

Something coiled behind the night sky in his gaze when she spoke, giving her a surge of confidence. She smiled.

"You have heard of them before," she concluded, crossing her arms over her chest. "And yet you follow the lie of the Sanctum, even knowing what they are?"

She watched confusion filter into his jaw and wondered if he'd made the full connection yet. The Divine Sanctum was a belief system based on the idea of Light and Darkness as the creators, something Sable's father had proved false with ease. If Abdaziel couldn't believe her father existed, he would not be able to recognize the item she needed to gain from him. But her father's existence alone was enough to prove his creators were a lie. The acceptance of her father would create a flaw in what this man had known for his entire life.

He tightened his fist around his mug. "I know of the race of legendary demons, yes," he responded slowly and with conviction, "but I don't see what an old, extinct group of fools has to do with the Sanctum."

That was the entire truth right there: the Calamities *were* the sanctum. They were the gods and the creators. They were all no more than demons. She had already discovered their true identities, but as he'd said, the current lore claimed the Calamities were destroyed. Except that the creators and their race of gods had the same characteristics, abilities, and *limitations* of those demons. His mind was moving though, and it shouldn't be hard to recognize the link. She could see it in his expression and didn't grace him with a response right away. *Let him spin for a while . . . will he float or sink?*

He cleared his throat, locking his gaze with hers and narrowing his midnight eyes into slits. "I'd like to know what any of this has to do with what I supposedly have from your father."

Her smile widened. "It has everything to do with him. My father is the god unknown and forgotten, replaced by fakes."

Sable braced for a bolt of rage. Some form of recoil. A violent outburst even. Anything but the laughter that erupted from him. His eyes glistened with mirth, and the sounds wrapped around her like liquid sunlight. The glow returned to his skin, creeping in with the rhythm of his laughter.

"You want me to believe you are the offspring of a god?" he asked. "Children of the divine race, even half-breeds, are incredibly powerful. You're only human!"

She almost chuckled but then stopped herself. "That's because he has nothing to do with the divine race. He is higher yet." She pulled in a long breath, reciting something her father had taught her in the beginning of her walk under his guidance. "*But as many as received him, to them he gave power to become the sons of God, even to them that believe on his name; which were born not of blood, nor of the will of the flesh, nor of the will of man, but of God.*"

He stared at her, his humor gone. She thought there was recognition inside his gaze, but that wouldn't make sense.

"I am adopted," she concluded cheekily.

His idea of gods were not known for such actions. They cared more for divine, inhuman creatures with great power and were not inclined to take in "children." Sable watched his jaw lock, squaring out his gentle sloped cheeks, then release.

"Unknown and forgotten," he echoed under his breath. "Alright, I'll bite. Tell me about this 'father' of yours. We'll discuss that claim of false gods later."

Sable finally allowed herself to relax a bit. She dipped her pinky into the teacup and stirred the brown fluid. In the back of her mind, Gabe's absence slipped into a place of worry. She wondered where he had gone and if he would return to her before this delicate situation turned dire. Had she broken something in their rebuild that could never be fixed? Would she escape this divine being's home to find out?

She focused on the half-angel, drawing her brows together as she tried to organize her thoughts away from the immortal trickster. With careful deliberation, she explained her father to the best of her ability.

"He is love itself. He loves with no requirement from us.

His love encompasses our good and our evil, and if anyone seeks him out, he welcomes them no matter their transgressions. He holds no grudge against us, and he will help anyone change their ways if they come to him."

Sable let a soft chuckle leave her throat as another truth came to her lips, one she still had a hard time admitting. "He loved me even when I was travelling with Kazious, a madman and a murderer who was hell-bent on making my father cry long before he ever adopted me. I spent three years watching people die as if it were the most normal thing, and he doesn't hold it against me. He . . . he understands." Tears could be heard in her throat even though her eyes remained dry. "He knew all that time that my heart was turned to stone. That I couldn't feel. That I wanted to, but I couldn't." She sounded far away but came back with a quiet scoff as she shook her head. "He even loves Kazious."

Abdaziel leaned back in his seat, his expression softening as he watched old wounds open in the girl. He sipped his tea and smiled gently. She was a child. Oh, she was a warrior and a grown woman, but even in the few moments he'd had with her, he could tell. Inside, she was a newborn still trying to understand what to do with her emotions. That was how he knew she told the truth. Her soul sang with it.

"Who was Kazious?" he asked, prompting her to crawl further into her pain, not out of malice but for the sake of drawing her out.

She pulled in a long, quivering breath. "Kazious saved me from a life of violation and shame, but he was far from a good man. He told me that my experiences gave me the intellect to be 'higher than the rats' he'd killed—rats being my entire village. I was too young to survive on my own, and I'd been in chains for the majority of my childhood. I knew I wouldn't make it far alone. So, he took me with him, albeit with reluctance. I traveled at his side throughout that bloody path for three years until he was imprisoned by the Tazera Illusionists, the immortal governance appointed to watch over the balance between human and divine."

The angel heard tears growing in her voice. He frowned. Soon they would reach her eyes. He was familiar with the end of that story, but he'd never tell her that.

"And this 'father' of yours?"

Her eyes flared, snapping her old wounds shut. She even smiled.

"He's going to set Kazious free," she declared with a resonance that raised the man's eyebrows. "Not just from the prison but from the evil inside him as well."

Yet the resonance faltered, her tone hiccupping on itself.

"You don't sound so confident about that," Zade observed. "How can you be so certain of this freedom yet doubt his cleansing?"

Sable released a heavy sigh, her brows drawing together into a glare. It was choked off by the resignation in her face. "Because it's a matter of choices, and if he won't let go when my father offers to save him, I don't know what will happen."

He leaned forward, watching her closely. "Evil cannot be released on innocent people just because it 'belongs' to a loved one."

Now her glare was real, lighting up the forges in her amber eyes. "I will not let him hurt anyone else if he is set free." Something broke in her tone, crawling away from her lungs and cowering deep inside.

"You're prepared to kill him," Abdaziel concluded.

Sable turned away, gulping down a breath that got stuck in her throat. She would never admit it aloud. She couldn't.

"I am continually proven wrong about you. I should apologize for underestimating you," he admitted, tilting his head in a slight bow.

Sable gulped down stones in her throat and glanced back in time to catch, and despise his gentle, admiring smile. "Anyways, that's why I'm here now and not with Kaz. I'm being taught how to be steadfast and strong, so my father can trust that I can lead him."

Abdaziel leaned back, the corners of his eyes pulling tight as if he were suppressing a laugh. This was too good. He doubted she would ever come to understand the irony, but he would try to explain.

"Do you not realize the entire point of his incarceration was for your safety?" he asked in a slow, tender way that almost sounded sincere.

She narrowed her eyes at him, which inspired a gentle smile that brought back the glow beneath his skin. He continued to answer the unspoken inquiry of how he could possibly know anything about that time with ease. "Gabe cares for few people. When you mean something to him that goes beyond his games, he will protect you even if it makes you despise him. Your friend sounds dangerous and unstable. I can see Gabe fearing for your life as you traveled with him, and he does keep powerful company."

Sable scoffed, crossing her arms over her chest. "What gave you the crazy idea the Immortal Trickster would care for a human?"

"Because he left you afterwards. If you were just a game, a part of his study, something his sights were fixated on for the sake of his insanity, he never would have turned away once he had you isolated and in perfect shape for his manipulation. But he did leave, and he stayed away until now."

Sable gritted her teeth, glancing away as she bit down on the ache dripping into her throat. "Well, I'm not the same little girl he thought he was saving."

"Oh, really? Tell me, what's so different now, other than trading in who you'll blindly follow?"

"The difference is that I'm not blind. I know who my father is and who I was intended to be. I will not be swayed from that, not even by one whom I love," she snapped, unable to contain the ache that reared up within her.

The words were sparked by a dark memory, the final day she'd seen her teacher. In the end, it was her father who had been the topic of Rose's betrayal. But no one, not even the loving woman who was the closest thing to a friend Sable had ever known, could deter her loyalty to him. That experience was her lesson about how strong her love for her father was. She clenched her fists to push away the blood in her mind. Her reaction did not go unnoticed.

"Interesting," he muttered, nodding. "Tell me more about him."

She tipped her lips up in a soft smile as her veins started to heat up with a soft pulse. It was a feeling she'd become well used to. The one which made others see her skin glow. *The helper. The holy spirit.* It was becoming excited within her.

Recognition flashed across Abdaziel's face, confirming her assumption about the light moving beneath her skin. Sable suppressed a laugh when he glanced down at his arm and back up. He said nothing, though, and she moved along, lost in the warmth of the only memory that had never brought a chill into her stone egg.

"My father is love itself," she repeated, almost inaudibly. "He loved me when I was a broken, blubbering mess of a child, and with that love, he guided me until I became this humble warrior sitting before you.

"He is good and just. He has no equal, because none are worthy of his glory. He's . . . he's perfect. He will forgive even the darkest atrocities so long as you will let go of it. He brings grace and order where only pain and chaos could reside before him. What else can I say?"

The man remained silent, drawing the information in with a frown. Sable fought the urge to fidget beneath his analyzing stare, finding it even more unnerving than Gabe's.

"What is it about him that changed you?" he asked finally. The question brought her up short. He leaned forward, folding his hands together to hold up his chin. "From what I was led to understand, you were quite the little spitfire as a child. I'd heard Gabe's rantings about you back then. How did this god's 'love and grace' change that? I would assume if he is the embodiment of such things, it would leave marks on anyone who's been near it, yes?"

She heard genuine curiosity in his tone as he theorized about her father, broadening her smile.

"He brought me back to life," she replied softly.

The subtle quake in her tone wasn't missed; she caught his flinch when he heard it.

"How?" he demanded. Then he seemed to become aware of etiquette again and cleared his throat. "If you don't mind my asking."

Sable frowned while she struggled for words. How could she explain without prying open her ribcage and flooding him with anguish from her darkest days? She let out a long, slow breath. Then she uttered words her father had given her before. One more teaching to give away.

"A new heart also will I give you, and a new spirit will I put within you: and I will take away the stony heart out of

your flesh, and I will give you a heart of flesh."

She was looking down into the cooling fluid in her mug, so she didn't see Zade's eyebrows rise.

"Where did you hear these riddles?" he queried with an edge of awe.

Glancing up, she shrugged and knitted her brows together. "He spoke these things to me when I asked him for understanding while he changed me. I was instructed to not forget them."

He stood with such quiet ease that it formed a knot of worry in Sable's chest. Then he pulled back the curtain beside them, showing her why he'd moved.

The other half of the room was a library. It had floor-to-ceiling shelving units bursting with books and scrolls and loose papers. She counted six units in total, filled on both sides and spanning the length of the room while each wall had another two against it. Most tomes were falling apart from what she could see, some held together by nothing more than string wrapped around the loose pages.

She moved to stand, but Zade raised a hand to still her, shaking his head. "Wait here. I know what you have come for."

He dropped the sheet back into place when he disappeared behind it.

Sable eyed her tea while she waited. She stirred it again with her finger, watching the surface ripple, the fluid now lukewarm.

A thick, old tome hit the table beside her cup. Its cover was made of hardened leather, and its thin, yellow pages were curling along the edges.

"Do you recognize it?" the man inquired, leaning his hip against the table.

She shook her head. "No. Is this what you had of my father's?"

He let out a soft laugh, his dark eyes sparking in the light. "You knew you were here for something of his, but you didn't even know what to look for?"

The remark drew her mouth down into a hard frown. "He told me where to find what I needed, not *what* to find," she explained. "So, what is this book?"

The redhead shrugged, smiling down at her. "I thought it was nothing more than a fairytale until about ten seconds ago when you quoted it verbatim—for the second time, I might add. And this is the only copy left. The rest were all destroyed long ago. So, why don't you take a good look and tell me what that is?"

She glanced down at it, running her fingers across the cover. Her chest grew hard and tight, but she couldn't decide if it was anxiety or anticipation.

"I don't think it will bite," he prompted, his peaceful wind returning to untie the knot behind her collarbone.

"Stop doing that," she muttered halfheartedly as she flipped the book open and began to read. *"He was appalled and afflicted, he did not open his mouth; he was led like a lamb to the slaughter, and as a sheep before the shearer is silent, so he did not open his mouth . . . ."* She pinched a chunk of the pages, flipping to another place at random and began again. *"Come to me, all you who are weary and burdened, and I will give you rest."* One more time, she turned the pages to a place at random. *"Before I formed you in the womb, I knew you, before you were born I set you apart . . . ."*

She stopped reading aloud, furrowing her brows as she bowed her head closer to read the text more thoroughly.

Her lips moved to shape the words, but she did not speak them out loud. Again, she flipped through the book to lean in and read.

Understanding washed over her and the warmth in her veins was almost *singing*. She gasped. "This . . . this is . . . ." Sable stopped to gulp down a huge breath, so she could calm down again. "These are his teachings! This is a collection of people recollecting their experiences with my father, he's spoken many of these to me! This must be what the Calamities buried."

Abdaziel frowned and crossed his arms over his chest as he analyzed the girl's excited fiery eyes. They raced across the pages faster than he thought possible. She would read a few lines on a page, flip a few pages, and then find something else to soak up, all while telling him what the words were saying. Either reading them aloud or commenting on how she had received the same teaching. He was irritated by the book, but he admired her childish joy. A moment earlier, one threatening movement would have had her pressing a blade to his throat without question. She wouldn't have hesitated to defend herself, not caring if she would win, and she was cautious of his every movement. Now the warrior was gone in the breath of a page, replaced with the excitement of a child welcoming home her long-lost father. There she was, sharing this groundbreaking discovery with an inhuman man whom she had feared less than a few moments earlier as if it wasn't ripping a hole open in his entire world if it was all true.

"Stop," he croaked, almost begging. "I have heard enough."

Sable stuttered to a halt and looked up at Abdaziel, whose face was twisted in confused irritation. He cast his dark eyes to the ground, working his jaw as he decided what to say next.

"How do you know this text tells the truth?" he asked slowly and deliberately, as if hoping she wouldn't miss the sincerity of his question.

She tugged gently on his arm and pointed at her current page. "Look at this," she instructed. "Read this aloud for me, alright?"

He leaned close to the text and did as he was told. "*The eye is the lamp of the body. If your eyes are healthy, your whole body will be full of light. But if your eyes are unhealthy, your whole body will be full of darkness.*" He looked up at her. "What does that even mean?"

"At the moment, it doesn't matter," Sable replied, flipping pages in a less random manner. She searched the texts on a few pages before finding something to satisfy her. Nodding to herself, she began reading again. *"Your eye is the lamp of the body. When your eyes are healthy, your whole body also is full of light. But when they are unhealthy, your body also is full of darkness."*

He turned to catch the glow in her large serious eyes. "Why did he repeat himself?"

She almost smiled when she shook her head. "That's the thing: he didn't. This is the account of another man who heard the same teaching. Let me show you."

She flipped back a few pages to where he could see a clear beginning to that section, like the opening of a chapter. *"Many have undertaken to draw up an account of the things that have been fulfilled among us,"* Sable read, *"just as they were handed down to us by those who from the first were eyewitnesses and servants of the word. With this in mind, since I myself have carefully investigated everything from the beginning, I too decided to write an orderly account for you."*

The man had narrowed his eyes to read over her shoulder, double and triple checking the introduction. She glanced up, her smile like that of a patient teacher. "This book appears to be a collection of smaller manuscripts that all talk about experiences over thousands of years with the same god. The very one who has been with me for thirteen years. This last part focuses on a man that my father has told me about. His son—not adopted but his actual biological son."

Abdaziel stared at her for a long moment. He didn't appear upset so much as strained. A hard breath fell from his mouth. "Okay, so what about this makes your other claims true?"

"In any of your stories, Light and Darkness have limitations. The history itself says they created the race of gods as an answer to the universe tearing itself apart to accommodate their creations. The gods were designed to fill the anomalies, because they couldn't sustain reality itself. My father is not bound by this physical world though. He has no limitations, and as far as I know, that means he has no equal. He is the only one who is not bound by physical laws. I already knew all this, but you can find it in these texts as well."

He wore a hard frown, soaking in the information with serious consideration. He remained quiet for a short period, during which Sable observed the gears working in his expression.

After what felt like hours of tense silence, he closed his eyes and released a sigh. "I hope you realize I'm not about to believe this offhand."

Sable shook her head. "I never expected you would. I didn't come here to change your mind, nor does the truth need a defense."

His soft smile returned, giving his face a slight glow. "You are wise, and I like that."

"I'm not so sure if it's wisdom. I have simply lived long enough with darkness to know what light is, and I will not be swayed easily from it."

He released a full, joyous laugh. "You would not be nearly as interesting if you could. The book seems to be rightfully yours. You may remove it from my archives."

The compliment caught her off guard. Still, she nodded her thanks. "I wouldn't have left without it anyways," she mumbled.

"You say that like it would have been a bad thing." His easy laughter tumbled out again.

Her cheeks heated up, and she locked her jaw beneath his stare. His midnight-blue eyes sparked with amusement at her discomfort. She turned away from him, returning her gaze to the book on the table and gulping down a long breath. His smile widened.

Abdaziel leaned down as if glancing at the book as well, but his hand came to rest near hers, and she felt his face draw close. "Can I ask you something?"

His whisper sent warm air down her cheek. She didn't respond, her fists clenching. The change in him was tightening her belly into knots.

"What are you doing at Gabe's side?" he asked softly.

She turned up to see him bent down over her, fire racing into her throat at the threatening position. Still, she narrowed her eyes and refrained – *just barely* – from throwing a punch.

"I'm doing what no one else seemed to have the patience for," she responded through her teeth.

He straightened up, letting loose another chuckle. "I can't tell if you're brave or just naïve. You would truly risk your life to remain beside him, even knowing he could kill you one day?"

Her flaming eyes narrowed to slits. "Without hesitation."

"You're not blind to his insanity. You know what he's capable of," he mused, almost too quiet for her to hear, as if speaking to himself. He shook his head. "Gabe drugged you to bring you here and then left you in my care. He knew I wouldn't bring you harm, but you didn't. For all you know, I could have been your absolute worst nightmare in the flesh." He tilted his head to the side, and his tone became almost mystical, "you are so fragile . . . so human. What makes this worth it?"

She stared into his gaze, finding no threads of malice or ill will. He genuinely wanted to understand her. Seeing that allowed her tense muscles to loosen, if only a little. Perhaps that twinkle shivering in the blue darkness of his midnight gaze was a thread of hope for their immortal trickster.

"He can't be expected to show others what he himself has never known," she whispered, her animosity fading even from her voice. "He wants to be trusted, but he has never been given the chance to learn trustworthiness."

Abdaziel's face hardened as if she'd slapped him.

"Do you truly understand the danger that you're in though?" he asked, his voice strained. "Do you know about the passenger in his mind? The other Gabe, the demon that would tear you to pieces and laugh at the gore if he ever took over while you were there? Do you realize the time bomb with whom you travel?"

Sable placed a hand on his chest and urged him back another step. He crossed his arms, his face tight with anguish. This was not the first time he'd given this warning.

"I know," she admitted. "I have heard the stories of him. The god of chaos, they call him. The calamity trapped inside him from his demented creator. I know those dangers, Abdaziel. Be assured: I did not make this decision blindly."

"Then why are you shouldering this burden?"

A smile teased her lips as she glanced toward the window. "Because my father can save him. We love him, and it hurts to watch him struggle. I would rather die than abandon him."

He couldn't respond. His mouth hung open, but no words would fill the silence.

A thud struck the door, jolting them back into the world. They turned to the noise just as the door flew open, and the very topic of discussion burst through, wild eyed.

"Speak of the devil and he appears," the half-angel muttered.

Gabe's eyes scanned the small space until he found the pair at the table. He bolted toward them. "Sable, I royally screwed up. I'm so sorry!"

The sound of a splintering crash filled the small room, spewing shards of glass across the table. Sable snapped her attention back to the sound, her vision blocked by a bloody hand inches from her nose. A thin piece of wood tipped with a grey pyramid of razor edges peaked through Abdaziel's palm. She watched a thick black substance ooze out around the bolt intended for her.

Why must everyone be filled with such darkness?

Another bolt shattered her untouched mug, spilling warm tea across the table.

CHAPTER 11

"How exactly did you manage to lead the *only* idiot who wouldn't care about fighting you and I right to the exact person you think you're going to protect?" Abdaziel shouted.

Two more bolts flew through the window, but Gabe had already yanked Sable out of her chair. Her knees hit the ground, and she hissed. She had to use every ounce of willpower to stop herself from punching Gabe as he dragged her toward the wall and shielded her with his body.

"I had no idea he was hired to kill *her*!" He yelled over his shoulder.

Gabe grabbed her face in his hands and turned it to meet his galloping eyes. "I'm going to protect you, but we don't have time to argue about how. You can hate me later."

She opened her mouth to retort but snapped it shut

when the black smoke began to wrap around her. It felt cool against her skin, not lashing out this time but she could almost feel how reluctant it was to refrain from doing so. He poured it out through his hands, covering her in a cloud of liquified illusions. His blue eye twitched with a breath of pain as the bolts rained down on the house.

"Gabe, get her out of here," Abdaziel instructed, forming a flaming blue ball around his fist as he hopped through the broken window.

A moment later, Gabe lifted her into his arms. Her skin skittered, nerves screaming in a familiar way, but she locked her jaw tight enough to shoot electricity into her skull. They burst out through another window, blood splattering across her cheek as Gabe's arm wept red around shards embedded in his skin.

"Where's my gear?" Sable asked.

"Are you serious? You are not fighting this guy!" He shouted as he sprinted across an open green field.

She growled, letting her punching instinct reign with a vengeance. His chest made a thud he didn't seem to notice.

"Stop treating me like a damsel! I can handle myself!"

Gabe slowed, closing his eyes and letting out a breath. He came to a halt, chancing a glance behind them. They hadn't been followed, and the lightning cracking down told them Abdaziel had covered their escape.

He set Sable down and took three steps back. She eyed him with suspicion, noting how that was becoming a regular occurrence. *Since when does Gabe understand personal space*?

"Listen, Sable. This guy is not like Abdaziel and me, alright? He's here to kill you. That's his job, and he's *very* good at it. Me being here is not going to deter him either. Please, understand."

Her fist made a crack against his cheekbone. She rubbed it, swearing under her breath as he blinked in surprise. He glanced down at her, tilting his head to the side when she struck out again.

"You know that doesn't hurt, right?" he asked, not bothering to deflect the kick that struck his belly.

She gave up, clenching her fists at her sides. "It doesn't matter who that is; they're here for *me*. I can't leave someone else to fight *my* battles, Gabe!"

An irritated growl was her only warning before he grabbed her arm, yanking her toward him.

"You are *not* like us Sable," he snarled. "You will *die* if you fight him, and I can only do so much to protect your suicidal ass!"

"Then just do your best and shut up!"

To her surprise, he released her. She didn't question him though, just took off running.

Her heart rose into her throat as she crossed back into danger, the egg thrumming in her chest. She sent up a quick prayer. "Master, I entrust my safety into your hands alone. Guide my battle and protect me, lord."

Footfalls behind her told her Gabe was not leaving her alone, but she didn't mind the company as long as he wasn't going to stop her. She climbed through the shattered window and ducked down beside the wall. Crashing thunder rocked through her bones from the power striking on the other side of the front door hanging ajar. She held her breath, waiting for it to burst open. Power cracked the air, and she could swear a fire was roaring out there.

Gabe scrambled in, crouching beside her and pointing to the hallway. "Your gear is in the bedroom, tucked behind a door."

She moved to get it, but he grabbed her wrist, careful with his strength this time. He gave her a gentle tug to bring her gaze back to him.

"Let me go get it. Just stay right here, please," he whispered, almost begging.

Sable mirrored his frown, but she nodded. She thought back to what she'd said to him, *This right here is why no one can trust you.* Those words did not reflect her true feelings. She did trust him. It was his power that was frightening, and rightfully so. He should be able to understand the difference, but she hadn't explained that. She understood his concern for her as well. After all, Gabe was enough of a threat if he lost his temper with her. His mind could stop her heart, and he wouldn't even have to ask it to do so. Not only that, his protective side alone already had her wrist throbbing.

Abdaziel was unknown to her, but the ethereal waves her gift showed her earlier had told her enough. As for the assassin outside, she had no idea how strong the danger was. She was caught inside a battle of divines and once again found herself reminded of how easily her life could end.

Those thoughts caused the black cloud around her to shiver like it was *excited* in the terror. She closed her eyes, exhaled long and slow, then brought her hands up to her chest and began clawing at this *evil* encasing her body.

Off, off, off, get off, she demanded in her mind.

Another crash of power jolted her nerves at the same time Gabe returned to her side. He frowned down at her, his eye seeming to have twitched. She looked to her hands to find her fingertips bleeding with many little pinpricks in them. The power had a deep gouge clawed out of it.

In the silence of Gabe handing over the leather and metal guards, he slowly raised his other hand. The illusions shivered again and pulled away from her, the process making her cringe as it sucked away what little energy she had and left her body chilled.

"At least I can feel somewhat better with you slightly less vulnerable," he mused humorlessly.

Sable didn't reply as she slipped her cloak over her shoulders and then proceeded to place her armor pieces on with smooth precision. Gabe didn't give her a choice in his help when he tied the strings for the guard her weak hand would have struggled with. She didn't miss the way he flinched and glanced over his shoulder toward the clashing and thunderous sounds outside.

"Are you afraid for me, or of whoever is here?" she asked, grabbing her bow and nocking an arrow.

"First, I'm not afraid; I'm agitated," he clarified, following as she positioned herself just below the first broken window. He put his hand on her wrist to get her attention. "Second, this thing wouldn't happen to be enchanted or perhaps made from some ancient powerful tree bark, would it?"

"What the hell are you going on about?" she snapped.

His glare returned. "Because your arrows won't do anything but draw his attention if they aren't special!"

Sable locked her jaw, listening to the crackling outside. Gabe drew closer, dropping his tone to a sincere warmth, begging her to listen. "Trust me, this guy and Abdaziel have a history together. This is the only person aside from myself who he actually *enjoys* beating. Please, don't loose that arrow, or so help me I will snap this bow in half."

So much for sincere. She shot him a glare, the fire in her eyes burning like a volcano. "He can't be completely immortal. You said so yourself: everyone can die."

It was his turn to glower. "Do you have a death wish?"

Sable let out an exasperated breath and rolled her eyes. She peered over the windowsill at the battle outside, ignoring Gabe's protests.

The redhead had a pale light glowing in his palm as the other man seemed to be falling from the air, a long blade in his left hand. Ropes of fire followed on either side of the man in his descent. Abdaziel's back was to her, but she saw his shoulders droop to a calm stance, reaching his glowing palm into the air toward his adversary. She half expected to see a flash of power when they met, but there was none.

He caught the blade in his palm, his glowing fingers wrapping around it. The columns of fire on either side of the assassin spilled down to cover Abdaziel. She held her breath. The flames were too strong to see the man inside them, but she didn't hear any agonized screams. The ground beneath him shuddered, bucking so strongly that Sable felt it in the floor under her knees.

A wave raised. It was clear though, visible only by the way the flames curved as it pushed back on them. It rolled the angry orange backwards, throwing the man controlling the flames to the ground and pressing down on him. The sword remained in Abdaziel's hand. He stood unchanged from when he'd caught it. With a quick gesture, he flipped the sword, so he could hold it by the hilt.

The man on the ground began to laugh. Cracks splintered into the force holding him, revealing its shape was that of a dome with a flat bottom crushing him. A strange, hollow song filled the air, piercing her ears, and she fought the urge to cover them. The dome shattered, allowing the man to scramble to his feet as Abdaziel brought the sword down. It grazed the man's cheek, drawing a thin white line of fluid where there should have been blood.

"You would never guess they used to work together," Gabe mumbled at her side, giving up on trying to stop the girl.

Sable listened with a distracted fraction of her senses,

analyzing the assassin for a place to shoot. "It's not hard for comrades to turn on each other once the common denominator is removed," she replied.

The assassin had jet-black hair that fell into his face, the back groomed shorter and spiked up in all directions. He was built like a genuine warrior, his arms about the size of her head. His jaw was strong and square, but his cheeks were gently sloped until his grin took over. It defined the ridges of his cheekbones and rose into his eyes, sparking their violet shades with something like glee.

I wonder . . ..

She chewed her lip, debating as the men fought. It would be a gamble, but she had to do something.

She leaned back, repositioning her legs, so she could brace herself. Her gaze remained fixed on the selected target, and as she raised the bow, she inhaled a long, slow breath.

"And just what the hell do you think you're doing?" Gabe yelled, throwing his arms up in a helpless gesture.

He was beginning to know better. She almost smiled. "If you want this shot to hit its mark, you best keep your mouth shut," she whispered.

The men outside were powering up ropes of elemental magic all around them. Abdaziel was attacking with the other man's sword while the man defended with his arms, avoiding being sliced up due to a pastel purple coating he'd drawn over his skin. It was cracking with each blow though, and his flames didn't seem as hot and angry as before.

He shoved aside Abdaziel's last attack and flicked his wrist. The half-angel fell to the ground with glistening lilac threads wrapped around his ankles. The assassin grinned as he stalked toward the fallen man.

Sable drew her bowstring. Her wounds screamed and frothed blood as the muscles in her back fought against the power of the pull. She ignored the aches, drawing into her anchor point and biting her lip to stifle the agonized groan in her throat.

She exhaled and released.

The assassin stopped walking. A trail of white, milky fluid dribbled down his cheek as the towers of fire dropped into the earth. He appeared shocked, his jaw slack, the power fading into a hush that overtook the battlefield.

He fell to the ground.

The threads on Zade disintegrated, and he rose to his feet with grace. He turned back to the girl, his midnight eyes connecting with the raging forge of hers through the shattered window.

"Please, tell me he's dead!" Gabe called out, his deep tone strained with worry.

Even though he'd addressed the angel, Sable felt his eyes boring into her. He was taking an account of her wounds, which were bleeding again, staining her pale flesh. Her shoulder was so furious with her that she had a violent quake racing down the length of her arm and she knew he was watching it. She cast her eyes to the ground, sitting back on her haunches.

"He is," the redhead confirmed. "For now."

Sable tensed. *What the hell does that mean*?

Gabe stood up, leaning against the windowsill and crossing his arms. His lips were pulled down to a hard frown that darkened his eyes. "Stick that stupid sword in him too, just for good measure."

Sable's guts rolled and bucked as she listened to their exchange, whether due to the life stolen or the terrifying confusion, she had yet to decipher. She placed her weapon on the floor with a stiff hand that she half expected would creak like an older door.

"That was a clever shot," Abdaziel said as he came through the front door and glanced down at Sable. "I have never been fast enough to go for his eyes before."

"The eyes are the lamp of the body," she grumbled.

She pulled in another long breath, clamping down on the bile that was trying to rise.

Intense eyes analyzed her when she scrambled to her feet, picking up her bow with her good hand and flinching when she straightened her back. She watched him glare down at the weapon but instead of speaking his mind, he turned his attention to Abdaziel.

"How long do you think we have?"

"Long enough for you to tell us what the hell just happened," Abdaziel replied in a cool, level tone. "Where were you, and how did you manage to lead him here?"

Sable knit her eyebrows together. "What are you guys talking about? He's dead, isn't he?"

Gabe closed his eyes, sighing in a way that sounded more like a groan before turning back to her. "That guy out there is named Kivas Sabotage. You wouldn't know the name, 'cause he's not in the spotlight as often as the rest of us freaks. He's a glitched-out hybrid between two different half-breed races, and that asshole doesn't stay dead, alright? So, we need to be long gone before he gets back."

He tilted his head and gave her an almost malicious smile. "Oh yeah, and if he had any plans of sparing you, they went out the door when you shot out his eye."

"Sounds lovely," she muttered. "So, I guess he was the one you ran off to, right?"

Gabe shot daggers at her, but it was Abdaziel who spoke up, disgust evident in his tone. "No. He goes to Edge when people don't respond with absolute praise at his sick games. But I wouldn't put it past the little snake to turn on his friend if he knew someone had a bounty on your head."

"It wasn't like that," Gabe protested.

Sable shook her head, closing her eyes and holding a hand up to the ache pooling in her forehead. "Both of you shut up! The bigger question is, who wants me dead? Gabe's actions aside, 'assassin' means that man was hired, if I'm not mistaken."

Both men nodded, but Gabe stepped forward, as if going to Sable's side. He stopped an arm's length away, his intense gaze falling on their host.

"It was the master of souls who hired him," he breathed, sounding ashamed to admit it.

"Why would my father have any interest in a human girl? And why would he hire someone so far out of her league?" Abdaziel inquired on a shaky whisper that made the sore woman smirk.

They were taken aback when Sable let out a dry chuckle.

"Master of souls," she echoed, mocking the title. "Maybe it's because he's finally heard what I've been trying to reveal to people. . . and he's threatened by someone who knows the truth about him."

Gabe frowned. "You sound like it's a good thing the ruler of the afterworld wants your head on a platter."

She scoffed. "He's far from a ruler of anything."

Across from them, Abdaziel's gaze was unreadable. His

silence drew Sable's attention and she arched a brow at him. In response, he raised his hand to his chest.

"I think I may owe you an apology. I am not admitting that what you claim is true, but I know my father is not one who cares about the affairs of humans. He barely conjures up the effort to care about divine business." He let out a long breath. "After listening to you, it appears as if there's a great deal of suspicion on his shoulders if he's hunting you."

She smiled and waved away his apology. "It's alright, sir. It's like I said before: I never expected you to believe me offhand."

"I missed something here," Gabe concluded, pointing between them. "What the hell are you guys talking about?"

Sable shook her head. Abdaziel followed her lead and remained silent, his eyes glowing with amusement.

"You two should be on your way," he advised, waving at the door. "You have what you came here for, and I will do what I can to keep Kivas occupied for a while when he returns."

Sable nodded. "Thank you. And I pray you meet blessings for your help today."

She was already at the door before Gabe stopped her with a hand on her shoulder.

"You haven't moved your drawing arm since you let that arrow fly," he observed, making her tense. "Abdaziel is a healer. Will you let him restore you before we go? Please?"

"Gabe, we should respect that she will not appreciate the touch of any power that does not come directly from her father," Abdaziel cautioned.

That put a smile on Sable's lips. She turned to face him, surprising both with the glow that illuminated her.

"Despite who your father is, I know your powers come from the one who gave you life," she said, her glow beginning to swirl and pulsate the way his would.

Gabe stumbled a few steps back when the warm light increased, snatching his hand away from her. He eyed her with a thread of possible terror dancing behind his gaze.

Sable stood before the half-angel and reached out the hand that she could still lift. Her orange eyes were swaying with a fire that was entirely different from what used to form blades before. "My father still loves your loyalty to what is good, and with his love, I will trust the power he gave you—if you choose to use it."

Abdaziel appeared stunned, staring down at her as if the floor had just fallen out from beneath him. He brought his hands up, one to grasp her paralyzed hand, the other pressing against her shoulder blade. His touch was careful, treating the wounded girl like a precious glass figure.

"I will find the truth," he promised as warmth spilled from his palms. "I will find out why Kivas was sent after you, and I won't rest until I have answers."

Sable couldn't reply, shocked by the warm dripping syrup that spread across each fiber of her aching muscles. The wounds in her arm and shoulder sealed up with no fuss, the syrup pooling behind them as her skin knit itself back together.

"You are a fascinating woman," Abdaziel complimented with a soft smile. "Not even your mortality can deter your will to fight. The least I can do is fulfill these promises."

The stars glistening inside his deep-blue eyes spoke of a terror she understood quite well. It wasn't easy to face the vale and tear it down. *But the truth doesn't tend to care about feelings.*

She returned the smile and nodded, "if it will bring you a step closer to release from deceit, I will be grateful."

"Okay, that's enough fuzzy feeling sharing for today," Gabe interjected, with a dramatic movement of his arms.

He went to the door, waiting with his arms crossed over his chest. Abdaziel glanced up at him, drawing his lips into a hard line as Sable tested her arm and rolled her shoulders.

"You aren't travelling with any ordinary human, Gabe," Abdaziel warned. "She may be aware of the danger that lies in keeping your company, but I will hold you personally responsible if harm comes to her. Do you understand?"

Sable stepped away, hanging her bow across the scarlet-bound sword fastened on her back and picking up her father's book from the table. She held it to her chest, frowning at their host.

"I can take care of myself," she asserted as she moved to Gabe's side. "Hold him responsible for his actions alone."

Gabe grinned beside her. "About that 'no ordinary human' thing: I've known that since she was a kid." He glanced down at her dark curls, a spark of pride in his brown eye. "She can't stand to be saved."

She almost laughed. Instead, she shook her head. He didn't know her at all anymore.

CHAPTER 12

"You're not going to knock me out again, are you?" Sable asked after they'd returned to something almost resembling a road.

"Nah, I don't think he minds if you know where he lives now that he's met you. I'm actually pretty sure he'd like to see you come by again," Gabe replied with smooth scorn.

She nodded, looking ahead at the setting sun. His attitude seemed lost on her, and he frowned at the evening glow on her pale cheeks.

"Hey," he said, waiting for her to look back at him. "I know I could have handled the whole situation better—with bringing you here and all. It's not something I'll make excuses for, but I'm sorry. I never meant to deceive you or frighten you."

Sable shook her head, releasing a short chuckle. "I'm

traveling with the Master of Illusions. A little fear and deceit are only the beginning of what I signed up for," she responded, earning an arched eyebrow from him. Her eyes hardened though, and she stepped toward him with a glare. "I can forgive a blunder with good intentions, but don't think that gives you a free pass. Friends don't take advantage of each other's weaknesses."

Gabe chuckled. "Friends? I thought I didn't have any of those."

"You won't if you continue drugging them."

He shot her a half-hearted scowl, but her snicker told him she did not hold it against him anymore.

They resumed walking, a gentle silence taking over. Gabe let his mind wander back to the child who had fascinated him thirteen years earlier. His "stone witch." He was well aware that she was only a broken girl who had learned to survive through things children should never face. She wasn't special to him because of that; it was hardly unheard of in a world of monsters for kids to harden themselves out of an instinct to preserve their tender minds. No, it had nothing to do with Sable's "stone egg."

He'd originally been following the madman, Kazious. A mind divided between a man, an angel, and a vampire was not something Gabe could pass up. Especially when that very man had set out to make the heavens cry. It interested him now to see how one man's delusions about a single god's heart could lead to a precious treasure being fooled into believing she followed the same entity. It was even more interesting how the one that her companion wanted to hurt turned out to be the one to whom she had become loyal.

No, it was nothing so trivial as her simply being broken.

Sable had caught his eye the day that she had chosen to die.

Obviously, he couldn't let her. She was far too young to be giving up on the potential in her intelligent mind. The part that intrigued him was that she couldn't seem to accomplish it by her own hand. She had sought out danger and given herself over to those who would destroy her.

Even with all her emotions and torments tucked away inside her chest, where she didn't have to face them, a single thread remained that fought for life. He had known many humans of all ages who lost all emotion to pain, burying it somewhere far away alongside their will to live. Never had he come across someone who fought the need for death with such ferocity that they ventured their lives into malicious hands.

He looked down at Sable, her dark curly hair bouncing on her shoulders, her pale skin glowing, whether by evening light or that strange power deep inside, he wasn't sure. The warrior she had grown into may have become a bigger hassle, but he preferred her fighting to stay alive.

Sable interrupted his musing. "Can I ask you something?"

"Anything," he replied.

"How does your story really start?"

Gabe laughed at the seeming randomness of the question, ignoring the way it punched him in his chest.

"Where is this coming from?" he inquired with measured humor, holding back his tone for an edge of secrecy and not being subtle about it at all.

She frowned, her eyes far away and deep in thought. "The stories say you were once human. Your legend says they thought you were the child of a demon until somewhere along the line, the world learned you were created by Anzillu."

"You should know better than to listen to every detail of a legend. They're born out of half-truths and raw fiction," he warned with a smoky cadence.

"That's why I'm asking. I want to know who you really are, Gabe," she said gently as she tilted her head up to look at him.

"Why so interested suddenly?" he snarled, unable to hold back the acid that spilled up his throat.

Sable softened her face, and cast him a look of absolute sincerity. "You know my full history. Can't I have the same courtesy of what the truth is behind you?"

He let out a long sigh, closing his eyes for a moment longer than a standard blink. "Fine," he relented, casting her a smile that stung with deceit at the edges. "But no pity or crying, and whatever you do, do *not* suddenly fall madly in love with me. Deal?"

She chuckled. "I'll do my best not to care."

Despite the joke, he dropped the smile and humor from his face. His hand reached down into the brutally destroyed heart in his chest. He brushed the blade of memory buried there, slicing himself open for her and releasing the agonized, stale words he'd only spoken to one other soul in this world. He hung his head, balling his hands into fists at his sides. His face twisted into a grimace as the memories were dragged from the deep crevices in his mind.

"To be perfectly honest, I don't remember much about my life as a child. I can't even remember my mother's face. It seems the world knows how my life began, but no one can actually go back that far, not even me. Funny how that works, hey?"

He chuckled humorlessly to himself, shaking his head. Sable clearly understood his question was rhetorical. He continued in a low, rumbling whisper. "They seem to miss the most important details though. The first is that I was taken from my mother at a young age, and that torment was what created the immortal. But the second piece is perhaps the most vital. It's that I had a . . . a sister."

He paused, turning his eyes to the sky. Sable looked away from his misery when he swallowed a hard gulp that caused him to flinch. He could safely assume she understood what that felt like. Shards of glass slicing up the throat when the hardest part of the memory was leaked into the world for the first time. It was ugly and bitter on the tongue.

"We were twins," he continued. "She was all I could focus on through the pain after they took us. I had this foolish notion that I was somehow protecting her as long as they were directing their attention toward me. They could beat me, starve me, burn me, rape me . . . none of it mattered, because I thought it meant they were leaving her alone.

"But ten years is a long time for a child who just barely remembers what his mother's loving embrace felt like and doesn't understand why all these people would want to hurt him so badly. It seemed like all they could do was torture me and relish in my screams. Eventually, I just . . . stopped. I stopped making a sound. How was I supposed to know they had so much more time than what they spent with me? It was like an eternity of fire. It felt like it never ended. How was I supposed to know?" His voice cracked on the last few words, pain washing over his face.

Sable reached out to cover one of his fists with her hand.

Gabe released another exhale that caught in his throat like a whimper. He forced his fist to loosen, so his long, spidery fingers could lace around her slender, shorter ones.

"I guess I should explain this a little better. They were a cult that was called the Children of the Afterbirth. You see, my mother was blessed with children despite having no husband. No one stopped to think about which god she'd devoted herself to, that Anzillu might touch her with something. No, this cult took it upon themselves to explain the phenomenon.

"I was told for all those years that I was the product of a whore and a demon. Yet somewhere in their twisted logic, they decided my sister was still pure. We were royalty, you see. I was the royal beast, and my dearest sister, she was the royal priestess.

"I didn't know how long they had us for until after I escaped. The only reason that I held on was because of that delusion of keeping her safe. It wasn't until the day of the ceremony when reality finally struck me down.

"They had branded me like a bull that morning. Imagine a pain so strong that your mind goes white, and your entire body grows cold thinking it will fight it off. Even today, the mark still burns. It was the symbol of the royal abomination."

He brushed his fingers over the scar at the base of his neck. It was the symbol she'd seen when he was taking care of her wounds the night she'd sliced open her own heart for him. Her eyes glittered, and she gulped down her emotions as he'd requested of her. He almost wished she'd let the tears fall, though. Regret laced his heart and added to the agony he was pulling out. He moved to continue.

"I never realized there would be a time when we would see that hell coming to a voluntary end. I should have, considering how they worshipped bloodshed. Funny how the day that I finally stood on death's doorstep was the one when I woke this power to stay alive."He pulled in a long, shaking breath that cut him open at the collarbone before he continued. "I was shackled when they brought me into their sanctuary. My sweet baby sister. . . Castle. She still looked like a child, but she was taller, filled out just enough to be mature but not enough to know she was an adult. She lay there on a stone slab staring at the chandelier hanging overhead. She knew what was about to happen. I could see it in her golden eyes . . ..”

His chin wobbled, and Sable squeezed his hand. He stared into the distance, seeing not the setting sun but the girl who plagued his heart with a mystery. “I will never forget the resolve in her face or the way she turned from me when I called her name. She was ready to die.”

Gabe stopped walking, casting his eyes up to the sky as he gulped more glass down his throat. “You could argue what caused it, I guess. Maybe it was the finality of those years weighing down on my shoulders, and they finally snapped, realizing all that anguish I suffered thinking I was somehow protecting her was wasted.”

He glanced down at Sable as fluid built up inside his eyes. The blue orb sparkled like an ocean. “She . . . she had so many scars, Sable. They'd used her for blood sacrifices all that time, and I thought I'd kept them away from her.” His voice rose several octaves of despair that scratched from the base of his heart. “That day . . . it . . . it was going to be her final one. I put it all together like a clasp snapping shut in my mind.”

He swallowed hard and straightened up. His jaw clenched and then released. He forced some stability back into his face. “Let's say that was the trigger. All I know is that one moment I was chained, defenseless, staring at doom itself, and then it was like I blinked, and everyone was torn apart. I looked down at my shaking hands to find them so thick with blood that they dripped globs of red to the ground. It was just me in the center of a massacre, and I don't know what happened to her.”

His mouth went slack. He wanted to say more, but his jaw refused to move. Sable's fire forge gaze was burning him with her sympathy and for a split second, he wanted to hate her for it.

He whispered the final words of the story in a jagged voice that barely brushed the air.

“Gabe . . . what was that?” she urged as gently as she could.

He let out a sound that was almost like an animal's whine. “I said I . . . I probably ki—” He took a deep breath and shuddered as he let it out. It tasted like razorblades. "I probably . . . probably killed her too."

With his power floating around them and his psychic fingertips brushing the edges of her heart, he felt within him the way those words snapped something behind her ribs, and a chill crept inside her bones.

"I doubt that," she whispered. "You loved her. Even in your blackout, you wouldn't have hurt her. I know it, Gabe. You wouldn't have."

He laughed. It was raw and ragged, and it stabbed her. "You think too highly of me, Sable. After all, I'm no more than the results of a god's failed experiment. Or did you miss that part of my 'legend'?"

She frowned. "I don't give a damn about how you came to life, Gabe. I *know* you."

He looked away from her penetrating stare. She was glowing again, and though that power frightened him in a way he's never known before, he couldn't bring himself to pull his hand from hers. He wasn't ready to be isolated with his pain just yet.

"When did you realize that you'd awakened something; that you were no longer human?" she prompted.

Gabe regained part of his trademark humor, quirking his mouth into a grin as he looked at her. "Well, technically, I never was. I was just in a weakened state, but to properly answer your question: I tried to throw myself off a cliff. When I survived, I realized something was afoot!"

He tugged on her hand as he resumed walking, bringing her along with him as his eyes narrowed into annoyed slits.

"Of course, it wasn't until the first time Kiro Baroch broke loose that I finally found some answers. Lucifer's right hand was sent to deal with him, since it was Edge who had locked up the essence of the God of Chaos in the first place. Once he allowed me to reclaim control of my body, he taught me how to form blocks in my mind to keep him back. After that, it was him who explained how I'd been created by the God of Abominations, Anzillu. The irony wasn't lost on me either.

"Then he told me about Kiro, how he had been defeated and his essence hidden away until I was brought to life with it. Anzillu had thought to bind up my power and hide his mistake." Gabe clenched his fist around Sable's fingers. "He never anticipated that my anger would shatter his locks!"

A growl came from deep within his chest and for a moment, the breath of an instant, he felt her begin to pull back. Reality cracked into his chest. His emotions slammed into a brick wall, and he slumped, his shoulders drooping. He stopped walking, and his hand went limp in hers. She clutched it tighter as she stood in front of him. His lips were pulled down into a hard frown.

"Now I'm a legend that children have nightmares and nursery rhymes about, a trickster who likely murdered the one person who kept him sane throughout his own torture, and I still haven't figured out how to *fucking die*!"

He saw the exhaustion in him through her eyes, the shape of his misery pressing down on his shoulders like a mountain.

"Maybe it's good though," she offered, pressing her free hand over his heart. "If you died now, you would only know more pain. There's a home of light waiting for you, Gabe. Please, don't leave me until I know I'll see you again. Please."

He was taken back by the fresh glitter of tears in her eyes and the one that slipped away. Something inside of him snapped as he stared down at Sable, and despite knowing she would fight it, he caught her up in his arms. He clung to her and buried his face in her dark curls, as if she were the last thing keeping him rooted to the earth. He would forever cherish the moment her hesitant arms slipped around his waist in return and he let out a laugh that could have easily been mistaken for a sob.

"I don't intend to leave you again, Sable," he mumbled into her hair.

CHAPTER 13

The sky was bleeding as the sun dipped low. It was no more than a crimson arc on the horizon. A crisp wind greeted the coming night, pulling a shiver from Sable's sensitive human body.

"Do you want to make camp for the night?" Gabe offered, eyeing her bare arms beneath her armor.

It would have been nice to have her sweater back, but she wasn't sure what had happened to it when she was taken to Abdaziel's home.

She furrowcd hcr brows as a realization struck her and a thread of panic swelled up. "How far did we detour from the forest?"

Gabe let out a laugh that rumbled like a thunder cloud. "About a day's travel, if we're going to walk there like this."

Her heart skipped a beat, and she frowned. *We've*

already wasted a day! She couldn't afford another one. The city could already be under attack—or worse. They could all be dead by now. Her lungs squeezed behind her ribs, and she had to breathe out through her nose, long and slow. *What if I've failed them?*

~ *Were you not just hours ago proclaiming the greatness of your lord?*

He came to her mind with humor on his velvety tone. Her eyes widened a fraction and she realized how long it had been since she'd heard from him.

~*Nothing happens that I don't already know will come to pass, my child. Those people need you, but I will deliver you into their hands on time.*

But we've ventured so far away from your destination. How can the enemy be stilled?

~ *You do not need to understand. Only trust in me. You must keep moving.*

His voice was so gentle, she felt it release her lungs and loosen the stone on her chest. *Just like Abdaziel.* A smile found its way to her lips for a moment before it fell again.

She turned to Gabe, rising an eyebrow. "Your powers wouldn't happen to involve anything that could help us travel faster, would they?"

He choked on his laugh. "I thought you didn't trust in my powers."

"I don't trust in unclean power. Your illusions are not what you think they are. But I know you have gifts that are outside of that darkness," she explained with a quiet respect.

He worked his mouth into a toothy grin, but she saw a twitch of pain behind it.

"What exactly do you know about the power that I possess?" he asked with genuine curiosity.

Sable frowned. "Why does that matter?"

"When you're wielding a weapon, the efficiency of that weapon is the first thing that people will question. Your intentions the second."

She nodded. "I know your psychic abilities surpass that of the false deities. I also know your mind can mimic almost any power that you witness, including the elemental control you have. Some legends say you can create and destroy just like the gods, but I get the feeling that's exaggerated by the black power you wield. I know your illusions don't come from the same place that your mind gift does. Is that what you wanted?"

Gabe's jaw hardened at the mention of his illusions and their source, but he still nodded. He shouldn't have been surprised, yet she could tell that her words picked at something inside his chest. Something dark and smooth like silk flashed across his eyes.

"Will you answer my original question now?" Sable prompted.

His smile returned, almost smug. "I could get us there in a plethora of ways, many of which require that which *disgusts* your precious master though, I'm afraid." Sable opened her mouth to protest, but he rushed ahead to continue, "so, it'll depend on whatever *Daddy* allows you to partake of," he snarled. "Cyclone or illusion: one can speed us up, and the other is instantaneous." He snapped his fingers to emphasize his point and stepped into her space, lowering his voice. "I guess it depends on how badly you want to save people, Sable."

His gaze bridged on murderous as he clenched his jaw. He was hurting, and a small part of her understood that, but her instincts were battling the urge to flee from the immortal's anger. She hardened her expression, drawing on the stone egg for its solid texture and allowing it to spread as she stepped toward him. Her position dared him to do something with his sudden rage.

"*I'm* the picky one, Gabe. If you have a problem with *my* decisions, you can come to *me* about it. Hiding behind your hatred of my master is not only beneath you, it's insulting," she growled, raising her chin to challenge him.

Gabe bent down to bring his face inches from hers, his lips twisting into a sinister grin. She saw something splinter inside him, her gift activating out of recoil and showing her the hissing snake deep inside. She smirked despite the coil twisting inside her chest.

"Since when did my Stone Witch care about the appearance of a power?" he hissed. "Or did you *not* travel through a bloodbath for three years?"

Kazious invaded her mind, flashing between memories and the nightmare that morning. His smiling lips showing her soft care, even as his bloodstained hands clenched her throat. The egg in her chest burst open with the screams that followed him into her thoughts. Her stomach twisted, the dead haunting her. She thought she was going to retch. Before she knew what she was doing, her clenched fist was smacking Gabe's cheekbone while her other hand unsheathed her dagger.

"Why do you think death makes me sick?" she hollered, snapping the dagger up to his chin while her striking hand grabbed his wild hair and yanked him down to her height. "Let me explain it to you loud and clear, you ignorant dick!"

She did not recognize the rawness of her rage. All she could see was blood spilling across her mind. Her tone dropped low and venomous, giving the snake within him pause. "When you see the true face of evil behind all the pretty, seductive masquerades of darkness, the *first* thing you will do is vomit out the contents of your stomach. Then, if you're blessed enough to walk away with your life *and* sanity intact, you will *never* interact with *anything* that so much as resembles such a monstrosity again. *Do you understand me*?"

Her throat closed off with the onslaught of red pouring from the egg inside. She released Gabe, turning away and gasping for breath. Her chest bucked with violent recoil, demanding to suffocate her for all the lives she'd watched meet their miserable ends.

Monster.

Her hands shook as the dead chanted behind her eyes. She clenched them shut and let out a sound somewhere between a broken sob and a scream.

Monster.

The broken children giggled, stabbing their claws into her brain.

Monster, monster, monster . . ..

"Caillea?"

Witch.

A pale thread of slicing metal locked around her heart, cutting it open and spilling yet more red.

"Is that all I'll ever be?" she gasped, shuddering.

She wasn't sure whether the question was meant for Gabe or the voices.

He was at a loss, his frustration draining with the color in his face as he stared at her quivering back.

"Let's get moving," he urged, pressing a hesitant hand against her shoulder. "Let's just forget about this."

His touch sent lightning skittering across her shattered nerves, and something inside the panic attack snapped. She spun around, her hand clamped around Gabe's throat before either of them registered the movement.

"Answer me!"

His eyes widened, the two stark colors contrasting each other in the dusk and pulling loose the wire cutting into her.

"You're not a witch," he said, raising his hands in surrender. "You're a warrior, Sable, a beautiful warrior who rose from the ashes of a broken child."

She clenched her free hand into a fist at her side, willing just one breath to sneak down her throat. It didn't work though, and the red stains on her skin darkened.

Gabe frowned at her, remaining still while her fingers tightened as if she were capable of hurting him. He wondered if she wished in that moment that she could.

"You're just saying that now, because your stupid mood swings are making you feel guilty," she mumbled, losing contact with her rage as her guilt threatened to crumble her bones.

He reached out to her, so slowly that she registered his hand's destination and allowed him to press his palm against her cheek. His brows came down together while the silence poured over them; the ever loyal mediator, begging for them to fix the rift between them.

"Sable, I don't have any reason to lie. You should know that. I'm saying that because it's true. I still call you Caillea not to insult or hurt you. The word is so much more than 'witch.' That's a crude translation. It is a title of power, a power that is stronger than any others but is wrapped inside pain and blood. I call you that, because you have come through so much pain, and it never destroyed you. I know other divines who could never stand up to what you have faced down. You are so much more than a witch."

She heard the words, but they didn't register in her mind. Sable found herself blinking her eyes with a fervor, as if she could blot out the blood dripping down behind them.

During the silence, Gabe tapped his finger against her

wrist. "Speaking of strength," he began, locking his gaze on hers, "if I were an ordinary man, you would have killed me with this grip."

Reality came back so fast, she felt it snap into focus, sucking a long breath into her suddenly greedy lungs. Her nerves didn't quite settle, but she snatched her threatening hold away from him.

She turned away, gasping for breath and raising her eyes to the sky. Behind her, Gabe rubbed the red tinted blotches on his neck, frowning at her.

"Sable, it's alright to feel that guilt. It keeps you good," he whispered as he stood behind her, placing a hand between her shoulder blades. He took it for a good sign that she didn't recoil.

"You're wrong. It's not the guilt that made me this way. It was him, and I was supposed to release all of this to him years ago." Her voice shook with tears that she refused to set free. "He told me once that it isn't mine to keep. It will destroy me if I hang on to it. It smothers the light inside of me."

"Sable . . .."

She spun to face him, and he drew his hand back. The coals were raging inside the forges of her eyes as her face twisted with misery.

"I don't know how to let it go," she admitted, dancing on the edge of a sob. "He says I've already been forgiven for not saving them, but I can't wrap my brain around that. How can so much blood just be wiped away?"

"I don't know, Sable. I don't think it can." Gabe remained cool and collected despite the hard chill of his words. He sighed, looking up to the sky with a small smile. "But I don't know this god of yours. He seems to be the only one that I haven't met. Perhaps he knows something we don't." He glanced at her from the corner of his eye. "Do you trust him?"

She was brought up short by his words. Had Gabe just admitted that her master could truly be who she was trying to tell him he was?

"Without a doubt," she replied, still processing Gabe's words.

He chuckled. "Then for now, I'm willing to trust your judgement."

"What?"

"We're in a hurry to reach the forest, correct?" he asked, relishing her dumbfounded expression.

"Um . . .." Sable blinked a few times to catch up to her friend's shift in mood. Again. "Yes," she said finally. "The town inside will be attacked next, and if we aren't there when it happens . . .."

"You'll never forgive yourself for the carnage," Gabe finished. "Alright, wind it is."

She looked up at him, confused even further. He met her with a childish grin, pointing toward the horizon, where a small, grey cyclone was racing toward them.

"You've got to be kidding," she grumbled, triggering mischievous laughter.

At least traveling inside a tornado wouldn't be the weirdest thing to happen to her lately.

CHAPTER 14

The night was silent when they reached the edge of the forest. Gabe's tornado had picked them up in gentle arms, depositing them just off the road. They walked from there, soon coming to realize the quiet would not be interrupted this time.

Sable's heart sank with each undisturbed step. *We're too late.* Nausea rolled through her, and she clenched her fists.

Black ink spilled over the grass, forming thick puddles in some places. Even the leaves that still remained on half-naked branches were dropping with the fluid.

"Well, this is disconcerting," Gabe mumbled.

They followed the tree line, stepping around the thicker puddles, webs of the sticky substance grabbing at their legs. No one came to greet them, not even the creature Gabe had befriended.

As they reached the top of a small hill, Sable stopped mid-step. Her jaw hung slack while Gabe stepped up to her side, a hard frown pulling at his mouth.

Scattered across the field were trees snapped from their trunks like twigs and thrown haphazardly away from their companions. The tree line pushed back far enough to reveal the great wall they'd missed before. It was shattered; thick slabs of white marble the size of mansions and houses thrown into the field as well. Some parts of it were crumbled into dust like a crushed sand castle.

Where the gap opened in the thick stones lay a beast like a giant horse, its blackened muscles steaming in the cool night air. Sable wanted to tell herself that she'd seen its belly rise with a breath, but she knew better.

"What happened here?" Gabe growled, clenching his fists until his nails opened shallow cuts in his palms.

"We . . . we're too late," she almost whimpered.

He gestured toward the ground, calling up a gust of wind that yanked him into the air. Sable continued toward the destruction, choking on the bile rising with flashes of flames and cackling demons. Gabe landed near the beast, racing toward its head. He covered his nose with his right hand, his blue eye glistened in the moonlight, the only color penetrating the blackness of the night.

She finally caught up to him, her throat closing off against the stench of copper and mold permeating the air.

~*The trail is fresh.*

Her master guided her attention to the demolished trees that gave them a perfect doorway into the Caladhvik forest. Blackened footprints led her gaze farther up the trodden path until the forest reclaimed its safe beauty.

"We have to move, Gabe," she urged, already climbing up the glistening white marble. "They didn't make it far; we can still stop them!"

"And how exactly do you know that?" he snarled, right on her heels despite his protest.

"Because my master just told me the trail was fresh, you putz!"

A stone under her foot gave way, sending her tumbling down the jagged edges. She didn't flinch when the backs of her thighs were bitten open, breaking off into a sprint the moment her boots touched solid earth. Branches whipped at her cheeks as she ran, a solid fist clenched about her heart to direct each twist and hurdle over obstacles.

Her mind drew up the crackling of fire in her ears, the blackness of the night adding to her memory of the storm clouds hovering like a plague over the towns she'd just barely saved from destruction. How many had died before she arrived? That blood soaked her hands. How many more while she fought her way through the apparitions? They deserved better. How many in the seconds it took to draw her arrow and release it? Her stone egg became an anvil, crushing her chest, and she swore she heard the bone crack.

The next horror was somewhere ahead of her, and she wasn't about to let them reach that city!

~Are you prepared to lead the broken and the lost into my arms?

How strange to ask at a time like that, when she was more worried about saving their lives than whether they would listen to her message. The question made her legs stutter beneath her, almost causing her to lose her footing on the crunching leaves below.

~Are you ready for what is coming?

No peace filtered into her chest to relieve the pressure. Confusion swirled instead, thickening the shell of the egg. What was coming?

~Are you sure you're ready to face the one thing that will turn Gabe's loyal eyes from your lead?

Oh.

That's why.

It wasn't her master's voice.

"Gabe, they're in my head!" she called, slowing down as her eyes lit up to survey the surrounding trees.

The unseen adversary in response to being discovered, sent a little girl's laughter spilling through her mind like liquid sunlight, and every nerve ending along her spine lit up with fire. The sounds bashed on the inside of her skull, making colors dance in her eyes. She raised her hands to her head as if she could ease the thundering inside. Her legs tumbled over a log and sent her crashing to the ground.

"Get out!" she wailed, bending over until her head hit the cold dirt.

She heard branches crack to her left, but she was paralyzed by the incessant laughter pounding like little fists on her mind. Footfalls caught up to her, and all she could do was hope that it was Gabe. The sounds of mirth spilled out all around her, seeming to dance in the air and agitating the ones inside. They drummed down her ribcage and thundered across her back, hammering nails inside her skull.

A thread of clarity slithered through the attack on her senses. It nudged her lips open, gently and slowly, so as not to allow the anguish to catch onto its presence. An understanding came from somewhere deep in her heart.

He gave authority to all who call on his name.

"Help me, Yeshua HamaSchiach!"

Silence dripped down an instant later with such grace that the absence of the laughter seemed to drum against her bones.

She opened one orange eye and then the other. It *was* Gabe beside her, much to her relief. He stood stock still though, as if he'd been cut from the same marble as the forest wall. She raised her eyes until his face came into view. Her relief washed away in an instant.

All the color had drained from his cheeks, defining their hollowness like he was no more than a skeleton, and his eyes widened.

"Gabe?"

He didn't respond. His Adam's apple bobbed as he gulped down a hard breath.

"C-c . . .." he raised a hand like he could reach out across from him, struggling to get the word out that choked him. "Castle?"

Sable turned to follow his line of sight.

A familiar salmon-colored scar drew her orange gaze first and foremost. It rose up the girl's slender neck, crossing over her jaw to press a permanent dimple into her cheek. She smiled at them, her thin pink lips turned up in a gentle slope. Two large golden eyes glowed in the wicked night, taunting Gabe with a familiar dance of mischief. She had thick, chocolate-colored curls that tumbled about her shoulders, ending just before they could hide the undeveloped swell of her small breasts.

Black ribbons tied to each bicep contrasted with her

porcelain skin, draping down over her slender arms. She wore long bright skirts of blues and greens that were tattered, torn, and ugly. Her shoulders were bare beneath the edges of her black cloak, but her chest and abdomen were covered by a thick violet scarf that she'd wrapped about herself and pinned at the sides.

Sable frowned, opening her mouth to address the girl, but stopped when she was met with a giggle. The girl raised a slender finger to her lips, closing one eye like a prolonged wink. And then she blinked out of sight.

"I don't believe it," Sable muttered, picking herself up and dusting the leaves from her legs.

A gentle breeze lifted her dark hair as she turned to her friend. "Gabe—"

He knelt down, one arm shaking as it snaked around the little girl's waist. Her smile widened when she looked up at her brother, tilting her head to the side and revealing more of the scar that twisted down her shoulder.

"I've missed you," Castle whispered, her voice like warm syrup.

She pressed her hands against her brother's chest, curling into his embrace and leaning her cheek against his collarbone. Sable's gift shuddered awake as she held her breath. Black needles covered the girl's palms, and Sable watched as each one speared his chest when he pulled her close. He brushed a hand down her hair, his jaw hardened and his eyes closed. The snake inside began to hiss and dance; Sable heard the little boy wailing again.

"It's been far too long," the child who was not a child cooed.

Sable's heart squeezed into her esophagus, and the egg thrummed in time with the blood rushing through her veins.

"I thought you were dead," he mumbled, pressing his face into her hair.

This began to look familiar, but the serpent was growing so loud that Sable couldn't concentrate on anything else. Her hands shook.

Gabe, she's poisoning you! She couldn't make her mouth work, but it seemed his own gift had gone deaf.

The air became thick and warm, like a muggy summer's day at a bog. Sable had to move. She had to stop this.

"I'm so sorry," Gabe sobbed.

His agony broke the spell. Sable's hand snapped behind her and unsheathed her dagger. She stepped toward the pair, watching the snake inside him stop its swaying dance, alert to her presence. It didn't matter. She *knew* this girl better than Gabe possibly could. She'd shared meals with her for a decade. Trained with her. Lived under the same roof.

I gave you that cloak.

Her heart twisted in on itself while that memory cracked open. She yanked the girl away from her brother with one arm and pressed the dagger across her throat.

"Make one more move, and I *will* scar you again, Rose," Sable warned in her teacher's ear.

Her lips quirked into the sinister smile that Sable had grown accustomed to over the last few days with Gabe.

"I'm surprised you're still alive, Sable," she replied, seemingly unfazed by the knife against her jugular. She looked into her brother's glazed eyes. "You have a horrible taste in companions."

She vanished again within that next moment, like she'd turned to mist and floated away on the night's breeze. Sable stumbled back a few steps in shock, catching her balance and staring down at her dagger.

Gabe slumped against a tree. His hand brushed through his wild hair, pulling stray locks from his face. He breathed heavily, like he'd just run a marathon.

Sable kicked her foot in the dirt, swallowing hard. "Are you okay?"

He let out a dry chuckle. "That was one dirty trick. And I fell right for it."

She knotted her brows together in confusion, tilting her head to the side and eyeing him. He looked exhausted, his skin pale with a sheen of sweat over it. His shoulders drooped, and his eyes were half hazed with fog. She chewed her lip, weighing the truth in the palm of her hand. It wasn't difficult for her to put it together: they had both seen the person they knew.

Her teacher. His sister. But how did it make sense?

She cleared her throat. "Gabe, I knew her, and anyone trying to get into your head would have never thought long enough to add details from my memory as well. That was no illusion; it was really Castle."

He scoffed the way she expected him to, but her frown urged him to inquire further. "And how exactly would you have known her?"

Sable pulled in a long breath. She'd never had to admit this to anyone before. She motioned to her shoulder. "I gave her that scar three years ago."

He eyed her for a long, quiet moment, narrowing his gaze until it felt as if he were stabbing her with his eyes. She decided to elaborate, if only it could help. "I knew her as Rose, and she never mentioned that she had a brother. She was the one who trained me. The reason I've been out here is because I was trying to find her again. I wouldn't forget her face in a thousand years."

"How did she go from 'teacher' to . . .." He gestured absently to his face and shoulder.

Sable turned away from him, lifting her face to the sky. "I saw hatred. She was drowning in it, suffocating under its weight, yet she was mutating it too. It was as much a part of her as the blood in her veins. She was nurturing it like a child. I wanted—I tried to save her from it. And then we fought."

His chuckle made her skin crawl, something slithering beneath it and reminding her of the blackened needles on his sister's hands.

"Rose is her middle name," he said, indicating that he believed her. His deep baritone squeezed her heart. "So, she was really here in my arms then?"

"Yes."

Another humorless laugh broke loose as he moved to stand. She glanced back at him, flinching when her gift still showed the snake. It was slithering around his abdomen, squeezing his waist, hissing at her. It almost looked like it was smiling at her. Something oozed from the tree he'd sat against. As confusion rolled into his gaze, Sable stepped back from him. Her hand rose to her sword hilt with slow trepidation.

The little boy could no longer be heard.

"Your eyes are glowing," he observed coolly, pretending once more not to notice that she was threatening him.

"You were poisoned when she touched you," Sable informed him.

Clarity stabbed him before she could draw her blade. He stumbled a few steps back, desperate to put distance between them.

"You need to leave," he said, his voice much calmer than the wild look in his eyes. "Get as far away from me as possible!"

"What are you—"

"Go!"

As if his agitation had spurred it on, his eyes glossed over with fog. He dropped to the forest floor like a sack of potatoes.

"Gabe!"

CHAPTER 15

"Gabe what's happening?" she shouted, shaking his shoulder violently.

His glossy eyes peered into a world a thousand yards away, and he didn't respond to her jostling. As his chest bucked to draw in air, she listened to his throat constricting and wheezing.

"Gabe, talk to me!"

To no avail. She pressed her palm to his sticky cheek, realizing too late that black tendrils were swiveling out from him. One latched onto her hand, tightening until she cried out and snatched it away.

A pale red line appeared, throbbing across her knuckles.

"Father, bring him back to me," she commanded while she crawled just beyond the reach of his dark power.

~He hasn't gone anywhere, my child.

Sable released a growl, watching her friend's power dance about him like snakes taunting her. "Then what is this? What did Castle do to him?"

Pressure built up in her lungs before her master could respond, spilling acidic fire throughout her chest. She gasped for breath but found no air would pull into her lungs.

~Get away from him, Sable.

If the order had not held such a father's concern, she may have spat at it. Instead, she found herself moving farther away, dragging her body across grass and dried leaves. Mud caked her as the pressure followed and strangled her. She tumbled over a fallen log and fell down a slight decline onto a bed of leaves. As if a veil had been pulled away, crisp forest air leaped into her throat, which she gulped down with greedy relief.

She crumpled into a heap on her hands and knees, pressing her forehead to the earth. "Father, I don't understand what's happening. What am I supposed to do?"

Tears snagged in her heart instead of dripping from her eyes. She glanced back at Gabe, who laid there still and suffocating.

~This is a moment of choice. I can only save those who will allow me to do so.

Her shoulders sagged, and she sat back on her haunches, turning her hopeless eyes to the sky. She already knew the answer to the question she was about to ask.

"Is he dying?" she whimpered.

~He is ill, my child. And his sister knew her power would cause that sickness to attack him.

A tiny thread of hope flapped. "If he's unresponsive, and I give you permission to help him, will that allow you to intervene?"

~I love him as I love you, and I do not wish to see him suffer. I will do what your prayer allows. By your faith, he will wake.

Gabe's scream split through her grief like a bolt of lightning. Sable gulped down a long breath and sprinted back to his side. She fell to her knees beside him, unwilling to acknowledge the dull ache that threaded through them at the impact.

Gabe's expression was wild, his eyes dancing off the trees above him to her face. His lips were drawn into a tight line, and his nostrils flared. He was breathing again, but his breaths were short and shallow, no longer wheezing yet still struggling. Sable placed a gentle hand against his shoulder, offering comfort to focus him. She cried out, though, ripping her hand back. Her palm was tinged bright red.

"What the—" She snapped back into focus and balled her sore hand into a fist. "Tell me what's happening!"

Terror galloped next to his anguish as he flinched away from her, his hands clutching his stomach.

"Does it hurt?" she asked.

His arms locked around her too quickly for her to register that he'd moved. By the time she tried to escape his hold, his mouth had clamped down on her neck where it met her shoulder. Her mind went black with a child's torment so sudden that she almost cried out again.

He inhaled from her flesh, bringing her back to reality with a sliver of her attention as her skin reacted in a peculiar way. A wound split open, but it was not a physical tear that would bleed. No pain registered either. It was a spiritual opening that spilled a thick, warm syrup. Gabe gulped as if this strange exchange was the only thing keeping him from starving.

She refrained from fighting him, closing her eyes instead and wrapping her arms around his back. The triggered memories clawing into her bones were more than welcome if this act would save him.

Ethereal hands ghosted over her arms and down her spine, coating her in grime that tainted every inch of her body. A little girl cried in secret once the violating hands had gone to bed.

She bit her lip, feeling the cold prick of tears at the corners of her eyes as Gabe gobbled down the essence spilling from her skin.

Blood dripping from wounds long sealed . . ..

Bruises throbbing in time with the blackened dance of Gabe's snakes biting her . . ..

Pain and pain and pain . . ..

He pulled away in a panic once clarity snapped back

into focus. Her neck and shoulder were bright scarlet where his fevered skin had touched hers. His mismatched eyes widened in horror, his jaw popping open and his hands shaking. If she hadn't been on her knees, the wobbling of her bones would have sent her down to them.

"Oh no," he mumbled, shaking his head in disbelief. "I'm so sorry, Sable."

Exhaustion tugged her eyes as she frowned. She opened her mouth, but only air would come out. Her chest tightened. Her exhaustion ate up any fear that could have risen, though.

Gabe reached for her, lowering her onto the soft forest floor that begged her to rest. His large hands were warm on her back, and once he was satisfied that she was somewhat comfortable, he drew one back. The other went to rest on her belly, slipping under the metal to bring its heat through her tunic.

"Don't try to talk," he instructed. "And don't move. If you don't rest, your body can recoil from that exchange. I-I could lose you. Okay? I'm so sorry."

He hovered over her, his face tight. Sable let her eyes wander into the sky, which she almost couldn't find between the trees. Her bones were heavy yet hollow. It was like they were made from thick leaden tubes.

Gabe brought his free hand to her cheek, his skin cool, already back to normal. "Speak to me in your mind, alright? I understand if you're scared . . . or angry." His voice vibrated her metal bones. "I'll explain everything, but I need to know that you're coherent, okay?"

She pulled a long breath in through her nose, blinking away her exhaustion. *I'm not upset. I'm confused. And tired. And heavy. But I think I'm alright.*

Sable saw him relax as a breath left him in a rush. He even smiled.

What just happened to you . . . and to me?

He closed his eyes, turning away while he locked his jaw. She didn't need to see his eyes to know they were full of shame. He glanced back at her again, and her gift saw the serpent fall still as it watched her, its head next to his. He frowned, and the little boy inside whimpered.

"You remember when I told you about Kiro Baroch, right? I was brought to life by having an evil god shoved into my soul."

It's not something one would forget.

He nodded. "Well, I can't actually sustain him," Gabe admitted. "I'm sick, Sable. His essence is like a magical poison, and when it seeps in enough, I have an attack as my body tries to get rid of the poison. Well, you know the dangers of that now.

"My body goes into an extreme fever, and the air seems to be sucked dry by my very presence. Sometimes I can function through it, but only when the episodes are mild. Otherwise, my insides light up like I've ingested magma. It wouldn't surprise me if my veins and organs are actually melting during such episodes."

He brought his hand away from her face and frowned at his palm. The dancing black power had faded back into him, but the snake was still coiled around him, poised for attack. "My shadows and illusions are hard enough to control when I'm at my best. When I go through that, they act on their own. Creating or destroying anything around me at random."

Gabe locked his gaze on hers, frowning. "I could have killed you, Sable. I know you wanted to help, and I appreciate the warmth of your heart, but don't you dare do that again. I wouldn't forgive myself if something happened to you."

I'm not helpless, you know. To her surprise, he rolled his eyes. *I'm not afraid to die, either,* she continued. *It isn't my choice how long I'll survive; it's my father's.*

Gabe didn't reply, but his strained silence tilted her lips into a gentle smile. She felt the exhaustion ebbing from her bones. It reminded her of one more question: *What did you do to me*?

He sighed, hanging his head and looking at her through his eyelashes.

"There's two ways to come out of an attack, depending on how they came." He held up his fingers and counted them as he talked. "First, if the attack happens due to an emotional or psychological trigger, like a panic attack, it can be settled like one as well. Otherwise, it's only by pulling out another's life energy that I can come back. The more mortal that energy, the stronger it is." He glanced away, lowering his voice to a whisper. "Essentially, I devoured a piece of your spirit to revitalize the balance inside mine." He remained silent for a long moment, gulping down a hard breath. "I'm trying to give that piece back now."

That drew her attention back to the hand on her stomach. His palm was warm, even through the cloth layers beneath it.

"You'll be alright," he assured her. He still wasn't looking at her, his voice strained. "I'll build a fire, and we can make camp here. Rest for now, alright? We'll deal with my sister when you're well again."

When he pulled his hand away, it left a chill that stabbed at her. She frowned as she watched him stand, her eyelids drooping once more with an uninvited rush of her earlier exhaustion. It pulled on her.

Gabe, you're worth the trouble.

Whether he heard the thought or not, she would never know.

CHAPTER 16

I stand in the center of a small town with wooden shacks and stone businesses surrounding me. My limbs are shrunken to their old childlike proportions just before the swell of breasts had begun to form. I am a child again of a dozen years. I can recognize this place as if I've lived here. Because in a way, I have. I have never left the horrors behind. I force this memory into my heart every time I begin to forget what I've done.

Or. . . more accurately; what I didn't do.

I sit observing my deranged companion in the midst of one of his many massacres. For three years, this is a memory as repetitive as the sunrise. Blood stains the air with a fog that stinks like rot and copper as bodies lay scattered in the streets. I am perched on a sagging wooden fence, my feet safe from the blood spilling across the dirt.

He smiles with gleaming teeth and a devilish glint overtaking the joy on his face. A grey tattered ribbon wraps around his empty eyes and disappears behind his silver hair. The long, straight locks are saturated with thick scarlet as it sprays against him.

I watch, hypnotized by the demon's feast. My stomach churns, though I can't turn away. The torture he inflicts adds to the scarring on my heart, and I need to watch. I have to carve the agony into my soul.

None of you will be forgotten.

But there are too many faces to remember. I am a liar.

His lips are pressed against the curve of a young boy's shoulder blade as the clawed tips of his fingers dig into the child's stomach. The body grows stiff before finally falling limp in the madman's hold. He drops the boy, throwing his head back and releasing a maniacal laugh.

A girl the same age falls to her knees, but her eyes are dark and hollow. She can't cry. Her mouth won't open to sob, and her empty gaze is frozen with overwhelming confusion. **How is this happening**? *she asks herself.* **Why**?

My chest aches as my belly twists and rolls with violent waves of nausea.

He reaches out to the little girl, the last human alive in this desolate place.

"Please," I beg suddenly. "Please, stop!"

I want to reach out, but the wooden fence has grown over my hands, trapping me in my helplessness. He pulls the girl into his hold as if it were a comforting embrace for her loss. Her face is pressed gently against his chest as his arms reach all the way around her. She tenses in his arms, her shoulders quivering as his tunic muffles the sound of the sobs she is finally able to release.

"Kaz, you don't have to do this," I try to shout, my heart pounding so loudly that I can't hear my own voice.

How did I ever let this happen before without so much as flinching? *My egg thrums with the thought, as if to answer by waving for my attention.*

His arms tense in a slow, deliberate manner as the muscles flex with inhuman strength. His nails dig into the girl's flesh, his left hand on her hip, his right engulfing her tiny ribs.

I start to fight at the living wood that has begun to

swallow my arms. It has reached my wrists, and I yank at them with such fervor, something in my muscles gives a wet pop when it tears. Deep in my skittering heart, I have lost hope. I can't admit this aloud though.

The girl whimpers, struggling now that she finally realizes she is caged. He pulls at her, his arms aching to cross over each other and move through her small body. A wail of raw anguish is swallowed up by his chest. Her hip bone shifts into her pelvis with a dull pop.

As my eyes fly open to the real world, I cannot tell if the scream belongs to my memory or to my own throat.

~~~

"Death haunts all of us in some way," Gabe muttered, staring into the fire.

Sable sat up slowly, feeling brittle and chilled. The girl's wailing still pounded on the backs of her eyes, the forge that illuminated them reduced to a pale thread of light.

"What?" she asked, blinking the sleep and ethereal blood from her eyes.

He glanced at her across the fire, his face solemn. "Your nightmare was about Kazious, wasn't it?"

She nodded, her throat closing off as the haunted, hollow gaze of the girl who had lost her brother stared up at her.

His turned to the dancing flames. "It seems like it never stops. The screaming and the memories and nightmares. It's almost like they die and then come back to haunt the minds that can know guilt. They want your life to join them, and they won't rest until they've destroyed you."

Sable frowned, her heart sinking. He wasn't speaking about her alone anymore.

"They can't have me. I belong to my master, and when he brings me home, I will be free of this pain." She knit her brows together, watching the fire. "I just wish I knew then what I do now. Maybe I could have saved their souls from the torment of Lucifer's trap."

That prompted a questioning smile. Gabe tilted his head to the side, arching one brow. "That's right; you put yourself on his shit list," he said, chuckling. "I guess it's time I pay a bit more attention to your claims. He's not the sort to be insulted easily, and in all my years, I have never seen him hire an assassin. I never would have expected to see Kivas
~~~

hired to kill a human either."

Sable smiled. "I'll give you the basics, and then you can inquire further."

When he nodded, she leaned back on her hands. "The deities you know are no more than a race of demons called Calamities," she began. "All worship of them brings power back to Lucifer and allows him to remain the puppeteer of our world. My father is the one and only being that Lucifer fears, because he understands my father's true power. He is the original creator, which means he is also Lucifer's creator. Lucifer has taken our world hostage, stealing them away from eternal life and salvation, yet the people rejoice within their captivity. This is why your comrade is hunting me. I'm possibly the only one alive who's learned the truth and I am not afraid to shout it off the rooftops."

Gabe waited a couple seconds to be sure she was done before throwing back his head with a hooting guffaw. "*That's* what you call 'basics'? Just 'your entire world is a giant lie'?"

Sable shot him a half-hearted glare. "You don't believe me?"

His face settled into a soft smile. "Tell me about these Calamities."

She was shocked he would allow her to elaborate, but she didn't hesitate. "You're familiar with an arch demon, yes? Your friend is one, if I'm not mistaken."

Gabe nodded.

She pulled in a long breath, forcing her thoughts to organize into a single file. "The arches were a mutation that caused their incredible powers to take on a mind of their own, which they have to subdue for the duration of their life to stay alive, only losing their lives when the power becomes stronger than their control over it."

She took another long breath and turned her eyes to the fire between them. "A calamity is basically the perfection of the arch demon. It is one with its magic and has complete control over it. Furthermore, it grows with the being's age the same as an arch demon but without the danger of it becoming too much to bear. Their power is essentially limitless. That's why it was so easy for Lucifer to slip them into places of worship as gods. If you don't know the real one, you would never comprehend how futile and puny a calamity truly is. And they would appear grand."

He soaked up her explanation in silence, a frown pulling on his lips. When she glanced up at him again, his arms were folded across his chest, his eyes on the ground.

"Are you telling me that your big guy is even bigger than the big guy trapped inside me?" he inquired.

Her jaw locked for a moment. *Kiro Baroch.* "The Chaos Calamity is no more than a bug to my father," she affirmed.

Gabe chuckled, but it had no humor. He shook his head slowly in denial. "You have no idea what he does."

"I don't need to know."

When he glanced back at her, his eyes were glittering. She wasn't sure how to take the new development, but her heart clenched for him.

"Do you believe me?" she asked, her voice almost drowned out by the crackling of the fire.

He let out a heavy breath, closing his eyes. Then he nodded. "I do."

She leaned forward. "You don't still think I'm the one being fooled?"

A sinister smile crossed his lips. "That cult of mine has grown to nearly control this world because of those stupid gods. I've kept tabs on them over the centuries, and I know they would never have gained such influence without Lucy's help." He sneered. "As far as we've been concerned, he's the ruler of this earth, the son of the supposed creators who hid themselves in a vessel to avoid abusing their power over us, leaving his word as law. There's no way their superstitious arrogance would have spilled over to so many people if Lucy wasn't involved."

He shook his head, his blue eye sparkling with murderous amusement. "I've met the gods who are worshipped. Every last one of them knows me by name, and I could never understand the worship of them."

His gaze settled on hers, something black swirling within his irises and making her uncomfortable even as he laughed sarcastically. "Now, an all-powerful, ever-loving *true* god, though, that's something that I still have a hard time getting on board with."

Sable felt her head spinning as his smile softened, all his animosity disappearing. His shifting moods were getting harder to track. She swore they were accelerating.

"So, rewind for me," Gabe said as he leaned back on his hands. "What is this trap that you mentioned?"

She chuckled despite her confusion. "It's the afterworld. Your current lore says heaven and hell are together as mirrored cities in another dimension that is controlled entirely by Lucifer. You believe hell is this place where broken souls are put back together, then passed along to heaven, where their memories are stored and they're reborn into new lives."

He nodded. "So then, what's your god's story about it?"

She wasn't surprised by his sarcastic tone. After all, his one and only friend was the devil's right hand, the original arch demon, the one whose powers were tied into the souls that were kept in the afterworld, too broken to be put back together. Technically speaking, his friend was alive entirely due to this very torment. With this understanding, Sable chose her words carefully.

"It is entirely against our design to live multiple lives. We were never created to be reborn. The heaven that creates what you call hell's ceiling is merely an extension of that terrible place. That entire realm is no more than a torture device designed to shatter the souls that are snatched into it. They aren't meant to go there, and that place is not even the real hell. Hell itself is a prison, and if Lucifer were there, we would hear no more from him."

"What about the angels who live in that mirrored city?" Gabe asked, arching an eyebrow.

"Any who inhabit that place are fallen and betrayed my father."

He nodded, smiling. "Have any of us seen a real angel then?"

"You have seen a real half-breed. But aside from that, I don't know."

"So, why would Lucy want to shatter souls? What does he stand to gain from it, and why does he take so long to accomplish it?"

Sable smiled. "Gabe, do you know how a demon is created if it's not through the sexual relation of other demons?"

The ensuing silence filled with steam and clicking gears. He did. He couldn't have traveled there on such a frequent basis without having stumbled upon the truth at some point. Not only that, it wasn't exactly a secret. For those who knew their lore, this was common knowledge.

"An unstable soul mutilates itself as it breaks," he said, "some so shattered that they either turn into a bomb of raw chaos, or Lucifer transforms them into a demon."

Sable nodded. Gabe shook his head, raising his hand to his face as the understanding came over him. She thought she saw shame flit across his face again for a moment.

"I had always thought it was a mercy when he changed them, so they could live on past their brokenness," he admitted, "like being reborn."

Her gaze softened, and she turned to watch the crackling flames. "It seems noble when you can only see the end. Once you realize he's orchestrated that very destruction, that's when you have to choose if it still is."

He dropped his hand, frowning at her. "No, there's no choice at that point."

That statement shouldn't have surprised her as much as it did, but she glanced at him with wide, astonished eyes.

In that instant, he changed again. The corner of his mouth turned up, and he looked to the sky. The smile was wrong, tainting his eyes with an inky weight that she couldn't place.

"So, this is what changed the young stone witch into a mature warrior," he mumbled.

"What?"

His tone was off too, by just a fraction of amusement. It lilted to the side like it had to be forced from a reluctant throat. Sable tilted her head, drawing her brows together. The air shifted, her gift shimmering inside of her tightening chest as her heart kicked up a notch.

Shadows danced from his chest, a stained blue light emanating from the shape of a child's hand. In that moment, she understood why her gift awoke.

He grinned at the moon above. "You're going to save this entire world, aren't you? One unclean spirit at a time until the world is pure, right?"

Her breath froze, the clarity spilling across her shoulders. Castle had never intended to trigger *just* his sickness.

Sable was no longer speaking with Gabe Arenreeth.

She gulped down a hard breath and tucked her hands

between her knees to hide their sudden inability to stay still.

"Tear apart the entire fabric of the world with your arrows and little righteous heart," he continued, speaking in a low rumble.

He chuckled, turning to her and leaning back just far enough to bathe his features in the shadows of the night.

The other Gabe . . ..

Abdaziel's soft voice spoke behind her eyes, void of the peace for which she longed.

The one who will tear you to pieces and laugh at the gore—if he ever takes over . . ..

CHAPTER 17

It was the change in his voice that gave him away first. The cold edge that evolved from causing incredible anguish and drinking it up like water. A drawl that was as familiar to her as her own name: the voice of a well-seasoned predator.

Sable turned back to him once she realized he had asked another question regarding the way she'd changed. She could not allow him to know she'd caught on to the shift. This was a game that Kazious had prepared her for well.

"You don't enjoy death, and yet you have grown to kill," he elaborated, smiling in an insincere way that instead of being kind, looked more like a wolf's snarl.

She frowned, leaning closer to the fire and resting her chin in her hands, pretending to ponder her answer as she tried to get a closer look at him. His face hid within the dancing shadows though. "I use my skills to protect. Sometimes protection of one requires the death of another."

"Is that so?" he replied, leaning toward her out of pure intrigue.

She had to fight not to gasp when his movement revealed the absence of beauty in Gabe's unique eyes. The colors were drained away, as was the ever-present amusement and all the deep scars hidden behind it. Every trace of it was smothered by the oil that had suffocated her the day she delved inside him.

"But you'll try to reason with your assailant and choose death as a last resort, correct?" he prompted, spilling out his false amusement in a forced chuckle.

"They don't generally give me the chance to explore other options," Sable replied slowly, her coil tightening as the stone egg on her collarbone began to tremble.

The whites of his eyes had filled in with the dead black of an abyss, broken only by shards of vibrant, electric blue surrounding the pupils. Behind them was no more than an empty void, cold and cruel.

The sticky tar she'd waded through with her gift stared at her with a hissing smile, threatening to swallow her whole. She had heard of his passenger even before the half-angel had warned her of his presence. Gabe's legend was clear about the atrocities that were committed by the deity trapped inside Anzillu's worst creation. Kiro Baroch was fabled to have been locked up behind a piece of Gabe's psychic powers, only to be seen when Gabe either strained his mind or was knocked out cold. It had been decades since anyone had seen evidence of him breaking out. How had Castle managed to weaken that barrier for him to slip out with such ease?

~That sounds like a question for Gabe. Bring him back.

It sounded so calm and simplistic, she choked on a sudden urge to giggle. Sable thought for a moment that he was joking.

She released a heavy breath as she stood, stepping away from the fire to lean against a tree at the edge of the fire's glow. She needed space from the monster in her midst. His intense gaze followed her every movement, drawing chills from her skin. She had no idea how to deal with one as powerful as Kiro. The masses called him the god of chaos for all the havoc he could wreak.

~Have I not moved mountains with your voice? Her master asked, amusement trickling behind her eyes.

She narrowed her gaze at the immortal, not quite catching his eye but analyzing each movement. *Yes, but this is different,* she replied. *I don't know how to fight this one without bringing harm to my friend.*

~He is not easy to bring lasting harm to, child. Do you trust me?

You know that I do.

~Then breathe. Do not fear the battle or fear for your friend's safety. I will guide you.

Not Gabe watched her with steady annoyance as his hands twitched against his knees. His back was hunched under pressure she couldn't locate even with her gift, but his stature began shifting. Growing.

Gabe's body is . . . too small?

She could have laughed.

The thought caused her to realize something though. A quiet twinge of hope fluttered in her chest at his mannerisms. Nothing had changed in him while he studied her with his black eyes, sending bugs skittering up her arms.

He couldn't hear her thoughts.

Even still, her heart began to squeeze and the hope fluttered away while reality pulled in way too close. She gulped down a long breath into lungs that stuttered and shied away from the coming confrontation. She felt the silence about to shatter, as if its strain were a palpable thing between her and her adversary.

He lowered his head, watching the flames from beneath his wild bangs. The sudden movement made her flinch, and she cursed under her breath. His black gaze reflected the fire like a tainted mirror.

"Do you realize the position you're in?" he rumbled in a familiar tone of gravel, clenching her heart like a vice.

He stretched out his hand, rubbing his palm with his thumb as if that would alleviate the irritation beneath his skin.

Sable choked down an inhale that her lungs almost refused. Of course she realized her position. What a dumb question; that's why she fought her buckling chest just to breathe. She trusted her master without hesitation, but that didn't mean her racing mind was going to cooperate.

Abdaziel's concerns rose in the back of her mind like an accusation. *What makes this worth it? Do you really understand the danger you're in*?

As if to answer, Kiro Baroch released a sinister chuckle. "You're bloody stupid. Do you realize that?"

He did not look up at her when he stood, but she couldn't tell her legs to move or her arms to reach for her sword. The coil in her chest yanked so hard, she thought her bones would be pulled out through her back.

"Here you are, traipsing through the woods with some ignorant, unstable *child* who houses such great power even his creator trembles at the mention of his name," he rambled, making grand hand gestures until he finally settled his eyes on her. His lips tilted up as he snarled. "Yet you sit here with such a pretty illusion of safety. You're a fool."

Oh.

He was well aware she knew he'd taken over Gabe's body.

Despite her frozen limbs, Sable prided herself on being able to respond with a steady tone. "I was well prepared for everything I would face when I decided to invite that powerful, intelligent man to accompany me on this journey."

Kiro threw back his head, barking out a thundering laugh that punched her ribs, reverberating up each bone until it reached her throat.

"Intelligent," he repeated with a mocking chuckle.

His thought was interrupted by a full-body flinch. He frowned, scratching his shoulder and twitching in the same way that his hands had a moment earlier.

"What's so intelligent about wasting away the centuries playing with vermin like you?" he asked, his voice just above a dragging whisper.

Sable watched him squirm, rolling his shoulders as if they were tense and needed a good crack. She tilted her head to the side, smiling calmly as he grew increasingly irritable in Gabe's skin. The display seemed to break the spell on her frozen terror.

"Problem with your host," she mused, slipping her hand behind her back to grasp her dagger.

He cast her a glare that chilled her blood. It was the first time they'd locked eyes, him pinning her with haunting obsidian. He was fixated now; she was familiar with that look as well. A flash of annoyance crossed his features before he reached up and shredded his shirt to ribbons. His pale, sickly skin glowed in the firelight, showing Sable the story written across his body that she'd heard only hours earlier. Silver and pink cords crisscrossing at random caused a thick ball to choke off her throat. This time, it had nothing to do with terror. She turned away, raising her gaze to the treetops out of respect for her friend's private and angry story.

"Like I said," he whispered, "you're a fool."

Warm breath crossed her face. His hand wrapped around her throat with bruising force, snapping the coil inside her chest and shooting an electric jolt into her arm. The short blade slipped into his ribs as easily as a sigh while the ground fell away.

He showed no sign of registering the stab wound. He lifted her into the air with one hand as she clawed at his wrist. Gabe's lips were twisted into a perverse snarl; the gaze of an abyss swallowed her whole and spat her back out.

"I wonder what you mean to him," he whispered, brushing her cheek with his nose.

Her mind started to retreat into the child who could face what was coming, dragging a wool blanket over her shivering heart while it wept.

"Do you think he'll rip new scars into his flesh for you? Does he care enough to feel guilt when he returns to his dying pet? Would he weep like a child?" he asked in a slow yet melodic voice, like a quiet song.

"Not a chance," Sable spat. "You should know better than anyone that he doesn't do 'caring'."

Kiro laughed, low from his belly. He shrugged as if he agreed. "Still, it would be rude of me to leave without giving him a humble gift." His hand tightened, choking off her breath as he pulled her closer, brushing the shell of her ear with his lips. "Let's allow him to decide your worth later," he whispered. "It has been a *long* time since I've been free."

The door her mind ached to crawl through was wide open at the end of a blackened corridor. The child self who had given up her body to wandering, filthy hands reached out to her as if offering to take over and ease the coming abuse. But she hardened her jaw and kicked the door shut, locking the tainted girl inside.

Sable would fight this time.

Kiro flicked his wrist and threw her into a tree. Lightning speared her spine, and she fought down a groan. She crumbled to the cold earth, her cheek pressed to the soft grass, closing her eyes for an instant.

Fight!

She scrambled to her feet, shaking off the haze in her head as she let out a laugh. "I think you're mistaken," Sable mused, smirking.

"Oh? Where is my mistake? Enlighten me," he invited, returning her mirth as he stalked her like a lion eyeing its prey.

"In thinking that I am alone."

Kiro barked a wicked laugh, giving her the chance to unsheathe the sword strapped to her back. She brought it down before her, the blade's folded Damascus design looking like tree branches spread across its deadly doubled-edged length. A golden glow danced across the blade, its weight familiar in her hand, though it had been so long since she'd held it. The precious gift was all she had left of her teacher. A symbol etched into the swaying curve of the hilt reminded her of an ancient name she'd received from the other Arenreeth twin. How many names did she have now? She wanted to tell Gabe about it, ask him what this one meant.

"You'll give him back," she told the demon. "You'll give him back, or I will take him back."

Kiro let a smile creep up his lips. His hands flexed again when he stepped toward her.

"Oh, this is precious," he declared. "You honestly intend to harm the man that you claim to protect? And with a stick no less!"

She didn't grace his mocking with a response, balling up her free hand into a fist at her side.

He bent his knees, dropping into a stance to begin their battle. "What will you do when you must protect the very man that will destroy everything?"

Sable scoffed. "For a parasite, you give yourself an awful lot of credit. You can't even access your host's powers!"

His growl was her only warning before he leapt at her. She closed her eyes and breathed in. The warmth came at her chest, the impact less than a centimeter away. Her feet followed the circle that evaded the path of attack, and she swung her sword up. Something dripped from her chest into her hand.

She heard his grunt and opened her fire-tainted eyes. No blood coated her sword, and its golden glow no longer reflected the natural fire behind them.

A strange, clear ooze dripped from his hip.

This is what trust looks like, she reminded herself in amazement. The sword was more than just a gift from her teacher. Apparently, it also happened to be the one and only time Rose and Sable's master had worked together.

She leveled the blade, its point steadied at his heart. Her breath tumbled out in an easy sigh.

"Oh, this is going to be fun," Kiro admitted, stalking toward her. "It is a rare day when my prey fights back."

"You talk like you've already beat me, and yet here I stand."

He lunged again, almost too fast for her senses to register. His lips were twisted into a sadistic grin, but Sable smiled in return. Her legs moved by a warm impulse, pivoting once more and slicing her weapon across his shoulder blade as he crashed into her empty space. The fresh wound crossed over a thick, upraised purple scar that spanned his back. The wounds made an X over his marred flesh, the one she'd opened spewing more of the black tainted goo to the earth.

He stilled with his back to her, straightening while another laugh rocked his shoulders. "You're going to die tonight," he whispered, his face turned up to the moon again.

His wrist struck her sword before she even realized he'd spun and lunged for her. He shoved her back, pinning her to the trunk of another tree. Her spine screamed at the impact, reminding her of how easily this could end. His face came within inches of hers as he breathed a ragged breath across her face.

"This fight is a joke, you realize." He moved closer, his nose touching hers. She inhaled rancid air, her skin skittering with an old memory, but she refused to flinch away. He spoke softly through his malicious grin. "I am a god, and you are no more than a roach."

Sable spat in his face. The warmth in her veins began to stir inside her chest. It raced into her throat and dived off her tongue.

"A true god cannot be trapped, you masquerading fool," she hissed. "You have only fists, where your host had magnificent giftings you can't even fathom. *You are no god!*"

A blue wave spilled from her lips, shoving him back. She seized the moment to raise her sword. It sliced across the underside of his arm, giving her the opportunity to dance out from his grasp. He faced her with a flash of confusion that melted away into cold steel. His eyes narrowed into obsidian slits.

"I don't need his pathetic powers, but I am certainly interested in the source of yours."

"My source is the proof that you are nothing but a glorified demon."

He smiled. The upward tilt of the left side of his mouth seemed more disconcerting than his blackened glare.

"I wonder . . . ." he murmured, stepping toward her. He appeared to glide into one more step before he vanished.

Sable glared at the empty space, training her ears for any sign of his reappearance. She breathed slowly, scanning the small clearing as the fire crackled. In the incredible stillness, the sparking flames were louder than they should have been.

Warm air spilled down her neck. Sable tensed but did not turn.

"What makes you so calm?" he whispered next to her right ear, his nose nuzzling her neck.

Centipedes skittered down her spine, yet she replied without wavering. "My life belongs to my master. Death means nothing to me."

His thundering chuckle rumbled inside her bones. "Death is not the part that should frighten you."

His spidery fingers grabbed her hips, and on instinct alone, her elbow shot back into his gut as she pivoted from his hold. His grin spurred disgust through her belly.

He raised his hands into the air, wiggling his fingers as if he'd just performed a magic trick. For a long second, everything went black. Electric pain across her face followed, and Sable stumbled back. She raised her sword and lunged for him, even as stars danced in her vision from his punch. He slipped out of reach, but as soon as her foot was planted, she spun on him again.

He caught her blade in his hand, his black tar gaze looking bored. "Seriously, this thing is—"

He snatched his hand back, glaring at the blue smoke rising from his palm. A bubbled mark rose from his palm, earning a studious frown.

Sable seized the opportunity to twist her hand up, slicing her sword into his neck. Clear, thick rolls of goo slopped down onto his shoulder.

"Interesting," he muttered, unmoved by the attack.

He was next to her in the blink of an eye. She had no chance to move before his fist struck her. This time, something in her side snapped and bent away from his knuckles. She couldn't bite down the groan as her lungs emptied and nausea chased the vacancy down her throat.

You're not like us, Sable! Gabe screamed in her mind as she choked off a violent cough.

"I think I'll enjoy your screams more than any other," the tumbling voice said, bringing her back to the clearing in the forest.

He grabbed the back of her neck with harsh fingers, yanking her head back and forcing her to look up at him. The smile remained on his lips, lying to her about a gentle kindness.

"You have a forge in your eyes," he said, leaning down. "I wonder if your anguish can light it as bright as your misguided bravery."

She bit back another groan as her neck pulsed under his hold. In that position, her sword arm was pinned between her shattered side and his chest.

His free hand brushed stray curls off her cheek while she struggled against him. His feathery touch seemed strange compared to the bruises forming beneath his other hand.

"If you're going to kill me, get on with it," she snarled.

He chuckled, and another blow hit her jaw, sending

black spots into her vision. The world danced, but he released her, much to her confusion. She understood when her crumbling descent met his knee, sending black terror galloping into her throat as the agony paralyzed her. The wet grass caught her, and she rolled onto her back, sucking in wheezing breaths.

Am I coming home? she wondered, even as she forced herself to kneel on clumsy legs on the damp earth. A hand knotted in the curls at the back of her head as he appeared again. Hot tears burned her eyes.

"Not so calm anymore," Kiro mused, shoving her face-down into the dirt.

His boot replaced his hand, holding her against the grass as she gasped in breaths that burned her lungs.

"What are you so afraid of now?"

CHAPTER 18

Her belly churned, and her head rolled. She didn't mind the cold, wet earth against which his boot held her. It refreshed her sweaty skin.

What was she afraid of now? Was that what he'd asked? How ridiculous. She feared many things. Fear was an emotion that humans knew better than anyone. That meant nothing though. She feared a prolonged and shameful death, but it wouldn't stop her from looking to her father during the agony.

"Father, if it is your will that I die here tonight, I only have one request," she mumbled into the grass. A cough wracked her body, jostling the lightning ball in her abdomen.

A knee at her shattered ribs shoved her over, throwing her down onto her aching back. He kneeled beside her, his black eyes glinting in the firelight. His lips were pulled up into a gentle, tainted smile. It added to the nausea on her throat.

~*Oh child . . ..* The voice came to her mind with such soft, resonating love that she almost wept.

"Have you suddenly lost your tongue?" Kiro asked, pressing his palm over her shattered ribs.

She groaned at the fire racing across her abdomen, and he nodded like she'd answered him. "Now we can begin."

He took her dagger from his side and flipped it in his hand with an over-dramatic flair. Sable closed her eyes, pulling in one long, acidic breath. Then she continued her prayer aloud, ignoring him. "I only ask that this not be in vain. Let this be what brings Gabe into your waiting arms. Promise that he'll make it home."

She recognized that Kiro had just questioned her, but his words were lost on her as she was dragged from her body. She fell into a warm cloud of light, unsure if she'd left her body or lost her mind. *Did he take me away before I could suffer*? She smiled at the thought. Her icy skin flushed with the life that had been fading from her a moment ago.

~*He doesn't know me yet. He needs you to be there when he returns.*

The voice wrapped around her like the father's embrace she'd never been able to experience physically.

~*Now is not the time to give in.*

Her chest pulled taught, and she had to fight the sob waiting in her throat.

"He's going to kill me!" she exclaimed, her cry choked off by the panic skittering into her chest. "He's too fast, and I'm only human. I-I-I can't stop him."

She pulled in long breaths, the stark truth sinking into her soul.

~*Not with your own skills or power. But you are not the one fighting, my child. You are doing no more than claiming victory over a beast with no power.*

"That doesn't make any sense," she mumbled around the egg strangling her.

~*Remember the first thing I taught you: my son paid for the salvation of anyone who calls on his name.*

"But Gabe doesn't know Yeshua yet!"

~You do. So why do **you** *fear a creature whose power was nailed to the cross he died on?*

She had no chance to respond before white hot agony chased her back into the world. A pathetic squeal tumbled out to greet the fist pulling away from her.

"Give . . . him . . . back!" she muttered through strangled breaths.

"Who? Gabe? He hasn't gone anywhere. I've given him a front-row seat," the beast replied absently.

Warmth spilled down her muscles and into her bones. She could almost swear gentle fingertips were kneading her insides. He pinned her arms over her head with one hand, dragging the tip of her blade down to scar the leather on one of her exposed sides.

How am I supposed to do this?

He hovered over her, climbing up her body and nuzzling into her neck. The sun itself burned inside her guts, devouring the agony of broken bones and bruises as it grew. She didn't have a single shivering nerve left to care that his tactics shifted from agony to another kind of torture altogether.

"You're glowing," he observed, ghosting the blade up her side. "I wonder if you'll light up or burn out when I'm done with you."

The forge in her eyes shifted into a glorious flame that threatened to leap out and devour him. Kiro grinned at the look, leaning back and settling his weight on her hips.

"So, there's still some fight in you," he commented with giddy excitement.

"I don't have to fight you," she replied.

Kiro tilted his head to the side, causing Gabe's wild, black bangs to drop over his eyes. In response, she closed her eyes and exhaled through her nose.

"You can't use any of Gabe's powers, because you have no authority over his body," she explained, even as his weight came down on her again.

The hand holding her wrists moved down her arm until he planted it on the ground beside her head. Her blade came up to kiss her neck while he watched her with an analytical eye. He wanted her to react to him. Her lack of fear or tears likely frustrated and surprised him. She felt his slow exhale across her face.

The energy blooming inside her washed into each muscle, bringing peace with it. Her mouth turned up into a trace of a smile.

"In fact, you have only the power that others will allow by their own ignorance," she declared.

Her veins thrummed with an electric song, and Kiro's silence skipped a stone across her blood. He stilled, becoming a statue atop her. This delighted her, and she leaned up just enough for the corner of her mouth to touch his ear.

"If you have no true power, then you have no claim to this body," she breathed against him. "I'll have Gabe back now."

She released her sword and shoved her torso up to crash against him. His surprise let her continue despite the electric fire climbing inside her belly as she reached out to grab his shoulder. She yanked him closer, meeting his black eyes with her fire. Her lips pulled up, and her other hand pushed against his chest, sinking beneath it with her gift in her palm.

As if the action were a trigger to strengthen the spiritual power coursing through her, her eyes widened, and she finally saw Kiro Baroch for who he was. He might have been a man once, but the black oil had mutated his form until it bulged in strange places off his arms and abdomen. His face was no more than a saber-toothed maw gaping out of swelled flesh, the top right side of his head sunken down. No wonder Gabe's body was uncomfortable for him.

The snake she had become well acquainted with over her journey coiled around him with its hissing head next to Kiro's high above her.

So, the serpent and the demon are separate, she observed.

Focus. She had to find Gabe.

Yet her gaze still slid back to the grinning face of the demon with no lips and jagged white teeth. This was the creature to whom she had almost lost her life. This was the nightmare that would have devoured her. A shudder passed through her, shifting the power of her gift for a moment of terror to sweep across her.

She felt the weight of her father's presence on her back and pulled in a long breath. Kiro's hands came down on her shoulders, the image engulfing her small stature despite the physical appearance being normal.

"You're in my way," she told the beast.

Sable pushed forward, her arm disappearing into the ink and oil as the snake coiled down toward her, hissing and snapping its teeth inches from her head. Her power shuddered when she flinched away, and her chest cinched so tight that she thought her windpipe had collapsed.

"Father, I need you," she begged, the tightness in her chest ripping open. How easily her life could end right there.

She wanted to cry.

To her astonishment, she saw another pair of hands come down over her own. They were like glowing bronze, and when they touched her skin, her body relaxed, softly whispering, "Ah, yes, this is familiar. This is victory and safety."

In the next instant, a quiet sob came from within Kiro's belly. Sable plunged. She choked on the oil that grabbed at her hair and pulled her down farther. Her eyes stung with the substance, unable to see anything but blackness. Her heart squeezed again, but she refused to acknowledge it.

"Gabe!" she cried, coughing when the thick goo attacked her throat. Still, she sputtered around it. "Come back to me, Gabe!"

Violent coughs wracked her as she continued her descent into the demented soul, the deep cries of a child ringing in her ears until she thought they would burst.

"You're stronger than him, Gabe! Come on!"

Long, spidery fingers touched her face and wiped the slime from her eyes. She caught a glimpse of one chocolate-brown eye before the black oil blinded her again. That look had all the sadness of the world trapped within; it was the most beautiful thing she had ever seen.

She clutched at the hand on her face, hanging onto it like a lifeline. The energy pooling inside her reacted to their union and clamped a thick rope around her belly, yanking her backwards and dragging them out of the depths of his tortured soul. Warmth spilled into her arm as they moved, and she wondered if he felt it too?

She was thrown back into the physical with an unceremonious jolt that sent her head reeling. He stumbled up and away on awkward legs. She crawled to a nearby tree to support her weight while she fought to stand on shaking legs.

A strange calm settled into her chest, easing her excitement and anxiety as if it had never existed. It pressed against her like an embrace, whispering that she had done good and assuring her racing mind that it was over.

Stark realization froze her solid a moment later. She hardly noticed him gasping for breath on the ground a few feet away. Her hands were trembling. She'd just faced the strongest evil the world had feared for centuries, and she had survived.

Sable's throat constricted, shooting fluid into her eyes. No mortal had ever lived to talk of facing Kiro Baroch. Then again, none of his victims had the loving creator standing behind them. A quiet sob broke out of her as she chanced a glance up.

Gabe's brown and blue eyes stared down in pained wonder. Her breath rushed out in a haze of relief that left her feeling lightheaded.

"Thank you, my lord," she prayed shakily.

He didn't respond audibly, but the fuzzy warmth inside her sputtered up like a hug from the deepest parts of her spirit. Tears spilled down her cheeks as she finally understood the power he'd given her. *The Holy Spirit.* A sudden irrational laugh tugged from her throat.

Gabe stared at her, numb to the strange wounds his body was already sealing. It was enough to give her a start, since he healed almost as slowly as a human. *The sword of the spirit.* Her blade lay in the grass, its glow already fading but still entirely unnatural.

She couldn't take her gaze from her friend though. Sable did not think there would ever be a time when she would be so glad to see those mismatched eyes staring back at her, as if she were a ghost.

The two stood in a silence broken only by the crackling fire, neither knowing what to do in the aftermath of a nightmare that should have left her with much less life and far more bruises.

Gabe looked at the purple ink with blackened edges blooming at her throat, knowing full well that his long fingers would fit each painted wound. Her hands were shaking as she stood transfixed by him, yet he found no trace of fear inside her fiery gaze.

Time suddenly rushed to flow again, and she collapsed to the grass with a harsh thud while fresh tears streamed down her cheeks. Gabe raised his hand like he would reach out to her but then dropped it, hopelessly. What could he do to comfort her after his own hands had caused her anguish?

"What did you do to send him back?" he asked in a whisper almost swallowed by the crackling fire.

Sable couldn't find her voice to reply, only stared at him with her huge eyes of flame.

"You should be dead," he stated.

She nodded slowly and mechanically with a slack and stunned expression.

"What did he do to you?"

Sable closed her eyes and drew in a long, agonizing breath. "He was going to torture me. He said he would leave you a 'humble gift'."

CHAPTER 19

"I knew it wasn't you, Gabe."

The sound he released was meant to be a mocking laugh, but it got strangled on its way, coming out like the cry of a wounded animal.

She stood up on brittle legs as if she would come to him, but his face darkened. His brown eye flashed black and amber like a warning that froze her in position.

"It was *my hands* that bruised you, Sable. *Mine* that would have killed you." His shoulders quaked as his voice rose to near hysteria. "Do you know what he does? He wouldn't have just beaten you! His joy is not in breaking the body but the spirit inside. He would have made you *beg* for the sweet release of death."

A small gale bit across her shoulders as he clenched his fists. He worked his jaw and turned from her, raising his face to the sky. The agitated wind chilled her fevered skin, but she did not move. The silence dragged on until its weight just about crushed her.

"He would have left you broken and dying," Gabe continued finally, "moving on after he'd had his fun and leaving you to die alone, frightened, and *stained* by such an unfathomable evil that even your righteous master would have had to turn his face. And he would have just moved on. You'd be nothing. *And it would have been my hands that did it.*"

He raised his palms before his face, releasing a growl from deep in his belly. He fell to his knees, striking the ground with his fist. Sable watched in choked silence, unable to comprehend how blessed her survival was. Gabe's shoulders shook, and he howled into the whipping wind, which grew in its own rage, circling them.

"Look around you!" He gestured with spread arms to the cyclone forming around him, his back still turned as he raged at the world. "Even when I'm myself I'm dangerous. This power grows with rage, don't you see that?"

Her curls whipped across her face as the gale rushed toward him from all directions. It danced in circles about his crumpled form and pressed against him, like it would hold him in a ferocious embrace.

He was so wrong.

Sable's lips pulled up into the ghost of a smile as she let the moment ease into her agitated bones. His wild hair danced in the winds greeting him, and she watched them caress the crumpled spider web of scars across his lower back. Even when he released a frustrated scream, she saw the tension in him begin to ease. It allowed her to pull a gentle calm over her egg.

"You give him such power over you, even now after you've regained control," she stated, taking a few steps toward him on legs much stronger than before. That wind lashed out when she drew close, which widened her gentle smile. "Do you realize he doesn't know how to access your abilities?"

Gabe froze. "What?"

She stepped closer, raising her hand to the gale as if offering her scent to a dog. It hesitated for but a moment before parting, thrashing a whip across her shins as a swift warning.

She stood behind him at arm's length. "He can't call the wind or read my mind."

His back tensed when he realized she was so close, his mouth dropping open as he turned to face her.

"He doesn't even have access to his own power, even though you do." She smiled warmly, crouching before him. "None of it respects him in this way."

The way she gazed at him with such incredible kindness, it struck him in his chest and sent cracks splintering across his bones. She gestured to the power, which began to show signs of calming.

"The wind is a wild thing, constantly changing shape and ferocity, never contained to a single place. It cannot be commanded. It will only serve through love. Why else would it be so desperate to come to you in this way, comforting your rage?"

As Gabe regained his peace, the wind softened, proving her point while he breathed slow, long breaths. It would not leave him, pressing against him in grave concern. He could almost hear it whispering against his skin.

"*Are you alright now?*"

He stared at Sable, speechless that once more she was teaching him about his own self in ways that he had never understood before.

Sable placed her hand over his heart and pulled in a long breath. "I wasn't the one who gave you back control."

Gabe's face became stony and confused. "Then . . . how?"

Her smile widened, pulling in a familiar glow. "What you have with the wind, I have with the one who created the wind."

Instead of scoffing, he was reminded of a time when he'd grabbed her by the arms in a rage and shook her. She'd tried to tell him where that power came from. All this time, she had been fighting with him to show her master was true and just. Since that night, she had done things and survived what no human should have been able to walk away from. *Let that incredible mind of yours prove which of us is true.*

He narrowed his eyes at her, suspicion replacing his guilt. "Do you realize I have never regained control before without at least one divine beating me bloody until my body couldn't sustain his manifestation anymore? And you want me to believe that 'faith' brought me back?"

The amusement that fluttered over her cheeks seemed misplaced.

She shrugged. "Would you prefer the story of a regular human woman defeating him with nothing but her witticisms and charm?"

He chuckled, shaking his head. "You're insane."

"Ha! You realize that's basically the pot calling the kettle black, right?"

He grinned at her response, but it was like a weak cloth that had been stretched too far. Their silence pulled the thin fabric of mirth away, revealing his solemn eyes. Gabe frowned. "I don't know how you did it. Maybe it *was* how you claim. I'm just glad you were able to give me back control. I don't know what I would have done had he—"

He couldn't finish, setting his jaw tight. Images flashed behind his eyes of the nightmare he'd expected to find: her beautiful curls matted with mud and a painting of glorified violation on the canvas of dull, pale flesh. Her glow stolen.

His hands trembled at the thought.

Sable came to him, wrapping her arms around his shoulders and pulling the immortal's head down onto her shoulder. She smoothed his thick hair.

"I'm so sorry, Gabe," she murmured in his ear. "I'm sorry that you are forced to suffer these burdens."

Silence overtook them as her shirt grew wet beneath his clenched eyes. She did not say another word, and he did not make a sound. Each drop onto cloth spoke more than enough for them both.

CHAPTER 20

"Are you sure you're going to be alright?" Gabe asked for the third time in the last hour.

The sun peeked through the branches above. Their fire no more than smoking coals. Gabe had taken to avoiding her, moving away in not so subtle ways as if she were surrounded by a force field that repelled him if she was too close. In a way, there was; a barrier built of shame and regret and dripped ink on delicate skin.

He was a monster.

"I'm fine," she replied, her scratching voice telling him otherwise.

Sable's bruises had darkened, some across her throat dotted with flecks of blue and black. She tossed back a swig of water, struggling to hide her wince when she swallowed.

"How are we going to walk into a battle with my sister if

you can't even breathe without flinching?" Gabe inquired, scowling.

She let out an annoyed breath and turned away from him, mumbling, "at least my ribs were healed when the Holy Spirit started to move."

He hissed, closing his eyes. "He broke those too?"

She nodded, her brows knit together in thought. He remained silent for a moment, struggling to keep the boiling lava in the pit of his stomach from rising higher. She didn't deserve his self-loathing induced rage. She was lucky enough to be alive still. How had he lost control over Kiro so easily? How had Castle been able to poison his psychic power so *flawlessly*?

Flashes of Sable's bruised and sweating face just hours earlier took over behind his eyes, clenching his heart to near bursting. Somehow she'd still been glowing despite the abuse on her body. The pale light had faded as reality crashed down on them.

The holy spirit. That's what she'd called it.

The spirit of truth that lies dormant within us all.

His eyelids rose again.

"Don't you think more could be done then?" he offered, speaking slowly, still deliberating as the words came out.

Sable glanced at him, shock evident in her widened eyes.

"If shattered bones were healed as a by-product, what could he do on purpose?" he elaborated.

Sable laughed, the sound choked off by a whimper when her bruises protested against the vibration. He realized exactly how absurd he must sound to her, as if there was actual hope behind his words. Her mind took a cautious step forward, and Gabe felt her heart stutter. *This is where the dangerous turn shows itself: hope is a fragile thing, and in the hands of an unstable mind, it could turn volatile in an instant if he lost that shimmering thread.*

He clenched his jaw and looked away from her.

"I guess we can find out," she admitted under her breath.

Something shifted in her even as the words came out. A familiar chuckle whispered into her mind, carrying with it the very answer for which she had yet to ask. The ethereal fingertips of Gabe's gift were collecting the revelations as they came, thus teaching him at the same time.

Her master began bringing to life for her the very stories inside her precious book that would show the ease and simplicity with which healings were accessed. Such miracles were like an exhale of the Holy Spirit, rising to the call of the need and requiring no more from the healed than faith in the healing itself. Her lungs stuttered as he fed the words into her mind, stories unfolding of so many occasions where the good son only questioned if they would believe. Each one with a simple conclusion when they told him they did: *And they were healed.*

Lepers losing their affliction. Blind men seeing for the first time. Even a woman who bled for years had done no more than touch his garment, and with the strength of her faith in him, she was healed.

He looked back at her with wonder and awe, just in time to catch her brilliant smile.

"He can," she concluded.

Gabe's jaw fell while his gaze darted from her eyes to her throat and back.

"He already did."

Her hand snapped up to her throat, her mouth dropping open. No words would form on her tongue as the absence of pain seemed to strangle her heart until tears pricked the corners of her eyes. Gabe sat across from her, becoming astonished at the frailty in his warrior. It was like she'd seen a ghost; the color in her face draining to make way for something ugly and raw taking over. For the first time, he could finally see the shape of her broken heart drawn across her features.

Considering the beast that she'd defeated less than a few hours earlier, he couldn't fathom how healing could have been the tool to turn his friend into this leaf. And what could have been so different about this from what Abdaziel had done for her?

As he pondered these things, his memory cast the child he once knew over her image. A little girl who had appeared much younger than her twelve years. Her curly dark hair had almost been longer than her short stature. At that age, her large eyes seemed too big for her, the flames too hot for a child's delicate face. She'd hated him for saving her life time and time again. Yelled at him even, fighting him each time that he had pulled her up into his arms and cradled her against his chest. How many times had he whisked her away from the end of her short life? How many times had she beaten her tiny fists against him for stopping her deranged attempts at suicide?

Yet, staring at the grown woman across from him, he finally recognized what had stood behind that rage like a menace with sharp, grinning teeth inside her mind. A creature that had been carefully cultivated inside of her by the hands of unclean natures.

Fear.

Such fear that it had a full humanoid shape, tormenting her from behind her eyes.

The girl faded into the warrior who stared in wonder at her shaking palms. Tears filled her eyes, and her bottom lip trembled. Not out of terror. No, she was far from afraid.

It was so simple that it broke his heart wide open.

Sable had never known gentle hands, save for the questionable nature of a madman and a trickster. How then could she have ever known that her father would be more than willing to heal her *outside of* pulling her back from the brink of death?

Gabe turned away, a frown pulling down his mouth as he gave her privacy. The ethereal hands dancing out of his mind brushed against a gentle voice carried in the wind.

He could almost swear that it whispered, "will you ever accept my love for you as it is?"

And for once, he wasn't fully convinced that it was meant for her mind alone.

~~~

They were packing up their small camp when the quaking began. At first it was no more than a light tremble under their feet, like a song vibrating inside the earth. Sable noticed it first, her eyes widening with recognition.

"Gabe, do you feel that?" she whispered, her heart squeezing tight with anticipation for impending doom.

He glanced back at her, caught once more by the red, dry eyed remains of the silent breakdown just twenty minutes prior.

"There's plenty of things to feel out here, Sable. Which one are you asking about?"

His flippant tone earned him a glare, but he grinned at
~~~

its flames.

The ground began to hum. It skittered up into her shins as she stepped forward. It lurched with a sudden urgency that buckled her knees and sent her tumbling against the trunk of a tree.

Gabe's humor increased as the earth gave a wild buck beneath them. Then another and another. He strolled over to Sable, who couldn't seem to collect her legs beneath her while she clung to the tree. Above them, the trees swayed and danced together, branches snapping under their wild movements. Gabe placed a hand on Sable's back between her shoulder blades, his other arm making an arched gesture above his head.

The falling branches began to splinter against a grey wall of angry wind circling in a figure-eight motion and protecting the pair below, tossing pieces of wood to the ground all around them.

"What's going on?" she demanded, rage singing inside her voice.

He didn't miss the anxiety gathered behind it. His mismatched eyes softened when he looked down on the warrior struggling to stop her legs from collapsing. Her cheeks were dusted with red, and a small scrape bloomed crimson on her cheekbone. The color irrationally agitated him. Her humanity, for one long second, almost sickened him to his core.

"Hang on," he ordered, not that she could do anything else.

Why couldn't she be like every other human he'd known, boring and *safe* in their house, fully aware that this world of gods and monsters was not for them? She would die on him eventually, no matter what he did to prevent it. He was so well aware of that fact that it rang inside his bones and screamed at him from something warm in his chest.

His gaze remained steadfast, like a guard over her, though his mind shifted. It sent out psychic arms high above the trees and deep inside the earth. His gut told him that this was no natural earthquake, but he would search everywhere nonetheless. He commanded the power to find a source, the arms shivering in response to his mental voice. They stretched above the swaying trees, spreading in every direction and allowing his mind to break apart into many sights. He saw the tree line through which they had entered, the grotesque aftermath of demented magic still lying there in the sunlight. He hardened his jaw, turning to another sight: the expanse of green that was dancing in the wild grumbling of the earth. He saw the shape of the tremors from the movement of the trees. Him and Sable were near the edge of the waves coming through the earth.

So, it's below . . ..

As if in response, his mind closed off the feedback from every psychic arm in the sky and opened all those in the blackness of the earth.

The shocks were getting stronger, white-hot lightning spreading up into Sable's legs with each buck of the ground. She cried out, but it didn't sound like anguish; the sound was more like an angry howl. Frustrated. She was frustrated with the ache showing itself as she lost her purchase and fell to her knees.

Gabe crouched with her, keeping one strong hand against her back like he was going to send his strength to her. A shot of fire raced up his throat at the thought. *Why did she have to be human? Why couldn't her god, with all his power, strengthen her weak body to suit the road she walked?*

She had the heart and the will for something so much stronger. It was almost laughable that her body refused to understand the quality of the warrior it would one day destroy.

The psychic hand he followed broke through a wall of earth, finding sunlight so suddenly that he let out a gasp. That breath was sucked back in though when understanding followed.

His sudden laugh drew Sable's attention. His lips wore a snarl, and he closed his eyes.

"It's her," he whispered venomously.

Sable didn't have to ask. *Castle. She's the one causing this earthquake.*

"No, it's worse," he responded to the thought, not even aware she hadn't spoken aloud. "She's shifting the earth itself. Breaking it open. She's isolating the city from us."

As if Castle had become aware she'd been caught, the world fell still again. Peace returned to the earth as suddenly as the chaos, creeping silence beneath the groaning trees that were still moving in the aftershock of the quake. Sable's heart reached her throat, strangling her as she forced her legs under her.

"We have to move," Gabe concluded, surprising her with its genuine urgency.

He all but dragged Sable along behind him. She could barely collect her shaken legs under her as she fought to keep up. Branches whipped at her, and the heat on her cheek told her that more cuts had appeared. He pulled on her to stay with him, but she wasn't as fast as him. A dull pulsating ache opened in her shoulder. Not a good sign.

"Gabe!" she cried, twisting her arm in his hold and trying with all her strength to yank it from him. "Let me go, and slow down!"

He made a sound in the back of his throat, close to that of a growling dog, but a moment later, he released her. The sudden lack of momentum sent her tumbling to the ground. He stepped away from her, crossing his arms and frowning as she struggled to stand up. When she turned her gaze to his, the forges were ready to eat him alive.

"What is going on with you?" she shouted, her fists balled at her sides.

Silence answered her, thick with contempt while he glared at her. She stepped toward him, jabbing a finger against his chest.

"We don't have time for you to go into your confusing mood swings right now! If you're so bloody determined to get there, then go." Her tone shuddered at the accusing words, even while she gestured with her arm toward the direction they were running. "If you keep dragging me along like this, you'll dislocate my shoulder or snap my bloody arm! If I'm slowing you down, just leave me here. I'll get there on my own."

That time he at least scoffed. Still, she received silence from her trickster. He wouldn't break eye contact, but his jaw remained clenched. She searched his eyes, her heart racing as if the ground still danced beneath them.

"Why are you angry with me?"

The question earned her an annoyed groan. He uncrossed his arms, his glare hardening into steel; darkening his brown eye until it reminded her once more of the endless black of an abyss.

"You said so yourself: I can hurt you. With ease. Without even being aware of the strength exerted to do it." His voice rumbled like stones that rolled across her skin, leaving quiet bruises in their wake. "I almost killed you within the last twenty-four hours. Twice. You wanted to kill me when you broke down yesterday, and your hold did *nothing.*"

He stepped closer, forcing her to look up as he towered over her. His hands pressed down on her shoulders. She fought every instinct that reared its ugly head, determined to stand defiant and not give him the satisfaction of seeing her flinch away from him.

"My sister is alive and well. I have spent twelve thousand years certain I killed her, and she is right there at the end of this race in a city you intend to save." His face softened. "You're going to make me choose whether I kill her for good or lose you."

She stopped breathing. His face hardened once more, and he seemed to become aware of himself. He looked down at his hands, his long fingers engulfing her shoulders. Then his eyes returned to her face, searching and prodding the bone structure like he would discover something new about her. Then his hands flexed. His fingers curled into her skin, tightening around her shoulders and drawing the warmth of anguish to the surface.

"Gabe . . .." She spoke his name like a warning, but he heard it like a prayer.

"You don't even understand how delicate you are," he growled, his eyes narrowing as they continued to explore her face.

You're watching for weakness, but you forget that I am not afraid of pain. She sent him the thought, silencing her tongue and taking the ache with a straight face.

His hold grew tighter. "You should be."

I will not fear you, Gabe. He wasn't testing her strength; he was testing the fragile trust she'd placed in the palm of his hands.

"You—" he choked on the words, closing his eyes and hanging his head.

You should. She didn't have to be psychic to hear what he would have said.

His black hair brushed her face, and she exhaled into it. The pulse beneath his fingers told her bruises were beginning to form under his hold.

"Gabe," she whispered into his obsidian spikes. "I don't want to kill her. I probably can't. But I also can't let people die just because of my mortality."

There it was. Hammer. Nail.

He laughed and then released her. He leaned back, running a hand through his wild hair. Sable frowned as she watched his nervous chuckles, tucking away the observation of the last few moments. His eyes grew lighter again, allowing something warm to spill across his cheeks.

"You'd risk your life knowing you're outmatched and that she won't hesitate to kill you," he concluded, shaking his head.

She nodded.

He pulled in a long breath that got caught in his throat. Then he nodded, swallowing hard.

"Alright then." He turned from her, placing a hand on his hip as he looked toward the direction they were headed. "I'll let you play the hero. But let me make one thing clear here and now: If your god lets you die, I will hold him accountable, and I will find him, and he will answer for it. Understood?"

She froze. "What—"

"Am I understood, Sable?" he prompted again, his voice low and dark.

"Gabe, where is this coming from?"

How had he shifted so far from thinking she was being misled to not only believing but also *despising* her father if she went home to him? She was going to re-create Kazious all over again.

"I can't protect you when you have this crazy notion that you'll give your life in a heartbeat for *anyone*," he snarled, still refusing to face her. "But if your god is as powerful as he's led you to believe, keeping you safe and alive should be as easy as breathing."

"But that's not—"

"Sable, shut up! I will *not* watch you die. If you can't tell me that he will keep you alive, then all of this right here, it's over."

"Why is this suddenly coming out, Gabe? Tell me that

first," she said, struggling to maintain a level tone.

He finally turned to her, his eyes half lidded and a hard frown pulling at his mouth.

"You are more family to me than the twin I'm going to have to kill for you," he admitted, the words grating on their way out like gravel crunching underfoot. "This whole idea of saving her from her hatred and all that, it's a dream. It's ridiculous. And it will get you killed. You may be fine with that. I know you've never wanted to live this long anyways. But I'm not ready to lose you again, and certainly not if it's permanent. I won't take you into that city if you won't tell me you'll walk back out."

"Gabe, you're right. I don't want to be here," she began with a quiet earnestness as she stepped closer to him. "This world has never loved or accepted me, not even other fellow humans. I *want* to go *home*."

Something in him snapped. "What the hell does that even mean, Sable? Do you hear yourself? When I'm the one who sounds more sane in the group, there's a bloody problem! If you want to die so badly, just say the word, and I'll do it myself!"

The shape of his words froze her egg solid, stretching spikes of ice down until they pierced her heart. She narrowed her eyes as the chill allowed her to think with less emotion clouding her mind.

"You can't even begin to comprehend the things that I have faced down since you last saw me," she hissed, drawing his glare to the rage building on her face. "I have survived things you couldn't even *try* to imagine. I don't know when I will be called home, but I do know that I will fight to my last breath. So, stop acting like I'm still the defenseless thirteen-year-old child you saved from a madman! I'm a grown woman and a warrior, and I will *not* be commanded by *anyone* to step down from *anything* no matter how strong they are! And if you want to test me on that, then bring it on. *I dare you* to stop me, Gabe!"

Her hand snapped to her sword hilt before he even registered what she'd said. The sound of it singing out of its sheath drew a grin to his lips, and a dangerous gleam lit up his eyes.

"You're insane," he muttered, gathering a red glow to his palms.

"Takes one to know one," she spat.

"What makes you think you stand a chance against me?" he asked as they circled each other.

"I did just fine against Kiro, and he had every intention of killing me. What makes you think you'll have the resolve after everything you just said?"

He laughed, but it held no true humor. "Maybe I just want to incapacitate you until I can deal with Castle myself and take her off your radar."

"And what about the next divine that shows up on it? Or the one after that? Are you going to babysit me for the rest of my life? Fight all my battles and keep me broken in the background like some twisted form of an overprotective big *brother*?"

He growled like a lion. "You are *no match* for the monsters in this world, Sable!"

"I don't need to be a match for them, because my father already took away all their power, you moron!"

"That makes no sense!"

"It would if you'd listen to me!"

He threw out his hand, the power sliding off and coming for Sable faster than she could lift her blade. It struck with the force of a full-grown man, throwing her back against a tree. The power latched onto her, seeping cold threads through her metal and leather armor, piercing her skin. She gritted her teeth, and instead of struggling, she dove her mind down until she touched the gift resting in her chest.

The spirit surged within her, winding around the strength of her gift and rising out of her. It pushed on the crimson power, spreading to counteract each place it made contact with her and shoving back.

Sable brought herself to her feet, raising her hand to the red magic and brushing it away like a measly pest. Across from her, Gabe stood with wide eyes. He could hardly believe he had attacked at all, let alone that she simply stood there with perfect, beautiful rage spilling out of her amber eyes. The glow he'd always seen on her bloomed out like a protective shield that covered her entire body.

"Do it again. *I dare you*," she said in a lethal whisper.

"How—"

She leaped toward him, her sword arcing down toward his jugular. His other hand, still gloved with red power, caught her blade as he stood there in shock. He pushed with his mind, shoving her back with a force she couldn't see. She stumbled a step but lunged again as soon as she regained her footing.

Another cloud of red shot toward her, but she sliced down with her blade. Gabe watched while his power disintegrated against the sword, unable to move as she continued toward him. The point of her sword stopped a hair's breadth from his bobbing Adam's apple. His mouth hung slack. If he were a man, he would have been defeated.

"I am never alone, Gabe, and though I am still a fragile human, his power is greater than *anything*," she explained. "Understand this: I can't guarantee that I will walk out of that city. But if I do not, it will be his will, just as it will be if I do."

He locked his jaw, turning his eyes away. Was that shame she saw in them? She couldn't be sure, but she slid her sword back into its sheath and knelt down to placed a palm against his cheek.

"I don't want to kill your sister, and I don't want you to either." Her voice was soft, like a cloud, pressing forgiveness against him. "We need to know if she's the one behind these pseudo-immortals, but I also know that she isn't evil. She's broken, just like you, and she's harbored a poison inside her heart for all these years. I never realized she was divine until we fought three years ago, but now that I know her relation to you, I'm certain her hatred is related to that cult. We have to *heal* her, not kill her."

His lips pulled up into a hard line, but he couldn't respond. He nodded though. The power around his fists eased back inside him, and he let his shoulders droop as the tension fell.

"Let's go," he mumbled, gesturing toward their destination beyond the trees.

CHAPTER 21

"Damnit," Gabe cursed, clenching his fists.

They stood at the edge of a chasm, the distance between the two cliffs almost enough to fit a village. Nothing could be seen at the bottom of the pit save for pitch blackness. Behind the cliff across from them, they could see the edge of the city. No wall surrounded it, likely no one ever thinking something could get past the guardians outside.

The stillness of the air unsettled Sable's heart. She glanced up at the immortal, her brows knit together.

"Don't tell me this could actually stop you," she jested, the humor halfhearted after the confrontation earlier.

He let out a long breath and turned his gaze toward her. His hand came to rest on the top of her head. The serious look in his eyes drew her coil back into its place.

"It can't stop me, but it can stop *us*. I can't cross this safely with you. I can't even guarantee my power will get me across on the first try," he explained solemnly.

"Oh."

He could get her killed if he tried to send her across.

"I've caused you enough pain," he grumbled, looking away from her.

She chewed her lip, pulling in a long breath to settle her nerves. "If you promise you won't let her hurt anyone, you can go, Gabe. I'll figure something out."

The hand atop her head rustled her hair as if she were still a child. She glared up at him.

"I'm not leaving your side, you suicidal brat," he declared, smiling like a proud brother. "What's your dad got to say about that?"

She almost laughed. That was the second time he had turned to her father for help.

Sable lifted her gaze to the sky, her mouth tilted up at the edges.

"Father, nothing catches you off guard," she prayed softly. "I give praise to your glory, and I submit myself humbly to your will. How are we to pass this challenge, my lord?"

He already began to respond before she even finished speaking. The light Gabe had grown accustomed to spilled out of her skin, making him stumble away from her.

~*Do you trust in me, daughter*?

Her face lit up with a glorious smile. "You know I do."

~*Then walk across the chasm.*

The light within her stuttered, her smile faltering. "What?"

He opened her mind again, allowing words to be written behind her eyes as he taught her what his book had recorded of him.

If you say, "the Lord is my refuge," and you make the Most High your dwelling, no harm will overtake you.

Her legs began to move as the verses came to her, pulling on the coil inside her chest until it untied the knot and led her farther.

No disaster will come near your tent. For he will command his angels concerning you to guard you in all your ways.

She heard Gabe whisper her name in gentle reproach. He couldn't fathom the sight unfolding before him.

Still, her mind saw the words that eased into her bones with a heavy blanket of peace. She opened her mind to her psychic friend in hopes that he would see what her father was pouring into her.

They will lift you up in their hands, so that you will not strike your foot against a stone . . ..

The gasp confirmed he'd touched the invitation in her head.

A bony, spidery hand laced with hers. He didn't say a word, nor did he turn his gaze from the blind trust on her face. For an ancient man, he was utterly and unfathomably uneducated on the concept of faith. But no one could deny the sight of the regular human warrior and her immortal trickster walking on nothing above a black gorge.

She opened her eyes only when Gabe urged her to do so. They'd made it two thirds of the way, and he wanted her to see the incredible moment she was creating. Her fingers tightened around his when her throat shrank to the size of a pebble.

She saw the other ledge ahead of them, but her eyes traveled down the cliff into the blackness below. Her heart rose into her shrunken throat, and she locked her jaw tight.

Gabe squeezed her hand, directing her attention back to him. He smiled, his cheeks slightly dimpling in a way she had never noticed before.

"He's really taking care of you," he whispered.

Sable glanced down once more, swallowing stones into her lungs even as she smiled. She raised her eyes again, seeking the destination ahead of them and pushing toward it.

Their feet touched solid earth, and Sable let out a gasp. From thin air to earth, nothing was different beneath her feet.

"I will never get used to that," she muttered, hugging one arm around herself.

Gabe chuckled. "You plan on making 'walking on thin air' a regular occurrence?"

Sable scoffed, shaking her head and smiling. "I hope not. But I meant . . . obedience despite appearance. He's always telling me that I can do things, and most of the time

I have no indication as to how, even after I've done it."

His smirk settled into gentle mirth as he put a hand on her shoulder.

"You've taught me something valuable about trust today," he whispered.

He gave her small fingers a squeeze before releasing them and turning to the sight ahead.

The edge of the city had small, scattered buildings built from white stones. They looked to be made of the same material as the wall inside the tree line, far behind them. The houses were closer together and taller as they neared the center and encircled two citadels that stood high against the backdrop of the glowing sky and green treetops. A golden sheen bloomed from those towering buildings like a cloud that expanded around the city.

"Well, I guess we have an evil twin to track down," Gabe declared. He let out a short laugh and shook his head. "I never thought I'd have the chance to live this particular story line."

"Why is there no one moving about?" Sable asked.

Gabe squinted, confirming her observation. The streets stood in silence, not a soul out for a stroll. Nor were any children playing in the streets or guards posted near the edge, as far as he could tell. He turned back to Sable, caught by the hard steel forged in her eyes.

"Hey, it's a holy city. Maybe they're having a service," he offered.

"Not likely," she replied.

As they entered the silent city, the quiet itself seemed like it wore eyes scraping against Sable's back while they moved. The walls themselves were alive and shifting to watch the pair. Where were the scorch marks from the raging flames? Where were the bodies?

None of this added up properly.

If they were too late, they should have seen evidence of the attack. If not, where were the people? *And what was Castle doing while we were catching up*?

"Keep your guard up," she warned, one hand already reaching for her sword. "She could be waiting for us anywhere, and who knows what she could have done here."

Beside her, Gabe grinned like a schoolboy.

"I doubt it's anything too elaborate," he said. "Perhaps

they just never thought to station guards, since that guy and his pony are supposed to weed out the bad guys." His tone dipped into something sarcastic and deadly. "Remember, only those who are blessed should be able to enter this 'holy' city."

She turned to him with a hard frown. "Don't think a place is holy just because people declare it to be. A thing is not made holy by popular vote."

"That's the point," he replied, rolling his eyes. "These people are blinded and vulnerable, because they think their gods have favored them."

Sable remained in careful silence for a long moment before replying. "Why do I feel like you're about to draw a comparison between them and me?"

To her surprise, he clapped a hand on her shoulder, his smile illuminated with a gentle assurance.

"I wouldn't dare," he said earnestly.

A soft smile stole her lips as she wondered why his words urged her toward a ridiculous act of weeping. Her stone egg thrummed with a steady warmth that was almost comforting. She nodded, turning away from him and swallowing hard. No one had ever reached the point where they'd actually believed her despite holding contempt for others of faith. It felt entirely strange, and she didn't quite know what to do with it. She had never done this before.

Sure, Castle had believed her and in her father, but she had made a clear distinction: keep him out of her world. That had only one of two options for falling apart. Either Sable would have eventually turned from her father for the sake of her friend, or the other . . . well, it shouldn't have needed to involve so much blood. She had only wanted to help.

Sable's heart clenched so tight, she thought it would burst inside her chest.

"Gabe, let's check these houses," she said, already moving away from him. "I want to know where everyone is."

He didn't respond, but didn't try to stop her either. Some part of her safely assumed that he knew something had changed within her.

She ducked inside a small stone hut, already aware of the ethereal stillness that told her no one was home. She found the chill of the wall comforting as she leaned against it and breathed. Her chest had begun to tear open. She couldn't stop it.

Many of Sable's aches were like well-polished stones. The torment she faced as a child, the scars written across her body, they were a memory that she touched often and would seldom find new cuts in her hand when she held them for a time. Her body had natural responses based on the abuse to which it was accustomed, but the memories themselves barely stirred a ripple in her heart.

Kazious was jagged still, but he was safe in her heart, tucked away behind her faith and her father's love. Waiting for her. The sharp edges of that stone were locked inside a warm barrier of peace. She would return to him; she had no reason to ache for him.

The guilt of the dead still clung to her skin like mud. It wasn't inside her anymore except for flashes of the dead in her mind at times. The absence of their distinct faces tormented her more than anything. The blood on her hands could not be washed away, and she had come to accept it like a tattoo only she could see. It hurt, but it was almost manageable.

Castle was another story. She was a dagger that pressed against Sable's collarbone, the point scraping on her stone egg and leaving white grooves in its shell. Her smile alone could crack bones with its simple ferocity, and the ache she left behind was a hole punched straight through Sable's abdomen. It began to hemorrhage, and it had gotten infected after three years of pretending it wasn't there. Functioning like a regular person just searching for their lost friend, as if that friend hadn't been scarred by her own shaking hand. As if that friend hadn't responded with such a violation of the mind that Sable had since been able to recognize the feel of a psychic hand like a tangible thing reaching inside of her.

As if Castle hadn't left her for dead in the same hour they had shared dinner together.

A ragged breath fell from her lips as agony washed over her. A full-body flame lit up and raged at the memory. Salted fluid appeared in her eyes, but she wouldn't acknowledge its appearance. She swallowed hard, balling her hands into fists. It was worse knowing Castle . . . who'd once been Rose . . . was right there in the city somewhere and that Sable would have to stop her if she couldn't save her.

"People are missing, Sable," she told herself, pulling in another long, slow breath. "Find them. Break down later."

She could have laughed. She'd been telling herself "later" for three years.

Closing her eyes, she gave herself a moment to settle into the ache, to let it embrace her like an old friend. Another ragged exhale filled the empty foyer. Her eyes glowed as they opened. She locked her jaw and swallowed the rest of the flames down into her belly. Her hand rose to the hilt of her sword. As it slid out, its song settled the stone into place over her flesh.

She moved through the house on mechanical legs. Her ears were trained for any small sound in the disconcerting silence. The walls still watched her move, but it seemed much worse inside. It was as if the room were full and she were in the way of a thick crowd. The weight of body heat and judging stares settled on her shoulders. Her breath came in short, thick gasps. The air was too thin for all its occupants.

But the house was empty.

No.

It wasn't just empty. It was so much more than empty.

Desolate. That was the word she wanted. Solitary and lonely. The sort of emptiness that left behind the physical shape of what had abandoned it. A stillness that screamed in agony for what once was moving inside it. This was utter abandonment, a place where the air itself communicated how unnatural and desperate the home was. It was as if she'd walked into a broken heart. It was a silence that whispered across her shoulders until she could almost swear the inhabitants were saying her name.

~*They're here,* he warned, freezing her blood into solid ice.

She stopped in front of a window that overlooked the street she'd left behind. There, with a familiar smile on her pink lips, stood Gabe's sister, her hands on her hips. A man much taller than her stood to her right, a murderous gleam shining on his face. His eyes were no more than coal-black voids.

Gabe lay crumpled at his sister's feet. Sable didn't know

if he was even conscious.

CHAPTER 22

Sable and Castle locked eyes through the window. Liquid gold and forge fire recounted in a moment the decade they'd shared together. Castle's scar seemed to glare at the woman inside.

"What have you done to him?" Sable shouted, stepping closer to the opening.

If she had to, the window was wide enough and close enough to the ground. She could be on the street in no time.

Castle's smile turned into a childish giggle. She raised one hand, gesturing for Sable to come closer, but Sable remained steadfast. Her gift stirred when the air shifted around them. As if a film were drawn up off her eyes, she saw the shape of the emptiness that had been the suffocating cloud inhabiting the city. She locked her jaw.

It was a squirming mass of shining, obsidian serpents.

They were contorted around each other, knotted in a great mass of liquid shadows that pressed on her from all sides. She didn't move, even as her instincts skittered down her sword arm.

"Don't worry about him," Castle said, her mouth twisted into a sinister grin that didn't match her gentle face. "I have a special plan in store for him. I've waited far too long for this to let his death come too soon."

She flicked her wrist, and the darkness shifted to follow her command. It rushed from around Sable, spilling out from the house and the surrounding streets until Gabe was enveloped in a cloud of night, void of stars or the moon.

Sable turned her mind to her father, sending a quiet prayer from inside her secret heart. *Keep him safe, please. Give me the strength to protect him as well as save her, Father. I don't want her hatred to engulf her. Don't let her kill her brother.*

Something snagged as the words found her prayer. Shards of glass settled into her chest, surrounding her stone egg like a protective barrier. It seemed counterproductive considering the edges were pressing against the shell, just like Castle's dagger.

One more breath.

She leapt down from the window, bending her knees when her boots hit the stones. The glow of the city's strange light seemed to pool across her sword as she stepped forward. She raised her hand, drawing the blade until it was pointed like an accusation at her adversary, who was once her friend and teacher.

"You know I can't let you do this," Sable stated.

Castle smirked, drawing her sword from its scabbard at her hip.

"I missed our sparring, my little forge." The words sounded like honey as she moved away from Gabe and the strange, murderous puppet at her side. "I warned you before, and I'll say it once again: I love you, Sable, but no one will stop me from destroying the broken little whelp who *stole* my death!"

Sable almost rolled her eyes.

"You sound just like him," she said, a sarcastic smile finding its way to her lips.

When Castle paused, narrowing her eyes, Sable took it

as a good sign.

"All the two of you seem to care about is dying. You've lived for twelve thousand years waiting to die and hating your immortality," she explained, a sliver of hope rising in her chest. "You can't tell me you haven't known a shred of joy inside those years. I spent a decade at your side, *Rose*."

Castle lunged, crossing the distance between them in the space of a breath. Their blades clashed, but Sable twisted and redirected the attack until their swords were down by her side. Then she flicked her wrist upwards, her blade rising toward her teacher's chest. She didn't want to fight. That was all she could think of as Castle danced out of the reach of her weapon. She couldn't bring herself to draw more blood. They circled each other with leaping strikes. Sable's heart raced with each reverberating clash of their swords. Her eyes still remembered the exact impression of her old teacher's speed and grace, allowing her to follow movements that would have caught her off guard with anyone else. She twisted out of the reach of her sword over and over again.

Her sensitive shoulder started to pound with each movement of her arm. She'd never had a battle tire her out so fast before and her mind began to shout at her that she was forgetting something important. Her next slash downward barely deflected the blow coming for her face. If she lifted her sword again, her leaden bones would surely snap with the pressure.

"Dammit, Castle, listen to me!" she finally cried out.

Said woman ignored her, slithering in for another attack, the smirk on her lips stopping Sable's heart cold when she blinked out of sight again. A bolt of lightning travelled down her arm and she cried out. Castle's sword sank deep into the wound Abdaziel had healed on her just the other day. The screaming of her mind halted with the cold rush of agony. As the woman pulled back, the blade's release from her skin forced her hand to open, closing off her heart at the same time. Castle came forward again, smirking like she'd won, but Sable had honed her skills in the last three years. She let her sword fall and clenched her teeth hard. Her hands came up in gestures that would have seemed random to anyone watching, but in the space of a gasp, something snapped in Castle's wrist. The dull pop was louder than a cry.

Both swords clattered to the ground, shattering the stillness as Castle was yanked up to her student's height.

"Castle, he wanted to save his sister; you can't hate him for that!" Sable shouted into the woman's ashen face. "How can you punish someone for an act of love?"

Gold eyes narrowed, and Castle locked her jaw hard. "Because of his act of 'love,' I will *never* see our mother again," she whispered venomously.

Sable's heart locked on those words as if her teacher had punched through her ribcage. She released the woman, her hands falling numb at her sides, and she stepped back. Castle fell into a heap on the ground on her hands and knees.

"You can though," Sable assured her, suddenly aware of the ache in her shattered egg. "I have told you before exactly where she went. Why can't that give you peace?"

Castle glared at her. She grasped her sword in her good hand and scrambled back to her feet. "Peace is a luxury I can't afford. She would have been better off if Anzillu had never created us in the first place."

She raised her hand, pointing over Sable's shoulder as she stepped toward her. "It is *her* vengeance I will take from him," Castle explained, taking another step forward. "*She* deserved a life where *we didn't exist*."

She lunged.

The words held such a weight that Sable could do no more than stand frozen in place for the mere second Castle needed. The blade pressed into Sable's shoulder before she could recollect herself.

Even then, Sable's mouth hardened into a line while she connected her gaze with the black flapping wings of a child's rage in her teacher's golden eyes. She was going to die - but she couldn't seem to care just yet. *But if you never existed, what would have happened to me?*

An electric jolt snapped down from the wound opening in her shoulder, and her hand raised to catch the hilt, wrapping around Castle's hand. Red-hot agony opened up, blood seeping from around the sword's edge. The rest of the blade scraped against her armor.

She snapped a hard kick against Castle's stomach. At the same time, Sable shoved with her torso until their hands were pinned between them.

"You don't think her love for you was worth her knowing you even for that short time?" Sable asked in a low whisper.

She brought her fist up to the other woman's cheekbone. Punching Castle was nothing like when she'd hit Gabe. Flesh connected with flesh, and something sickening cracked under her knuckles.

They're just like us. How did he harden himself then? Her mind settled back on curiosity, ebbing away from the danger and easing into a calmness that she understood. The twins weren't physically stronger than her. Gabe had done something to strengthen himself, but Castle could bruise and break and *bleed*.

She let out a long, steadying exhale. Then she punched again.

And again.

And again.

"Do you think your mom wished you away?" she yelled. "Do you think she didn't look for you when you were taken?"

Again and again she swung until her knuckles bled, and she wasn't sure if they were cut open or if it was Castle's red weeping face smearing onto her hand.

"What kind of mother would *regret* her *child*?"

The question tasted like acid on her tongue. *My mother did*. She shoved it away. She was an anomaly built out of the careful cultivation of a world living around superstition. This was Castle. This was a child who had been stolen away and turned into a monster. This was different.

Castle caught her next punch.

She heard the wisp of moving shadows before she remembered her dear friend had been imprisoned by the slithering wraiths Castle controlled. Now they were coming for her, and she was trapped against her teacher with a sword half-embedded in her chest.

"It's not about *regret,* you ignorant little girl," Castle breathed, much calmer than before.

Something slid across Sable's arm; it wet her skin like soft mist, but it shivered as well in a familiar way that reminded her of black ink washing over her body when Gabe had forced it to protect her. She knew better than to think it would hold back is hunger for pain this time.

"It's about the *torture* she went through. *Because* she

had to love *two bloody abominations*. And she . . ." *Snap.* "Deserved . . ." *Snap.* "Better."

Sable cried out, the bones in her arm crushed beneath the serpent encircling her limb.

The thick black mist shifted as something moved from within, pausing like a dog lifting its ears to a distant noise, and the deep baritone voice that came from there rang out against the terror in Sable's heart. She thought the sarcastic fool would never bring her more joy than at that moment.

"You know, I might have let you take your revenge quietly after that sob story," he said, wrapping a thick psychic arm around Sable's waist.

The arm tugged, and a moment later, her back hit his chest. His long arms came around her like a protective shield, and Gabe rested his chin on top of her head.

"But you've hurt someone I care about. And now I have to kill you."

CHAPTER 23

"Gabe, what happened to you?" Sable couldn't stop the urgent question from stumbling out.

Castle glared at the pair, silent for the moment as she assessed the brother she hadn't expected to get up.

"Sissy here doesn't quite understand what brought me to life in the first place," he replied.

She heard the grin in his voice and her throat constricted. *Kiro*. His black magic he called illusions.

Castle's powers had no effect on him.

"What about the man with her?" Sable asked, her fists shaking.

"You mean tall, dark, and very dead? Yeah, he was giving your dear friend his power while she fought you, so he had like, *no* power left to him by the time I got up. Buddy never stood a chance."

With Gabe's aloof attitude came a temporary disconnect in Sable from the terror of the last few moments. Her head reeled between the relief of him being alive and the agony of her pulsating arm. Nausea welled up inside her. Her skin was flushed and hot.

"Gabe," she breathed, an edge of desperation slicing her throat.

He moved his arms from her, running his hands down her shoulders in a way she assumed should have been comforting.

"Rest for now, Sable," he whispered into her curls. He stood up next her, his fists clenched at his sides. "What happened to the people in this city, Castle?"

It almost made Sable laugh again. Since when were people his concern? But she remained silent.

Castle smiled at her brother, the look made more sinister by the tumbling sparks in her brown eyes. She raised her hand, and the black shadows hovering, waiting, began to shudder.

"It's easier to control living ash than it is to control many minds," she answered in a silken voice.

Sable's vision reared its ugly head inside her memory. Her throat closed off, and her body grew ice cold. *They couldn't move. They couldn't scream. Only their eyes could show the terror as the flames engulfed them. Melted them. Destroyed them all.*

"No!"

They were too late. They couldn't save the people. They had failed.

She'd failed.

"Bullshit," Gabe spat. "Your entire goal is based around my death isn't it? What could the slaughter of an entire city accomplish? Trying to get me mad? Good luck with that."

Castle grinned, raising her hand to stifle a giggle. "Are you trying to act like you *know* me?"

Gabe crossed his arms. "I don't have to. I know Sable well enough to trust that if she thinks you aren't just a stone-cold hag, there's truth to it."

He's right. Sable stepped forward, her shaking arms reaching out like she would cross the space and embrace her teacher.

"Castle, you don't have to let this hatred lead you," she

said with a voice so gentle that it seemed to give the twisting darkness pause. "Please, let me show you peace. My master loves you so much, and so do I. Don't make me watch you destroy yourself for this."

Gabe stared down at the girl, his jaw slack and his arms dropping back to his sides. He gathered his clouds of red and black power as he watched her, stepping away when the tendrils reached for her glowing skin. She was on the edge of tears. It was utterly astonishing. Castle had almost killed her. Snapped her arm with ease, damn near sliced her in half. And still, she stood there next to him trying to redeem his twin.

"I already told you: I want no part of your peace," Castle replied, acid dripping down the words.

Sable closed her eyes and took a deep breath. Her arms fell. She turned, and when the forges reappeared, they were dim with resolve.

"Then you are too dangerous to be left alive," she whispered.

That was Gabe's cue. He sent out his mind first, pushing against his sister's back with a psychic wave that she couldn't sense until she'd already stumbled closer. His hands raised, and the power formed three solid metal spikes from each palm.

She smirked though, and at the last moment, her mind pooled psychic hands beneath her feet. She shot up from the trap, landing gracefully to the side of the attack. Her hand traced the obsidian edge before Gabe even realized she'd moved.

"It's too bad," she said, almost to herself. "This isn't the right stage for our final battle, Gabe. He'll have fun with you for now as I prepare it though."

He narrowed his eyes on her, shifting his hand to branch off another spike where her palm was. Blood dripped against the magic, but she was gone.

Again.

"Dammit!"

The whistle of a blade soaring through wind drew Sable's attention off the twins just in time to see that murderous grin again. The stranger with eyes like voids was barely an inch from her face with a curved obsidian dagger. *Gabe, you idiot!* The puppet still lived.

She stumbled away, her broken arm limp as she scrambled to unsheathe her own dagger with her other hand. Castle's laughter danced all around them, bouncing off the stones of the houses and pounding on their skulls.

"Not this again," Sable grumbled.

She heard Gabe cry out, and her heart sank. *Not his mind. Not his mind!* She couldn't deal with any of that right now. But she had no time to consider what Castle's laughter was doing to him as she dodged another attack. Her hip stung, and she realized his blade hadn't fully missed. Warmth dribbled from the wound, but she couldn't gauge its severity. She had to twist again. And again. It was a deadly dance all over again, but this opponent she wasn't familiar with, and he had a speed that her human legs couldn't match. The sting in her hip lit a fire in her blood though.

She clenched her teeth, lashing out with her blade at the same time as she spun out of another attack. Her blade plunged into his chest, sinking to the hilt. She almost found a leap of relief in her chest, but his arms locked around her back and pulled her to the ground with him. Chilly terror raced up her spine, smothering the flames her previous wound had lit up within her. *He should be disintegrating!*

They landed with a heavy thud, his arms like iron bars around her shoulders. Her shattered arm was pinned to her side, and she bit her lip hard to cut off the yelp waiting behind it.

Instinct screamed across her skin, but she needed to free herself. Her good hand was between them, and she snatched it up to the dagger embedded inside him. She gave it a hard yank.

It didn't move.

Her blood ran cold. He still wasn't fading into the dust like all the other pseudo-immortals had. He actually laughed beneath her, a harsh sound that vibrated inside his chest. She felt it more than she heard it.

His hold tightened, and she heard the easy pop of more shattering bones. Fire raced across her skin where he touched her, and a blackened memory roared behind her eyes. The little girl's whimper was swallowed by the demon's chest before Kazious ripped her in half.

Sable's eyes stung, and she let out a desperate cry. A

frantic surge overcame her, and she pounded his chest with her fist. The blade's handle mocked her as it held fast to his chest when she tried to force it back out.

His hands flexed across her back, and she felt the press of each finger against her leather, her eyes widening as sharp points passed through the leather like it was no more than paper.

Laughter and laughter and more blasted laughter. It choked her. Razors pressed against her skin, tearing it as she struggled in his hold.

"Look at how pathetic she is."

Castle's voice came like starlight from every possible direction. Even the road beneath them seemed to carry her words as she spoke to her brother. In Sable's terror, she wondered if he would be forced to sit there and watch her die.

A loud, strange noise grated on her ears like tiny knives, digging into her head with their claws and almost drowning out Castle's murmurings.

"I saw your mind when you searched for me today," she said from inside the stones. "I know her frailty *infuriates* you."

What?

She heard the scrape of his claws scratching something solid in her spine, the cool air diving far too deep inside her torn flesh. An absent corner of her mind realized the grating sound was her own scream. Even then, she couldn't snap her mouth shut, though the sound itself gave way to empty sobs. She couldn't even feel agony anymore; her body had become nothing more than a cloud of hot fog.

"It's too bad," Castle muttered. "Too bad you didn't know about the gift we have. About the bond. You could have given her your strength. You could have stopped all of this."

Silence filtered down over them like a blanket, and the reaper beneath her faded slowly; her weight crushing a sand castle instead of lying atop a monster. Her body lay flat against the heated stones before her sluggish mind realized the danger had been whisked away all over again. She wanted to make a comment about Castle doing that too often, but her lungs were choked off. The silence stung as her back dripped warm fluid, shy of the gentle eyes that bore down on her.

Her muscles quivered when she ordered them to move. *Turn over! Get up! Do something! Anything!*

But she only managed a shiver in her limbs. Her tongue felt thick while a dry sob snuck into her throat. She couldn't move.

She was defenseless.

How was this happening again so soon? Her mind was going numb, but all she wanted was an answer.

What did I do to deserve such pain? I've always done everything that you've asked . . ..

Hands came down on her, turning her over and spilling electric heat from her wounds. She had no chance to register her hatred of being touched before his eyes distracted her groggy gaze entirely. Clear ocean waves crashed in one, its neighbour filled with coffee swirling in gentle circles. Both were wide with worry as he leaned over her. Why such care at a time like this? She was human. She was weak.

Gabe doesn't care for weakness.

"Oh, shut up," he muttered.

Sable let out a soft laugh.

"Can you walk?" his baritone seemed so far away. "Sable, stay with me, okay? We've got to get you out of here while they're gone. Can you walk?"

His thunderclap voice rumbled deep inside her chest like a cat's purr.

But oh, how she wanted to rest for a while.

"I can't dance right now, Gabe. I'm ready for bed. Maybe tomorrow," she mumbled around the taste of copper on her tongue.

"Oh, you are a pain sometimes," he declared.

He scooped her up in his arms as if she were no more than a child. Just like old times. She giggled again. But where had her weapons gone? Her sword and her bow?

"Sable, right now, you need to focus on not dying, alright?"

But . . ..

"Uh-uh! No buts. Just stay with me, okay?"

Where would she go when he was holding her so close, as if he were the only thing keeping her anchored to this earth?

A far-away part of her mind wailed and went wild, screaming that nothing was "alright." It crawled to the forefront, begging her to ask: where had the agony gone? She should be crying out. Her back frothed out blood. As they walked, she felt the way her skin was billowing in some places, pulled into ribbons by the demon's claws moments earlier.

I'm not going to survive this one.

"Hush," came Gabe's gentle rumble. "I won't let that happen."

But she knew deep down in the pit of her heart that Gabe could not change anything if this was her time to return home.

Home.

A longing ache opened in her for that place. The realm where light was warm on her skin at all hours and pain no longer existed in her bruised heart. The place where she was celebrated with her strange eyes, long silences, and quiet wisdom, all of which had exiled her in this place of the living . . .

Her chest grew tight like a twisting spring. *Father, I'm ready to come home. I'm so tired.*

"You are a strange little woman," Gabe murmured, chuckling. He laid her down a moment later, chills rushing up into her wounded back from the dew-kissed grass. "Where *is* your father right now, Sable?"

Her lips were frozen, unable to frown. Such a strange, sour taste on a voice that had been so sweet a moment earlier.

"Now that your life is on the line and not just some random town or a madman you've foolishly decided to care for," he all but snarled.

Why was he so enraged?

"Now that you're here bleeding out. After all you've done for him and all we've seen him do for you, why has he chosen now to leave you to my care?"

Harsh hands unlaced her armor, pulling the metal and leather away from each other. The sound of torn fabric filled her ears as the shirt beneath was torn open and revealed pale, scarred flesh all over again. She was so cold; her cheeks could not even muster a blush. Yet, for the first time she could remember, her heart did not race when calloused hands touched her skin. In her mind, she reached out to him with words she hoped he'd receive.

Maybe he trusts you.

Gabe's hands were unbelievably gentle as he dressed her wounded hip, washing the grime and sweat from the wound's mouth. He pressed a strange concoction against it. His hands did not stray or bring unnecessary pain.

He laughed, muttering something under his breath that could have been, "Not likely." His hands and mouth could not seem to agree with each other as he continued to fume. "I have watched you wield a power that could not possibly exist. You survived the breakout of a deity and tossed his ass back into my head. You have walked on thin air . . . yet you remain so fragile."

He turned her over as he talked, so he could work on her wounded back. "You would think a god with that kind of power would have hardened your flesh, or at the very least, healed your wounds again. Why has he left you now? Why are you so weak still, after everything you've done for him?"

Sable did not acknowledge the sobering knot that began building inside her throat. Hope was a dangerous thing in the hands of those who did not understand trust. She tried her best to explain within her mind.

I am still entirely human. I don't obey him for the sake of receiving power or immortality or anything like that. I follow his commands out of my love for my father. I act as a vessel for his will to move through.

"Ah, so you are only a pawn?"

If she could have rolled her eyes, she would have.

Not at all. He loves me as he loves a daughter. The same way I love him. A pawn is no more than a slave. We have a relationship and understanding together that his will is just, and I want to bring it to fruition.

He boiled over in laughter like the ringing of a bell tower. It was a lovely yet mocking sound. Something changed in him as he released it. His fingers grew harsh on her torn flesh, causing a yelp to strain in her throat. Soft hair brushed her cheek as his lips came to her ear.

"Love would have never left you to the hands of someone like me, you lying fool," he snarled.

Her veins quaked and froze solid. Part of her mind

wanted to ask if this was *the other Gabe* once more, but she knew better.

"Love would not trust in me," he declared, his fingers tightening on the edges of the bleeding wound.

She tried to cry out, but nothing would move in her throat.

"Where is he, Sable?"

The words were so loud, they vibrated into every bone in her body, rising to spill from her eyes.

"Of all the people in this world, you were the last one I would have thought to play mind games!" he shouted. "Was this your vengeance for what I did to Kazious? Leading me all this way, pretending you'd forgiven me and *trusted* me, just to tear me apart all over again? Is that it? Answer me!"

Her heart galloped. She didn't know if she had the resolve for this.

Gabe, you're afraid, and I understand. He is always with me though. Please know that. Even when he remains silent, he is here. I have never lied to you. Please, hear me! You know as well as I do that none of what I've done would be possible otherwise. You can't tell me ***this*** *is what's going to write off everything that you've seen! I'm still human and* ***nothing*** *is going to change that!*

He scoffed, digging his hand into her bloody back. She couldn't muster the scream that thrashed in her throat. All that came out was a high-pitched wheeze.

Gabe, what are you doing?

Not like this. She didn't want to die like this. *Not by your hand; I trusted you! Don't do this!*

That earned her a dark laugh. "Why would you have to beg me for your life if your 'faith' was not an elaborate masquerade? Where is your god, Sable? He better show himself, or so help me, we will *both* lose you. I won't play this game anymore!"

Something tore beneath his hand, and as he ripped it back, her scream finally pierced the air, shattering it.

Her vision began to fade out, but she could still see a piece of the green grass swaying before her. She couldn't go like this. He was so close to the truth, she couldn't let him turn away now. Her life was safe in her father's hands. She would be fine.

But she would never see him again. The realization

could have made her laugh. How was it that even then, with his hand drenched in her blood, she still cared for him before herself? He was betraying her all over again. But she couldn't bring herself to hate him for it.

Gabe, I trusted in you even after what you did to Kazious. I trusted in you ***knowing*** *that you could do exactly* ***this*** *someday. I invited you to join me, knowing that you were dangerous. You could have killed me in any number of ways at any possible time, and still, I entrusted my life into your hands with every step we took together. Isn't this the very thing you have always wanted? Someone who trusted you despite your insanity? I* ***do****!*

"You were a bloody fool then!"

No. I wasn't. You're tormenting me, because you're afraid of the questions you can't answer. He's right here, Gabe. If you're so desperate to see him, call out to him!

His laughter triggered a sharp nausea that rolled over her as her muscles twitched with electric pain. She was fading, her mind giving way to the blackness overtaking her eyes. She turned her thoughts above as her heart squeezed too tight inside its confines.

Was this what you wanted, Father?

Her mouth released a sob that she didn't remember bubbling inside. Something warm dripped around her heart like a hand, softly taking her into safety. Fresh, hot tears streamed down her pale, chilled cheeks. Part of her wasn't sure if it was from the ache of her wounds or the one deep inside of her.

~Forgive, my daughter. Tell him what hurts there in your heart, and then it will be done for a short time. You will know rest.

His voice drew a gasp from her frozen lips, and as she fell into his arms, her soul began to weep. The last of her mind reached for her lost brother.

I hope I will see you again. Don't stop here. Find your answers, please. Know that I love you, and I forgive you, Gabe.

CHAPTER 24

The Mind of the Immortal Trickster
Gabe Arenreeth

Sable. . . You never should have asked me to join you. Of all the people in this world with misguided good intentions, you should have known better. How many years did you harbor that ache from your childhood? Yet still, you sat there that night asking me - the traitor - to come back to your side. You never told me that you had forgiven what I'd done to him, but you didn't have to.

It makes your final words here even harder to keep in my blackened heart.

Even when I had your life bleeding in my hands, you did it again. You forgave me.

"I hope I will see you again." You remind me.

I can't help but laugh. *You were insane.*

My hands are trembling, stained in a familiar color that

seems to be a recurring theme in my long life. I can't remain here with my *sin*. Your long hair is pooled around your shoulders, the ends wet with red. A chill creeps into my chest as I lift my eyes to the sky.

"I was fooled," I find myself admitting. The words taste like lies. "You had the last laugh, Sable. If revenge was the point of this game, you received it."

You will haunt me for the rest of eternity.

I leave you there, bloody and frozen with a soft expression I have never seen on you before. The peace which I will never know, but which you deserve the most. My dearest friend. *My Clo-Caillea.*

You should have known the game you were playing was dangerous. You should have been smarter than to play with the hope of something I cannot touch and dreams of a place I will never know. You had firsthand experience with the Immortal Trickster from a young age. Yet you were still a fool, thinking you would surpass my intellect with that bloody "faith" of yours.

I understand why Castle fought you now.

I commend your efforts, and I will enjoy unraveling the mystery you left to me for a while, but know this, Sable.

I love you too.

And I will not forgive you.

Let me be clear, if you are there watching, my friend: I do not enjoy pain nor death. Causing it feels grimy to my fingers and leaves dirt clogged inside my chest. It hasn't stopped me from the destruction these long years have seen, though. My hands have claimed many, and I have carved each memorial into my skin to let them live on unforgotten. That is where you will reside. Your screams will haunt my ears into eternity, gathered amongst the rest of my victims. You will become just another memory for the Royal Abomination to cling to: another reminder that I am a toxin to this world.

Damn you, Sable.

My body and heart are familiar with this ache; they know the routine like a dance. The chill comes up over me; a blanket to settle into my veins and close off my heart, turning it into a block of ice. Who needs to feel anyways? It's easier to go numb.

I stare down at the red stains on my hands. They don't

shake anymore.

"I trusted you." You whisper in my head.

Shut up, Sable.

I can't stay here. Part of me realizes that I should be turning my attention to the sister I'd thought I'd killed. But I don't care. She has been dead to me for so long; what does it matter that it was a lie? I need to escape from this . . . betrayal.

Turning my back, I close my eyes and let out a hard breath. Where will I go? My home is already plagued by ghosts soaked into the walls. I can't go there alone. Not with this fresh phantom following me and dripping guilt into my veins.

But do I dare bring this gore to the one friend I have left? Do I dare to paint him with my *sin*? He would bear any weight from my shoulders without being asked, I know that. He would never leave me alone to the hell inside me, and admitting that fact almost cracks the fresh ice because something whispers on the wind that you wanted to do the same.

I will go to him. It is selfish, and I understand this from the back of my mind, but I cannot be alone with you still whispering behind my eyes. You will drive me over the edge of my madness.

So then, how shall I escape?

My mistress, Wind has been forever faithful, but today I cannot ask her to come under my command. Not when I am this tainted shell of the man she remembers. Instead, I clamp one hand into a fist. Let the smoke rise. The power you loathe. The one you tell me is evil. That which you fear will now remove me from what I've done to you.

An absent piece of my heart wonders if you are watching. If you are already angry in your afterlife. If you even care.

I feel eyes on my back, but they are not yours. They are too old. Too wise. They follow the sound of whispering metal.

The dark power warms my blood as it moves, but not in a way that is pleasant. It agitates the flow and causes a strange sting inside me.

My heart quickens like I am being chased and I could almost laugh.

A presence stands behind me.
Not you.
Of course.
But familiar still.
The whispers sound like damnation.
Metal sighing as it brushes metal.
Will you kill me?

My bones are leaden as I gesture with the power which my coming savior had taught me to use, creating folds out of the air before me. I use my other hand to pull one side of the drapes back and reveal a familiar sight on the other side of the world. His hearth is lit with a fire that crackles in contained chaos. Its glow has never gone out for as long as I have known him.

Between the spike of my heartbeat and the phantoms closing in, I damn near leap through and close off the power before I can collapse. My legs are stiff when I ask them to move toward the couch. They are fighting against me too. I laugh to myself.

The weight of a stolen life can crush a regular man's shoulders. For me, it just makes every movement feel like I'm wading through sludge.

Let go of her, dammit. She played us like fools!

As I collapse onto the furniture in an unceremonious crumble, I hear the soft clap of his bare feet bringing him out from his kitchen.

"I didn't think I would see you again for a few more years," he admits, tossing a towel over his shoulder.

"I killed someone," I mumble from numb lips.

"You sound as if you can hardly believe you did it," Edge replies, sitting in the chair across from me.

He is shorter than me, much closer to your height, Sable, though he is far older than either of us. He knew Kiro Baroch long before the god or demon was trapped within me to bring me to life.

Though he has a face sculpted for mischief, he tends to demand authority instead when he draws his brows down toward his eyes. In the fire's light, the pale green color of moss glows with flakes of tumbling gold. He has a gentle jawline and thin lips, though when he grins, that mischief glows like a brilliant light off his sun kissed cheeks.

I turn away from him. "I don't know what came over

me."

Silence follows my statement. It echoes through the mansion and beats my chest with wild fists. I know what he is thinking without needing my psychic power to touch his mind. This quiet is a monster in itself, screaming inside my ears and slicing its claws deep into my ribs.

"Were you . . . yourself?"

The question shouldn't make me react the way it does, because I knew it was coming. Still, the rage that declared you a traitor roars at me again from deep in its crevice down in my soul.

"Of course I was! Do you really think Kiro would just relinquish control if he broke out? And even then, if that ever happened, do you honestly think one little human woman would have satisfied him?"

A crunch against the windows reminds me of what happens when I get angry. I sink farther down inside the ice until the winds outside settle. Edge remains quiet, frowning at me with narrowed eyes, heavy gears working behind them.

"Oh, come on, Edge," I plead. "I don't need him to do evil things. I *am* evil! I'm a goddamn abomination created for the sole purpose of *destruction*. If I want to rip open a woman's spine, I'll be damned before letting him take the satisfaction!"

"That's the thing, Gabe. You're violent, yes. But death is something you don't handle well, not even with strangers. I have seen you lash out plenty of times in the centuries we've known each other. Death tends to be the one thing that makes you hesitate to continue."

I narrow my eyes and move to argue, but he isn't even looking at me while he speaks.

"You've killed more people as a mental by-product of your study than you have with your own bare hands," he explains in a smooth, rolling voice of smoke. He sits back in his chair, clasping his hands in his lap. "So, what could have caused you to lose so much control this time that you crossed that line?"

I can't respond right away. The truth is shameful, and I hate its presence inside me. I let out a long breath. Your orange eyes are opening in the back of my mind.

"Does it have something to do with who she was?" he

prompts a minute later.

He has the same mind gift that I do, and I realize he's plucked out just enough from me to know the identity of my victim. I have never told him about my time with you when you were a child, but he knew about the imprisonment of your deranged friend. It isn't hard for someone like him to guess what you must mean to me. After all, I have never before left a human behind once my sights have been set on the intricate workings of their mind.

"This book that you brought, was it hers?"

I don't even remember taking the thing we'd retrieved from the half-angel. Sure enough, I glance back just in time to see Edge lifting it off the coffee table between us. The ice inside my veins becomes agitated, vibrating in a quiet hum.

"What is the importance of this?" Edge inquires as he flips open the pages.

Finally, I allow myself to grumble a response. "I'm not sure. She needed it for the gate, but that proved irrelevant once we returned."

He gives me a familiar look. It reminds me that he has no clue what I'm talking about. I have a tendency of not making sense.

"You're going to have to explain that a little better, Gabe. I wasn't there."

"Is this really necessary?"

"Yes. You're not yourself," he clarifies like a father trying to explain something to his child. "If this woman meant as much to you as I think she did, you need to tell me what happened. I'm the one who will have to help you deal with this once your heart thaws in a few years."

He has me there. The poor guy is always facing down my demons with me, though I have never asked him to. Of course he would know that I have frozen myself solid. I can't face what I've done. I'm a coward.

I lean back in my seat, gazing up at the ceiling.

"Find your answers, please."

"Can you hear her inside my mind too? Or am I alone at the mercy of that memory?" I'm aware that my voice is barely louder than a whisper.

"What is she saying, Gabe?" he inquires, as if his own psychic power is ignorant.

I can commend his lie. We've done this before. He will

pick apart my mind like a good therapist. Not so he can piece it back together though.

I doubt anyone can manage that.

No, he will organize the pain into perfectly placed dominoes. He will ensure each twist and turn inside my heart is as predictable as the metaphor implies. But for once, I want him nervous. I want my pain to be a mess that I must wade through to reach the other side. You are worth this much. I will etch the ache of you into my very soul if I must.

"Hand me the book," I demand in a soft warning.

His lips pull down, but he still tosses it into my lap. He watches as I flip through the pages.

I remember you reading it with vigor after Kiro broke loose. Your lips had been a hard line when you were concentrating, and with the glow beneath your tender flesh, I'd almost forgotten the bruises. Your excitement and your passion were brand new to me. I had only ever known the cold, closed-off, shattered warrior. You were beautiful when your god lit up inside of you.

I need to know what I've done.

Somewhere inside the thin, delicate pages is a place where you nearly wept as you read. I watched your hand come to your mouth in a little gasp that was more precious than any other moment in our journey.

But she played you; it was all a lie.

"Yes, you made a grand fool out of me, my Clo-Caillea," I mutter, chuckling.

I deserve to know what had you so convinced that I damn near fell into the deceit alongside you.

"Has it never occurred to you that maybe you just want it to be a lie?" Edge asks, breaking through my line of thought.

I glance up at him, narrowing my eyes. He is Lucifer's right-hand man. And Lucifer is the son of the creators, Light and Darkness.

Or so says our lore.

Why would he be willing to entertain the idea of another god that would prove his entire life to be a lie?

Ah, but I have not yet explained this piece to him. That's why he doesn't understand.

"That's just it," I finally snarl. "She would never have

been fooled so well by solid lies. There *had* to be some truth laced into the illusion. She wasn't naïve."

He laughs. "And that's what you intend to find in those pages?"

I nod, a smile slipping onto my lips that feels wrong and out of place. "I will find the place where deceit and truth collide. And then she cannot haunt me."

CHAPTER 25

"Who does that?"

My throat is filled with fog, and I wonder if I've lost my frozen heart on the floor. I continue to re-read the words, enthralled by their gruesome story. The thrumming in my agitated veins has increased to the point of nearly choking me.

I know what they speak of. I saw it further back, but how could he have known? My hand trembles as I flip back with an urgency that tears some of the pages through the corners. It doesn't matter, because I must confirm the two are the same.

Somehow, I seem to be losing my sense of rage toward that lie of peace and all-consuming love.

"Who did what?" Edge asks, glancing up from his own book, which he had begun to read.

I can't put it into words. It doesn't make any sense, and the confusion is rising up to my eyes without my consent. I read again just to ensure the words are correct, then flip back to the spot I kept further ahead. If I go over them enough, maybe they will begin to make sense.

"Gabe, what have you found?" Edge asks, bringing me back to reality.

"Come, read this," I instruct, desperate for another eye to see such a bizarre story.

The seat next to me pushes down, and I lean over, pointing to the page. I gulp down hard stones in a throat clogged by emotions that I'm not sure what to do with. My blood sings a strange song in its restless veins, and it sends misguided fluid upwards.

My mind can only create one word with clarity.

Why?

His appearance was so disfigured beyond that of any human being, and his form marred beyond human likeness.

Why would anyone do such a thing on purpose? Knowing it was coming and still allowing it? Somewhere inside my mind, the question rises and pulls on my guts. *Did you know too*?

I think I might be sick.

The frown on Edge's lips pulls farther down as he scans the words. He reads them aloud. "But he was pierced for our transgressions, he was crushed for our iniquities; the punishment that brought us peace was on him, and by his wounds we are healed."

Silence pours down on us as I make a frantic move to throw the pages back to where the story unfolds later. I can't even decide where to make my point, so I begin to explain with wild gestures. "He was insane! He knew. He kept telling them it would happen, and do you realize he even *prayed* to that god, just like her? Except that he *begged* to avoid being beaten bloody and killed. But he asked it on one condition: if it was their god's will. And later on, when everything was coming true that he told them would happen, *he let it happen*. Why? Who does that? What kind of purpose could a bloody, bruised, broken man serve for a *god*?"

I pull in a deep breath, desperate to make sense of my

jarring heartbeat. Again, I flip pages, searching and searching. Flipping further. Where had I seen it? The place that brought this tidal wave of strange emotions that whisper my mistakes through my mind. The place that dropped the floor out from beneath my feet. One line. Just one to bring this entire story to its knees at my feet, where the contents of my stomach will greet it soon.

For the joy set before him, he endured the cross.

There it is.

Fluid drips off my chin, and the page catches it.

"Wh-what joy? What does it mean? Who does this?"

I can't understand it, but I want to, because somewhere inside my heart, I know this is what put you into the palm of his hand. This man who claimed to be the son of your god, gave his life up willingly. For what? To prove the immense power your god had? Rising again days later, at a time when we didn't know our souls were recycled. Pfft.

"*It is entirely against our design to live multiple lives,*" you remind me in that memory before thc blackened stain of my own demon seeps over you. It is the first time I have called him that. It is also the first word that resonates in my mind with the truth behind it. I have to close my eyes and breathe long and slow.

So, what is the purpose of this? Why did he have to die? Why did he have to return? Where did he go when he stopped playing with his mourning friends and family? The rage is blotting it out. I can't understand. No matter which way I turn it, the story makes no sense.

"*There's a home of light that's waiting for you, Gabe.*"

My stomach twists. No. You're wrong.

"What is this?" Edge breaks through my reverie, pulling the book from my hands.

"I will snap every single finger that touches it if you try!" I snarl, snatching it back.

His mossy eyes narrow, sparking blue threads around the pupils as he settles back. He raises his hands in surrender before crossing his arms over his chest.

I close my eyes and sigh, releasing the tension in my shoulders. "It's supposedly a piece of buried history. It's about a god, one unlike any we are familiar with. She called him her father and her master, and she trusted in him wholeheartedly. Even when he told her to do things that she should have never been able to do. Yet, she was still afraid. It was amazing. She never doubted his orders, yet she had no clue *how* she was able to—"

Edge snaps his fingers a couple of times, drawing my attention. He frowns.

"Focus, Gabe. I don't need to know about how she was with him; she's gone." The words stab me, but he isn't done. He gestures toward the book in my hands. "Who is this man? How do the two things relate?"

I swallow a hard lump of glass. My mouth is dry.

"Well, apparently this is his son," I answer, shifting my gaze to the pages as if they might come alive and explain themselves.

They don't though.

"I guess her god has access to another afterlife," I continue, "different from Lucifer's and one that doesn't come with so much . . . brokenness. She called it 'home'. And somehow, this man was the one who essentially opened that gate for others to go there. I don't understand it though. The aspect that maybe his death led him there is fine. But how does that have any effect on anyone else? How does that let *her* go there?"

My guts are boiling inside, and I turn back to face my friend. He can't seem to figure out what to do with this either. His eyes have darkened to reflect the forest, where my shame still lies.

"She told me once that I could even reach that place. In fact, she . . .." Suddenly, I can't breathe. My lungs shudder, sending monsters to claw at my throat. I gulp down a couple of short breaths that are sharp and bitter lead on my tongue. "She begged me to find 'the truth,' so that sh-she . . .." I stop, breathe deeply. Force it out. "So she could see me again."

The words are shaking, and they taste like guilt. My dear friend looks at me with an unreadable expression.

I close the book, resting it on the table with trembling hands. It makes a hollow thud that reverberates through the ice inside me. I clench my hands into fists on my knees.

"Edge . . . she survived Kiro Baroch," I announce through my teeth.

He doesn't say a word. I turn to watch the crackling fire and recount it for him in a rush of words that are raw and jagged.

"I was drowning deep inside burning oil, confused and, I'll admit it, terrified. One second, I was talking with Sable, and the next, I was plunged into this torture. I didn't even realize what had happened until it was over.

"I remember seeing a light piercing the sludge just like one of her arrows. It struck me in the chest, filling me with a comforting warmth as if heated syrup had replaced my boiling blood.

"And then I saw her coming toward me, calling my name with tears flying from her blinded eyes. I reached out to brush away the oil there, and she gasped. She grabbed my hand like a vice, and these bronze arms wrapped around her waist. The next thing I knew, I was in control of my body, and she could barely stand."

Edge listens to my ramblings with patient silence. I face him again, but he tilts his head against the couch, staring up at the ceiling. I wonder if he is thinking of declaring my story false, and it makes mc laugh.

"She went up against Kiro," he repeats, rolling the words around his mouth. I don't blame him. It's hard to believe such a statement. "A human woman fought the god of chaos." He spears me from the corner of his eye, commanding me to confirm the words.

"Yes," I breathe.

"And survived."

I nod. "Yes. Badly wounded, but she gave me control again over my body."

"And yet *you* killed her." The words strike my lungs, deflating them and strangling me.

"Yes." It is no more than a whimper.

He lets out a misplaced chuckle, which, in turn, awakens the serpent that has been dormant until now. It coils inside my belly, and I wonder again if I will retch.

"Tell me you didn't miss the irony in that," he asks in his cruel way.

I turn to face him, stricken and wide eyed like a child. Yet still, I laugh. It rumbles from a broken place in my chest like a growl. The strength of it breaks a shard of my ice off from somewhere deep inside.

"I thought he would save her. I thought she was safe in his hands." I tremble as the truth flutters out; a traitorous bird.

"So, you believed."

It is not a question. He already knows.

I can't answer anyways; my lungs have stuttered to a halt. Wouldn't that be something, finally dying due to the asphyxiation of guilt? Ha, it would be too easy.

I bite down on the ache, crunching it beneath my rage. "But he didn't. That's the bottom line. She was fooled in the end, and so was I."

Edge gives me a thoughtful look as he decides whether to believe me. Your smile is painting itself behind my eyelids, and though I don't know where it is inside that statement, somehow, I know I have lied.

"You say this god has his own afterlife that Sable has access to through some sort of connection to this man in the book," he repeats.

"Are you trying to tell me that he wouldn't have minded if she died?" I ask, sneering.

He chuckles. "How long does it usually take for Kivas to return?"

I narrow my eyes, skewering him with suspicion. "A few hours at minimum. Sometimes days. The longest was two months and eighteen days. But Sable isn't one of those reincarnating Erset Latari, and she sure as hell isn't another bloody hybrid of one!"

Edge smiles at me, the mischief returning to light up the way his cheeks crease around his mouth.

"Of course not," he admonishes. "But if her god has a way of collecting souls to him, don't you think he would have the power to allow that soul to survive things it shouldn't?"

I bite my tongue, struck by the shape of something stirring inside his eyes. It cannot be hope. There would be no reason for such a foolish thing in him. Yet, I think back to that night when someone else had finally confirmed my suspicions of the deceptions holding this world hostage. I'd known for many years that my cult had never ended at my slaughter when I was still so young. My cult gained such power that they held more influence than the kings and queens in their comfortable castles, sworn in under gods and goddesses that are known like well-travelled houses. Ask anyone in the street, and they have met and exchanged words with their god of choice.

So have I. I have shared meals with all of them, except the wretch who created and then abandoned me.

It occurs to me whose hand would bear the blood if Lucifer's afterlife were truly no more than a torture device. All this time harboring my hatred for the divine race, thinking they were nothing more than glorified magicians. And all along, the one who would know for certain has been by my side.

~*He must know the truth. There is no other way it could have been done.*

How strange for that voice to ring inside my mind like a clanging bell. I wonder if Edge can hear it too, or perhaps what little sanity I still had has finally fled.

~*Be bold*, it demands. So clever and familiar, my guts drop into my toes.

~*He is as desperate as you are.*

Shut up!

"Gabe, why were you so desperate for proof of this god that you were willing to destroy the one person I can say beyond any shadow of doubt that you actually loved?"

Edge beat me to it. He carves open the ice that behind which I've tried so hard to hide. I can't face the void beneath it though. The loss of you is worse than the absence. And yes, they are different. The entire decade I spent avoiding you like a plague was easier than this, because you were alive. You were alright. I was giving you a chance to live a normal life after the madness and danger of staying by the side of a cracked man. The insatiable need deep inside my rotten heart to stay by your side could be silenced, because you were breathing and smiling somewhere else in this world. At that time, I could handle the lonely isolation, because I knew you were safe. But I killed you. Murdered you in cold blood. You are gone, and if your claims are correct, you will never return.

"She must have been so frightened," I mumble around the rock in my throat.

"Why?" It seems like an absurd question, but I understand it.

"She trusted me." The words are stale. I'm going to fall into a million pieces of jagged glass. I cannot bear this weight any longer.

"Why did you do it?" Edge asks, bringing me back to the answer I am trying to avoid.

"I snapped," I admit, running my hand down my face as if I can wipe away the shame. "I couldn't . . . can't . . . fathom how it could have been a lie. An illusion. How did she fake it? How did he fool her? Who was he? It was no more than a . . . a game."

Edge's lips quirk up in a humorless smirk. "I knew your love was dangerous, but I never thought it could be deadly."

My chest crumbles under his words. He leans forward, his elbows resting on his knees, his hands making a tent under his chin. Something has shifted in those eyes again. They are like venom.

"So, you knew beyond a shadow of doubt that he was real," the demon theorizes, more so to himself than me. "You knew he would save her, and you trusted that he would show himself by doing so. Essentially, you had faith in her god."

There it is. My guts roll, and I lock my jaw, if only to stop the way my chin tries to wobble.

"Tell me about your journey with her, Gabe," he commands gently. "Let's see how real he is, but we'll look at it from the outside."

This time, I allow it to pour out, spreading the stain of you through my veins as the words rumble into the chilled room.

I had faith in your god. And he failed us both.

I am so sorry, Sable.

CHAPTER 26

"Don't you think perhaps she *was* saved then?" he murmurs.

I stare at him for a long moment, waiting for the punchline. He can't be serious. He is Lucifer's right hand. If you were right, if your god is exactly as you claimed, and if he did somehow save you, the bottom line is that it would prove Edge's entire life to be *wrong*. If only he could see the mess I'd left of your body. I am good at one thing and one thing alone: ensuring that the end is exactly that.

"He would have to seal a hole in her back the size of my fist and return some muscle to their bones," I snarl.

I examine my pale hand in the following silence. The blood is gone, but I still feel it. I will forever.

"Doesn't this man who was beaten beyond human

recognition come back to life?" he prompts.

I snap my narrowed eyes to meet his. The question doesn't need to be voiced: we are both aware I never specified that part aloud. He frowns, all humor lost.

"I have seen this before," he admits in a voice just above a whisper. He points to the book on the table. "There was once a time when many of these manuscripts were readily available. Until *I* systematically destroyed them all."

His gaze freezes into a hardened, green lake.

"It's true then," I whisper, stones trapped in my throat.

He lets out a frustrated breath. He turns from me, his hands caught up into fists. "I can't tell you that. I don't even know the full story. What I do know are the orders that I've followed, and yet despite my effort to remove all knowledge of this one god . . . here we are."

The silence echoes off the walls. I pull in a hard breath. "The master of souls hired Kivas to kill her."

He nods, closing his eyes.

"He didn't contact him directly," I conclude.

"Let me guess," he begins, his smile returning. "She didn't need Abdaziel's help."

I remember the look on your face as you watched the immortals battle. That steady focus that consumed any sense of self-preservation. I can pinpoint the moment when you decided to target the most inaccessible body part on him. You were not without fear. I recognized its presence settled on your shoulders when you drew the arrow back. Perhaps that was what stilled my efforts to stop you. You knew exactly how weak you were in comparison to us. And yet you still chose to fight.

I laugh, shaking my head.

"He served as a good distraction," I muse.

Edge chuckles, clapping a calloused hand onto my shoulder. "No wonder you care for her so much."

But that can't be true. I killed you.

He becomes serious, his lips drawn into a hard line as his brows come together.

"Gabe, we have to face your sister," he states, slowly and thoughtfully, as if testing the words on their way out.

"That's a switch. What the hell for? Why do I care what she does?"

His gaze hardens to match the rest of his features. He

holds up his fist, and as he explains, he counts off his points by lifting his fingers.

"First, she's your sister. Not only have you spent the better part of twelve thousand years trying to remember if you killed her, but she *clearly* wishes you had. Second, she would know more about Sable's god than you, considering she had a decade to your couple of days. Third, if she's the one behind these things Sable's god was having her hunt down, don't you think you owe it to her to put an end to the mission she was on?"

I don't respond. I don't have to. He's right on all accounts. Of course. Between the two of us, my intellect may be far greater, but he is much wiser.

He must realize that I intend to keep my silence, because he sighs and stands up. It is mutually agreed upon that we will go. But where?

I stare at his back as he reaches out to build a power in his palms. Shimmering crystals form into a ball above each dark hand, reflecting the sunlight shining through his window. The crystals shoot across his skin, coating even his clothes and forming an ethereal layer of protection over him.

I wish I could crystalize my aching heart. The ice isn't strong enough.

I wonder what you would say about the arch demon accompanying me and what you would think of his powers.

"I guess I forgot to mention," he glances back at me over his shoulder. "When we find her, you're not allowed to do any of the talking. I am *not* facing the Calamity of Chaos just for you to confront her."

It is the first time I have ever heard him use that title. I feel sick, finding where you were correct yet again. I don't fight his restrictions. I don't think I have any good use left in me, if I ever had any to begin with.

"How will we find her?" I ask as we head out into the evening.

Edge puts his hand out before him. Threads of green and blue lights dance about his fingers. He shrugs, not looking at me. "Well, I know for a fact that no one can create without my boss knowing *and permitting* it. So, I say we start with him."

His plan is insane. I have to laugh, and it boils like

cracking glass.

"Careful, I'm starting to think I'm a bad influence on you." I crack a smile, and it almost feels as if everything is normal.

Almost.

He lifts an eyebrow, chuckling at my reaction and shaking his head.

"We've just spent the last hour discussing the great deception my boss has orchestrated, and we're about to walk right up to him and ask if your sister has any part of it, so we can hunt her down. *And you're laughing*?"

I toss a grin his way, but I'm sure he catches the fact that it doesn't reach my eyes. We both know this could be suicide. The difference is that he can die. I still don't know how to, and I doubt Lucy will either. I've asked him before.

The glowing lights leave his hand, wrapping about themselves and forming a small ball as they float away from their master. His obsidian blood drips to the grass, and the corner of his mouth is quirked up with our fading humor.

A faint crackling sound comes from the power as it pulsates with lights, growing and shrinking in time with the flashes. It's like a heartbeat.

And then it explodes.

The portal pulls itself open from the ripples in the air, drapes behind as if pinned to the sides of a window. We move through with no more words.

It has been a long time since I have come here. The last time I did, Edge was on the brink of death, and I dragged his body through a gate that I paid with blood to open. He'd taught me the trick afterwards once his boss recounted the tale of my "tantrums," as he called them.

Funny how I am now returning once more with the blood of a friend staining my hands. Except this one is gone for good. It also seems strange that I will step into Lucifer's throne room after all that I have seen of you and your god. I have to laugh one more time. If you can see me from his side, you must be furious with me.

Grey marble stretches before us. Edge trails his hand behind us, collecting the power back into himself as the lights split into their dancing threads one last time. They bite down into his palm, slithering beneath the skin to their resting place. More blood dribbles down to splash against the stone underfoot.

It reminds me of the danger in his power. You recited it well. The power has a mind of its own that he must keep subdued to use. It grows more powerful with age, and someday it will be too much for him to bear. It is the only thing that can kill him. As is the curse of the arch demon, though it is worse for him; he is the original. He is the source of power that all the souls are tied down to until they are sent to the mirrored city we once thought was heaven.

The souls heal faster with his presence here, but he can't bear their weight pulling on him. He has told me before that it feels like they will tear him apart every time he enters this place. And here he is, volunteering for it as if this suffering is second nature to him. He is a good friend. You would like him.

His hand slips around my wrist, and the contact brings me back into the hall. We proceed forward, but my heart is sinking.

The path does not end. It is wide enough for the two of us to walk, but then it drops off into yellow clouds on either side. I have never tried to find out what is beneath them. A few more feet, and more grey marble rises to create the walls locking us into this place. I don't have to look behind to know that, when I turn, I will not see an end there either.

It is this way whenever we come. A test he puts into place, I presume. This is where we first learned that Edge can tap into the spiritual essence at the core of my powers, allowing me to remain calm and focused as long as he keeps contact with me.

My mind can tell me with a breath of annoyance that it is an illusion. I should be able to pick it apart like child's play. I cannot for two reasons though, the first being the most important. *Lucifer doesn't know how powerful I am.* I have made a point of keeping my psychic power away from him. He only knows of my illusions. The second is simple: sometimes I try to avoid upsetting powerful people if it is in my best interest.

Beside me, Edge laughs. "I would think with how much he likes you, he would have changed this spell by now."

As if the master of souls is no more than a parent pulling pranks.

Alright, to an extent, that is a perfect description of the

anti-social hermit. He doesn't even have an active role in the running of this realm. His throne room is buried a few feet beneath a tiny cottage far from the city of hell. His way of observing what goes on is in a room with a wall of magical windows, each a portal that shows an important station. At times, I have come here with Edge, and we have kept such pleasant company with him that it was easy to forget he was a bloody god. And "bloody" in this context is entirely literal.

I clench my jaw, rolling my eyes at my friend. He continues to guide us forward, keeping gentle contact. Our shoes make hollow echoes that pool around us in mocking waves. It agitates the serpent, which opens its sleepy eyes inside my chest.

Suddenly, I am so struck by your familiarity with it that I almost stumble. This thing inside that I have spent centuries listening to, its hissing no less than venom in my brain. How did you see it with such clarity that your mind gave me an intimate tracking system of this curse? Not even the devil himself has recognized this unwanted guest within me.

Yet a simple human woman . . ..

"Gabe, don't bring her to this place with you," Edge rebukes under his breath.

He turns to look at me, but I can't meet his eyes. Instead, I close mine and exhale a long breath.

"We don't have time for this game, Lucy!" I shout into the echoes of disturbed marble.

Laughter extends around us, deep and resonating through the walls.

We turn back the way we came, only now the path has shortened, and we are standing before his throne. It is carved out of a marbled green rock, as if emeralds and diamonds had been smelted together.

He wears a tailored suit as white as freshly washed bones. Long, curling obsidian hair tumbles over his jacket in stark contrast. He is all colors that strike each other like stones. Flush pink lips in a perfect bow, smiling at us with dimples pressed into red dusted cheeks. Venomous eyes, sunken and hidden by defined cheekbones creating hard ridges beneath his humor. I find myself constantly amazed when I see him.

I realize he is amused.

"That can't be a good sign," I grumble, well aware that my rumbling thundercloud of a voice is enhanced in this place.

"To what honor do I owe the company of my two favorite monsters?" he inquires in a tenor voice like the velvet scrape of shadows in a haunted home.

"We're looking for someone," Edge says, steady and quiet like a good, obedient soldier.

Lucifer tilts his head to the side, glancing out of the corner of his eye. A dramatic show of listening for something. His lips no longer smile but form a taut line. He rights himself before I can think whether I should worry.

"I would have never thought you would complete the assassin's mission," he says to me. "I thought you loved the girl."

Praise followed by a stab, as is his custom.

I don't show that my blood has frozen with his words. *She's here?* Edge's fingers tighten around my wrist, but I don't notice. Blood rushes through my ears, and I grin, hoping he doesn't see the panic rising behind my eyes.

"You should know better than to employ that idiot. How many times have I proven to be much more useful and at far less of a cost?"

That makes him laugh. The sound thunders through the room, reverberating up my spine.

"Perhaps I misjudged your heart. Forgive me," he says through his chuckles.

It irritates me.

"My lord, if I may be bold to interrupt." Edge steps in, his hand bruising my skin.

"You may always be bold," Lucifer grants.

"Gabe's twin sister is alive and wants him dead."

I watch Lucifer's eyebrows rise, but mine come together into a glare. He hadn't reacted until the latter part of the statement.

"You knew she was alive," I whisper, stepping forward.

Edge all but jerks my arm back to stop me from taking another.

"I never thought she would harm you," is all he has to say.

I laugh, my fists clenched and beginning to draw black

smoke from beneath my skin. I am shaking, and I know I need to shut up, but I can't. I won't. You're dead, and my sister isn't my sister. She's an animal created by the hands of my one *good* deed. Freeing us that day destroyed you. And she is a part of it. And he *knew* all along.

"You're the reason she can make those creatures!"

He doesn't bother to respond, just smiles and shrugs.

I'll kill him.

The snake rises into my throat and takes over with a calm elaboration. "I wondered about that. How fast it took for you to silence Sable once she started telling people about this other god of hers. The one you're afraid of." I let a smile take my lips even as Edge tries to signal a warning to me with his grip. "Yet you somehow missed the creatures that she was fighting. It didn't seem like you. You're sharper than that. But now I understand: Castle has your permission to create. Tell me I'm wrong."

One more laugh spills out of him before he gives me the courtesy of an answer. "She isn't *creating* anything."

"Then what the hell do you call those things?"

A thin, scarlet needle pierces my chest somewhere between my shout and his frown. He made no gesture to send the power; it's as if it simply appeared there, embedded within me.

Before my eyes can travel down to the wound, seven more strike me. Something skitters out of the ends, and my blood begins to boil. I lock my jaw, shoving my mind downwards as Lucifer begins to talk. Each word sends another needle to stab me.

"My dear lost one, it would appear your brutal acts against the human are still tormenting you." He grins like a madman as blood dribbles around the projectiles. "Tell me, do you seek your sister for reunion or for vengeance?"

I can't answer. It takes all my strength to concentrate on allowing this torment to continue. My mind battles against my control, begging to protect my body and toss out all these needles torturing it. I can't let it though. He can't know. Instead, I press the psychic fingers against each point, if only to slow the poison. I force my jaw to unclench. He takes my silence as an answer.

"What you did to her lies on your shoulders and yours alone. Castle is of no concern to me, because she is *not* creating those beings. In fact; I have placed her under my protection *because* of her work. She enhances with well-honed skills what is already there. You could accomplish the same, Gabe. You have the same power. Take your guilt and use it for something other than hunting for your sister. It will earn you no favors."

I can't help the schoolboy giggle that escapes me. The notion that he would actually protect her seems outrageous.

"I would *love* to know how to buy you, my lord," I say, a snarl rising into my mouth. "And here I thought you had favorites. I don't want to kill her because of what I did to Sable." I choke your name down like swallowing razorblades. Still, I sprint ahead. "I want to beat her to a bloody pulp for poisoning me and not only triggering a bloody episode from that sickness of mine but also releasing the bastard in my head for a time too!"

His silence is pleasing, but I don't let it show. My mind is brushing against the needles, testing their depth and pushing on them just enough to ease some pressure. The itching flames have dulled, so I can think again.

"She went after your sickness," he repeats, sounding genuine in his shock.

Edge steps forward, seizing the opportunity to derail this confrontation before I lunge.

"That's right, and you have sworn your protection over Gabe for as long as he remains at your right hand's side," he reminds Lucifer with gentle boldness. "You *owe it* to us to tell us where she is, regardless of any use she may have to you."

Lucifer's eyes spark, agitating me with uncertainty. "Owe" is not exactly a word one should use when speaking to a supposed god. It doesn't always end well. Actually, it never does.

He smiles with something just short of glee and waves his hand to dismiss us. I let out a breath I don't remember holding.

"Thank you," Edge whispers as he bows.

His grip on my wrist is so tight that the bone whines beneath his hold as he all but drags me away.

"Be careful who you place your heart with, lost one. You may find that one day you will wake up, and it will be gone,"

Lucifer calls out, his voice following us through the portal.

I don't register those words until I turn to Edge, who's holding his palm up before his eyes. He has more blood in his palm than he did the first time we used his magical doorway. My jaw falls open as I notice a bead of sweat trailing down his cheek. He is breathing heavily, and his wounded hand is shaking, which is out of place in the stillness of his home.

I have never seen Edge fear his master.

Until now.

CHAPTER 27

"You could have started with the sickness and saved us half that chapter," Edge growls.

"Where do we go?" I ask, skipping over his advice.

Many would think we were dismissed with nothing. Given mercy for our impudence. But I do not. I have seen that exchange before. Lucifer transfers the knowledge from his mind into Edge's in an instant, dismissing him with everything he needs to know for his job.

"First, I think you should know he was bluffing." He waits for my eyes to meet his. "She wasn't there."

My jaw locks without my command, and I have to turn away. "How do you know that?"

I don't have to ask, because I already know. He sifted through the souls tearing at him, cluttering against his energy even with the great distance between him and the city. I laugh, glancing back at him.

"You didn't need Lucy in order to find my sister," I supply to his silence, a smile finding my lips. "You wanted to know if Sable had gone with her father just like she said she would."

He stares at his hand, frowning at the blood in the creases of his healed palm.

"She did," he whispers, sounding as if those two words are strangling him. "She's not there. Either she lives, or her soul has fled elsewhere."

I can't feel my legs, and maybe my heart has finally stopped, because I feel my chest cave in.

"There's no way that she lives," I say a little too quickly. I think I'm falling, but perhaps it is just the room tilting around me. "It was all true. Every last—"

An ugly sound breaks from deep inside me, and my stiff legs collapse to the ground. I clutch at the ache that is dripping acid into my chest. I can't see; your eyes are blinding me with their glowing love.

"I hope I will see you again. Don't stop here. Find your answers, please. Know that I love you, and I forgive you, Gabe."

"I fucked up," I mumble, my tongue swollen. My hands rise to clutch at my head. "I'm so sorry!" I scream into the carpet.

Edge is there, placing his hand on my shoulder. I can't handle the warmth in his palm soaking up all this anguish and whisking it away. I shouldn't be given such freedom. But the calm spreads across my shuddering back. The vibration in my chest settles into a steady pulse, like blood throbbing under the bruises of my *sin*.

You deserved better.

I pull in a long breath that gets stuck on the gaping hole at the base of my throat. Edge must sense the blockage, because he brings his other hand down to squeeze my bicep. The warmth pools into my muscles, following every fiber until it reaches the place that is infected with your smile. His hair tickles my cheek as he bends down to put his bandage over my pain.

An exhale shudders through my lips as I breathe out the agony the way a dragon breathes fire. The next inhale dances back just a little before flowing down into my lungs.

I square my shoulders, locking my jaw while the tears dry against my cheeks. My chin is still quivering, but one more breath dives down without a hitch, and I think I can manage. I collect myself, pushing away his hands.

"Alright, where's my sister?" I demand, ignoring the scratch of my aching heart dragging behind my voice.

"A village just to the west of that forest you guys went to. She lives in a small cottage at the edge of a grove between herself and the town," he says while furrowing his brow.

"Uh oh," I mutter. "We're serious. Why are we serious?"

He glances up, refocusing on my face. "She has no defences, either magical or mechanical. Nothing. Her home is completely vulnerable."

I can't help but laugh. The rumble feels good inside the freshly sealed wounds in my chest. "That's not an obvious invitation for a trap at all."

He nods, but he doesn't find it funny. His lips pull into a tight line. My heart skips a beat as I wonder what the problem is.

"Why would he lead her there only to continue onto the next attack?" he inquires under his breath, so quietly I'm sure he didn't mean to say it aloud.

"What are you talking about?" I ask, a nervous knot tightening in my belly.

He shakes his head, looking away again. "According to your account, the town that was attacked when you two met is the same one she lives outside of."

And the one that I was manipulating with the man Sable killed as my pawn. I let out a tired breath, closing my eyes.

"That's how Lucy figured out she knew the truth that he buried. It was a trap she'd dismantled, and I was probably the one who was supposed to deal with the pseudo-immortal—"

"Which you would have traced back to Castle at some point during your mind games with him," he finishes with a voice of stone.

I snap my fingers, grinning. "And then she would have killed me."

He raises an eyebrow and I shrug. "Well, tried to"

It was a good plan. But Sable's master knew better. He probably saved me.

Chills race down my spine.

"Right then, I believe we were killing someone," I declare, swinging Edge's front door open.

"Oh, that sounds like my specialty," a smooth voice chuckles from the other side.

Edge is between us before I can fully register that the assassin is there. Edge's back is tense, though he wears a mask of calmness while he crosses his arms and glares at the intruder.

"What are you doing here?" he growls.

I chuckle before the new visitor can answer and raise a finger to my blue eye. "I see she left you a gift. Looks good on you, Kivas."

He returns my compliment with an inappropriate gesture, making me laugh again. His eye is a pastel lilac shadow of its violet neighbour. An angry white scar spiders about the edges like a monster trying to climb out of an abyss.

"Where's your *pet?*" he spits, his lip curled up to the side.

My heart twists with understanding, but it's buried under the bandage my friend placed there. The humor alone is enough to tell me that he knows I finished his job.

"Which begs the question you have yet to answer," Edge interjects, plucking the silent exchange dry of its facts.

"I'm here because Gabe is paying for my eye," he answers through his teeth.

I lift my hands as if in surrender, baiting him. "I don't even know how to use a bow."

Edge shakes his head and rolls his eyes.

"Can you get your revenge some other time? We're in a hurry." His glare explains more than his lighthearted words. "Unless you want to help. Just like old times when you guys used to be guardians, remember?"

The offer elicits a snarl until he looks more like a feral dog than a man. He stands closer to my height, so while my comrade stands between us, his focus remains on me.

But Edge demands respect and attention in a way that can't be ignored, especially by someone who's met his correcting rage before. His body language is that of a commander, and when he speaks again, his voice forces the assassin to look down into narrowed eyes.

"Right now, you can't stand Gabe, correct? You hate

him, his insanity, his games, everything to do with him these days makes your blood boil. Right?"

Kivas isn't sure where this is leading, but he nods slowly.

"So, how would you feel knowing there is another angrier and infinitely more *focused* Gabe on the loose right now as we speak?" Edge continues. "Also, one who already released Kiro Baroch once."

The silence is amusing, though a voice in the back of my head warns me that it shouldn't be.

Kivas closes his good eye as he pulls a long breath in through his nose. The other wounded deep marble remains on me. Or perhaps it is just my height working against me. Visibly calmer, his fist drops to his side.

"That would be a higher priority," he allows reluctantly.

His sense of honor makes him easy to control and I commend my friend for learning my tactics so well.

"Then let's go." Edge points behind the man, urging him to turn.

His good eye pierces straight through me first. My humor drains as the color leaves his cheeks. He isn't afraid of me, because we have a strange kinship in this frenemy relationship. We were once brothers in arms, just like him and Abdaziel. All of us on a team protecting someone we each loved in our own way. I won't kill him. I might beat him bloody and bring him close. But he is aware that I have the strength to destroy the very thing that allows him to return to his body over and over again.

Another me has this power and would have no qualms about destroying him.

"Who are we after?" he inquires when we make our way into the cold night.

I cross my arms over my chest and a grin creeps up my face. "We're going to kill my twin sister."

CHAPTER 28

Edge raises his hand to draw the portal, but I stop him. I want to say I don't know what came over me, but that would be a lie. He has done more than enough for me since I came to him with innocent blood staining my soul. I can't let him continue to draw his blood for my sake.

"Let me have the honor," I say while the power in my blood already begins to nibble on my veins.

He raises an eyebrow but allows it. I am not generally "caring" when it comes to him, at least not in any way that he can see. A gentleness has pulled into me though, and I don't know where it is seated inside. I know it is your fault though. I can't take back the life that I have stolen, but I can let it live on in what I do.

The portal opens before us, revealing the early morn of

a familiar town. We step through, and the moment my foot touches the grass, I choke. You laugh inside my mind, telling me not to give up the fight so easily when I am angry about your use of that word that started this whole thing: faith.

The village is still in a state of disrepair. I have to remind myself that it has only been a few days since I left there with you cradled in my arms. It feels like a distant memory, as if decades have passed. I breathe through the thick mist Edge placed in my chest.

I won't let her hurt them, Sable. I will let you rest in peace with your father, knowing his will is still going to be fulfilled. I'm so sorry.

One more long breath limps down my clogged throat.

"There's a clearing on the other side of that batch of trees along the edge," Edge says to my right.

He points toward the right side of town. My heart sinks into my toes, but I was prepared for this. It is the place I finally spoke to you after thirteen years of keeping my distance.

I should have stayed away.

I work my jaw until the stone growing beneath his ethereal bandages stops growing on my collarbone. The bone creaks beneath its weight.

Inhale, long and slow.

"Let's go," I say, my tumbling baritone grating out like a prayer.

A hand on my shoulder stops me. Black smoke billows off my clenched fists, but I don't turn to attack. I battle that instinct, smothering it.

"What was she to you?" Kivas asks from behind me, his voice quiet and careful.

What does that matter at this second? You're gone. And I have to finish your job.

"You have changed," he says, his lips in a tight line. He's been listening to my inner blubbering all this time. "What was this Sable to you?"

I close my eyes at the sound of your name from someone else's lips.

"She is the sister that I spent my eternity searching for," I admit, looking up to the grey clouds closing in on us. "I would give my life if it would bring her back."

Kivas removes his hand from me, turning back to face the village. "That's all I needed to know."

I understand the question now. He isn't coming into this battle if he can't be certain we will remain on the same side. He needs to know that I have the resolve to kill this adversary. I've let him down before, so I don't hold his hesitation against him.

"Do we have a plan?" he asks as we tread toward town.

"Immediate and unforgiving death," I reply with a nonchalant shrug.

Edge pipes up with a tone that tells me to shut up. "She likely has her house full of those pseudo-immortals, guys. We need answers before we charge in."

I let out a chortle, but it sounds closer to a snarl. "Speak for yourself. I can't fucking die. No use in being careful, old man."

"Will you get your comrades killed though?" he snaps.

I stop, locking my jaw and glaring at him. Kivas steps away from us. It is the only indication of my lethality. My hands quiver at my sides as I hold back the power slithering into my palms. Crimson and obsidian snakes slide around my fingers like jewelry.

Flashes come uninvited into my mind. *That man is attacking you, and his mouth is a distorted grin that's too wide for his cheeks. I can't move to save you; my mind is pulsating with fire inside each psychic arm. I feel the shape of my gift and curse inside my skull. The head of an octopus sits inside my brain, and it's on fire. You are screaming, and my sister's cackles are shattering my bones. I look to you as blood drips down your attacker's arms. The ground falls away.*

What freed me?

I don't know, but I'm beside you in the next flash. Enraged. ***Why are you so weak? It hurts me.***

But I get it now. I understand. Death is not something you feared. It is only the end of a purpose. You have gone home. And I am trapped here in the world of the living.

As always.

Edge is right: if I am reckless with my trap, I will get others killed again.

Kivas is arguing with Edge. He seems to agree with me that we should simply kill her. No ifs or buts. He is probably right. She poisoned me on our first reunion and subsequently weakened my barriers on the god inside me. My illness is the only thing that might be able to kill me. On top of that, Kiro is the only being I know who can give Edge an equal fight. I would say I am his equal too, but we will never know, because I have made a point not to fight him. The point is that I am a time bomb waiting to be set off. The weakest link.

I gesture toward the ground, calling the wind beneath my feet. The men fall silent for a moment before Edge shouts my name. I have left them behind though, rising into the air and speeding toward the trees.

I wonder where I will go if she kills me today. The thought is unwelcome. Will I be returned to the world that Edge and I visit on a regular basis; Lucifer's afterlife, which tortures souls? He would have a heyday if he ever received my soul in his records.

It occurs to me that I may never see you again.

The thought so jarring that it almost crushes my windpipe. My heart is filled with wet sand, weighing me down and threatening to pull me from the gale's hands. In the next instant, I see my sister's home. Something inside me loosens with relief. She is outside the small shack. At this height, I can only see the tumble of her long curls and the flap of wind in her dress. She is waving at me.

I land at the edge of the treeline, crossing my arms over my chest.

"Are you ready?" she calls to me, a soft smile touching her mouth.

Her hands are clasped behind her back. In the sunlight, I realize the black ribbons tied at her biceps are threaded with royal purple words. It is a language I don't recognize. She is in a strapless emerald gown that pools around her bare feet, so I can only see the tips of her toes peeking out from beneath it. It has jagged tears in the sides, revealing a sliver of her muscled thigh. Her golden eyes are lit by splashes of sunlight. They look like tumbling fluid stirring around the pupil.

"Ready for what?" I ask, taking a few steps closer.

She skips back, mirroring my advancement. Her smile widens into a toothy grin. It doesn't suit a face marred like hers.

"For a proper reunion, of course. I have dinner on inside. We'll have a picnic in the trees. Just like when we were kids."

I can't breathe. Her words cause eyes of fire to shudder behind my own.

She sees my hesitation, smirks, and crosses her arms. Another mirror.

"You brought company," she states, tilting her head to the side and letting her gaze travel. I assume she is watching them advance toward us as she continues. "But as long as none of you disrupt my home, I can be hospitable.

My mouth is dry again and I frown at her.

"What exactly was it about a human that you couldn't be hospitable from the start?" I demand, my fists clenched with dark magic. "What about her made you so volatile, yet actual divines that have more than enough power to disrupt your home are being welcomed?"

I can't fathom it. I'm shaking, and your fire is eating me alive from the inside out.

Castle chuckles, the sound as smooth as melted honey dripped onto a bell. "None of you are willing to try convincing me of redemption. I see no reason why we can't be civil before the inevitable. I am your enemy, and you will kill me if you cannot use me. Tell me I'm wrong."

That sounds familiar, and I have to smile. *She's crazy. Just like me.*

"Not really," Kivas says, frowning as he replies to my thoughts.

She turns a welcoming smile to him, and something sparks inside her golden gaze.

Kivas' frown hardens at the sight of her.

"You are wrong," he informs her. "One Gabe is hard enough to keep track of and stop from blowing up the universe on a bad day. We are *just* going to kill you."

The light returns to her gaze, holding fast this time and I recognize it: hope.

"That's exactly what you want," I whisper. My jaw locks as I step toward her again. "You *want* us to kill you!"

She closes her eyes and lets out a long exhale. When she opens them again, they remain fixed on the grass.

"I was the lock on your powers," she admits, her voice

catching on glass in her throat. "When you broke free, it was me that you shattered. And when you became immortal, you forced me to become immortal as well. You *stole* my death!"

She throws the end at me like daggers, but she can't look at me. A grimace takes over her face as she sinks into her precious anger. She falls silent, letting the truth drag the tips of its claws against the edges of the hole in my chest. The bandage is slipping off.

"So, you'll either kill me and receive your revenge, or you'll die trying," I surmise, my mouth twisting into a sneer.

Edge lands on my other side and slips his hand around my wrist, pulling back my power with a silent warning.

Despite the action, he chuckles "Tell me you didn't miss the irony this time."

"Not at all."

Castle has come back from her pitiful act, analyzing the three of us while her lips pull down. As she turns to address the final visitor, recognition settles the tension in her shoulders.

"Your boss won't be very happy with you," she warns.

He laughs again. "You lost his protection when he realized you wanted to murder his favorite immortal."

Castle tilts her head in thought at the new information. Her hair falls away from the scar pressing into her cheek. "I guess having his right hand would have been better insurance."

"You're really not that bright," the assassin says, drawing her attention out of the corner of her eye. "Are you sure you're Gabe's sister? I mean, I may not like the guy, but his intellect isn't exactly that dull."

He is baiting her. Kivas has a simple code in his line of work. If someone must die but he deems them with some form of innocence, he will make it swift and clean, but only after granting a final wish before they go. That is why many have dubbed him the "Hollow Angel." Yet if he concludes that someone *deserves* their death, he doesn't sit around waiting on it, though he may take longer to kill them, make a mess of them before they are released. It depends on his judgement of them. The bottom line is he wants this to begin.

She doesn't take his bait though. Her humor returns as

she turns to face him.

"I am my mother's daughter," she says. Then she gestures toward me, her fingertips brushing the front of my shirt. "He also happens to be my mother's son. But I will be damned before I call him my brother."

Despite the biting words, she utters them with perfect calm. No malice. No rage. It is like a basic fact that shouldn't have to be explained. Her tone punches me in the ribs more so than her words.

~Ask about the well.

Excuse me?

~Let her know that Sable still loves her.

The only outward sign that I hear the words is the widening of my eyes. I become aware of the distinct shift in the hand at my wrist tightening.

He heard it too.

Oh boy.

My guts twist as I handle the trigger in my mind. Castle will snap. I may not know her, but I understand now what love does to a rotting heart. It stings like a poison, but that is the wrong word to use, because it isn't *bad.* It's just lethal . . . in a gentle way that makes it alright.

"*I trusted you . . ..*"

Ah, there you are. It's been a while since you last invaded. I can't make it up to you, Sable. I betrayed you in a way that is unredeemable.

But I can finish this.

I pull the trigger. "Castle, do you realize that Sable still loved you even after the incident with the well?"

She freezes, her head snapping back to face me. A marble statue of a girl stares with her mouth open as if she will say something. What can she say though? This is something between her and the woman I killed. I don't know what happened in the well. She has no way to retort. It will mean nothing to me.

"How do you know about that?" she asks, finally finding her voice.

I roll my eyes; I can't help it.

"The voices in my head wanted you to know," I respond, flashing her an insane grin.

She narrows her eyes. I am not about to admit who that voice sounded like. I can't. He would never help me after what I've done.

The octopus inside my head demands my attention with such sudden urgency that I almost laugh. It is like a child slapping his dad's leg and yelling "Papa!" over and over again.

I slip up into it, settling inside the great head of my psychic core. It shows me something bizarre in my sister's psychic ability. Her power is like snakes. Like my snake. Except mine is singular and separate from my mind gift entirely. In this view, she is like Medusa, hundreds of small serpents slithering out of her head until the folds of the air are squirming and distorting.

The part that gives me pause is that one of them is longer than the others, but this one does not come from her mind. It rises from her belly. Along with that, its head cannot be seen. Its curved body is stretched toward her little shack, and as I follow it, my heart sinks. Somehow, I know what is waiting there in the doorway. His mouth is pulled up into a familiar crazed grin that lights my veins on fire. All the ice inside me melts. The head of the snake gnaws on his chest, drilling its little head inside the cavity. It begins to sway, sending a rippling wave from her body to his.

My mouth falls open. *She isn't creating anything.* Lucy repeats in my head.

Oh no . . ..

"We can share our immortality," I whisper in horror.

Time shudders back to life.

Castle is gone. So is the man. I drop down into my body with an unceremonious jolt for which my power apologizes.

Edge's hand leaving my arm is the only warning I get before a body crashes against mine. We hit the ground, and my attacker scrambles off. A flash of light blinds me for a moment as I remain stunned on the ground trying to understand what is happening. Something clashes to my right. I know that sound: Edge's crystal short swords hitting metal.

My sister appears in front of me for a second before the familiar sting of a blade piercing me registers at my side. I almost sigh, but that place has been struck before, and I remember the pain that follows breathing. I clench my teeth instead and strike with my fist. My knuckles bounce off a bone while my other hand yanks out the blade.

I am standing before I remember telling my legs to support me, the dagger flipped in my hand, so its blade is snug against my forearm. She isn't there though.

A grunt to the left draws my attention to where Kivas has just landed on the ground, clutching the wound in his chest. He isn't going to die by it, but he is annoyed by the pain. I know the feeling.

She's here once more, her mouth smiling as her head bounces up under my chin. My teeth clack together and shoot colors up into my head. The little shit isn't even using her abilities. She's fighting like a bloody child.

All I catch with my fist this time is empty air. I let out a growl. "If you want a fight, get over here and face me like a warrior!" I shout into the chaos.

I don't know where her minion is, but the constant singing of Edge's blades provides a good guess.

My anger must have worked, because she reappears behind me this time, her arms cinched around my waist. It could almost be considered an embrace if I don't know better. Her palm lies flat against my belly, and I realize too late that she's done this before. I stab downward with her blade as the boiling starts inside my organs. It's just like Lucy's needles. An absent part of my mind wonders if he taught her this trick or if it was the other way around?

She doesn't flinch when the blade sinks into her arm. It shouldn't surprise me.

I descend into the blackened power inside me, letting it spill out through my pores. My jaw locks as its burn adds to what she's done, but I must end this soon, or the sickness will kill everyone if I have another episode this soon after the last.

"What did you do to her?" I demand as the black smoke billows off my skin. "The well. What was it, Castle?"

Her reaction is not what I hoped. She laughs, yanking one of her arms away from this strange embrace, only to return with a new blade that slips between two of my ribs. I lock my jaw.

The power is ready though. I flex all my muscles at once, squeezing it out of me and groaning as it rips through all the little holes in my skin. The magma racing through my veins coats me in the aftermath, but her squeal is worth it.

Her arms disappear, and I turn to face her.

Something changes in her. She is on the ground, glaring up at me through the burns on her face. Her skin is charred, some places black, others scarlet. I don't acknowledge the way that her pain becomes a poison in my heart. I have had enough.

Reaching down, I yank her up by her shoulders. Obsidian clouds surround my fists and leach onto her skin while her golden eyes widen with recognition and sweet terror.

"What the hell is this?" she asks as she struggles.

The illusions make my hands stronger than stones, and she has no leeway. This becomes apparent to her in an instant. I realize when she draws up her hands and claws at my chest that these illusions are not part of her design. They are mine. It gives me a sense of satisfaction. We are not entirely alike.

"It's your doom," I purr into her ear.

My fingers dig into her shoulders. I have done this once before, I realize. You were much weaker than Castle is though, and yet she shows more terror than you did. This understanding brings a clarity to my mind.

These illusions held no power over you.

Because of him . . ..

It hurts again. The bandage is torn away. My nostrils flare. With the pain, the power rises until it almost covers her head entirely. She chokes and gasps on the smoke when it sizzles against her burns, irritating them.

"You can't let him into your head!" she hollers through the magic. "He will strip down your powers to nothing! He *let* her die, remember?"

Her wailing doesn't elicit the anticipated reaction. It doesn't give me pause, does not turn me away. All I know is awe. Even Castle knows Sable's master. And she is *terrified* of him.

"This power is worth nothing! It couldn't keep her alive," I snarl, willing the black power to wash over my dear sister's entire body.

As the power moves, its flames inside me find the hole you left behind, and they spill down into it. Black clouds and goo cover Castle's body, while inside, the light you buried deep down that crevice pulsates like a bruise under the stinging bite of my illusions. The dark magic thrashes against the walls of the abyss. It aches for something that you would loathe me for. It will leave nothing behind of this entire adventure if it is given free reign.

A pathetic sound brings me back to the suffering woman. Castle has torn open my chest, and her hands are glowing red. She is whimpering. The sound draws a sadistic chuckle from my throat, though it is almost unrecognizable to my ears.

She meets my eyes, and something behind her gaze blooms inside the swirling gold. Her hands fall still. She moves them back, holding them up as if in surrender. It only raises the grin on my lips, and I tighten my hold. My nails have broken skin, the blood dripping into my greedy magic as it hums against her flesh.

"You say you want me dead, because our mother was cursed by our very existence," I sneer, my lips brushing her nose. "Well, we are double cursed then, because we destroyed Sable's life too."

Your name doesn't carve into my chest, and maybe that should warn me that I am diving too deep into my madness, but the blood that is spraying from her back when the power slices into her is too distracting. I relish her anguish as your screams echo in the back of my mind. Castle is right about one thing: we both deserve to die. Neither of us should have ever existed. It would have been better that way.

With this reverie, it catches me off guard and stills my blood when she stops struggling. Especially when her lips twitch into a smirk as she lifts her tired eyes to meet mine from beneath long lashes. She isn't crying out anymore, but she breathes heavily.

"If only you'd found me on your first trip this way. I could have shown you how to make the connection that would have saved her," she mocks.

I roll my eyes, trying to ignore the way that her words slice into the void, just like she wants.

"As if that interaction would look any different," I hiss, ripping my hands away from her and commanding the power to follow me.

She falls to the ground, sprawled out and bleeding. The black cloud is excited. As it engulfs her, I can almost feel the drip of your tears at the scene. The ache inside me suddenly has nothing to do with the effects of my illusions.

Castle hasn't given up though. She cackles into the grass. I hold out my hand, calling the darkness from her body to gather into my palm. It tears at her clothes and skin when it follows my command.

"When you killed her, you would have killed yourself in the process," she spits through heavy breaths. "We can't make other immortal beings, but we can share our power with them. It is a back and forth pooling of the power, and if we don't bring it back to our side before they die, we go too." She lets out a hoarse laugh that turns into a cough. "And it would have been a wonderful show indeed!"

I have to snicker as I step on her back and hold her to the ground. "And now here you are. Challenging me yourself, and you barely left a scratch," I mock, ignoring the fact that I can't recognize my own voice anymore. "You'll get your death wish granted, but I'm still going to be here. You were too weak to think you could do this on your own."

An obsidian sword finishes forming in my hand, and a faraway part of my mind wonders if she can survive everything I have. Will this even harm her? I am almost jealous when the recognition in her eyes tells me it can.

Her weakness will set her free, but I will remain alive. Trapped in a malnourished body of incredible power. Everyone else able to move on and know peace somewhere. I am always trapped . . ..

The distinct song of metal sighing against itself brushes against my ears, and my heart sinks. I know that sound. It is the punishment that the half-angel, Abdaziel, suffers for the mixing of his blood. One metal wing that wraps around his rib cage when it is not in use. The one that rips through his spine every time he draws it out to fly or defend.

But why is he here? And how did he find us?

Below me, Castle's sharp eye catches my hesitation, and her lips pull up into a wolf-like grin. I search for the new visitor, finding him soaring above the battle, something sinking in my chest. My power becomes heavy, weighted on my mind. Something presses against it, but I can't bother with that.

He lands near the house. Someone is in his arms. His good wing is curled around them, so that only a few dark locks are billowing against the soft baby blue of the feathers.

I half register Castle's psychic fingers digging into my mind. It doesn't matter, because at the same time, his arms have pulled away, and his wings settle behind him.

The person turns.

My heart stops.

I am seeing a ghost.

Two glowing forges meet my eyes, but I can't handle this right now. It's impossible. It's a sick joke. How could he have even known? How?

Your eyes widen as my hands shake. The sword disintegrates, and I think my chest is going to burst. You raise your hands as you sprint toward me. I forget where I am while the organ in my chest stutters to life, begging to take you up in my arms and never let go.

"Get away from her!" you shout, but it doesn't make sense. "Gabe, you can't fight her!"

"Sa—"

The fingers inside my mind become claws, and then my eyes go blind.

CHAPTER 29

I am dripped into fire.

The screams don't stop, and I can't move my hands to cover my ears. They are remnants of memory; some even belong to me. Others come from the archived memories of the calamity breaking loose and terrorizing entire towns for his pleasure. Some are the results of studies gone wrong. Those have a special place separate from the others, a reminder of the delicate minds that have become the tools to understand my own. All are no more than a constant chaos that bats at my soul, staining it with every soundwave.

My eyelids are leaden, and I can't raise them more than a crack. Blurred faces surround me. Their empty eyes are eating me alive.

"Castle," I grumble, somewhat surprised that I can

speak, "what is this?"

Her laugh comes at me from all directions, as per usual. The figures shudder, bending to lean over me. Their hands raise in unison, each holding a different type of tool, but all intended for drawing agony. I gulp before I can stop myself.

"Are you afraid?"

I can't find where her voice is coming from. I think it is behind, but there is only dirt beneath me. Perhaps it is above, beyond their heads high up in the ceiling.

No. It isn't there either.

She isn't here.

My attention is attached to the movement of one figure. His tool drops toward my thigh. It stings like a quiet burn, pressing against my skin with tiny pinpricks, moving in a sharp, jerking motion that his hand has difficulty controlling. His arm seems stiff as it continues to move the humming device against me.

"What is this?"

My question is met by another hand coming down with a tool that is as familiar to me as my own hand. It bites into me with licking heat over my ribs, and I smell my skin melting. I know exactly what this is; I could never forget that stench.

She is tearing open my memories. This is them. The cult.

"Is this the best you can do?" I can't help the question.

This is a well-polished stone. A memory handled with purposeful frequency. If she is trying to torment me, she will have to dig much deeper.

"Let's get on with this," I say as the rest of the tools come down on me at once. I don't flinch, nor does my skin seem to be as receptive to their torment. I wonder at the numbness even as I mock them. "You're putting me to sleep here."

The image goes black. Sounds of anguish still grate on my ears though. These are not part of her manipulating hands picking at my mind; they are a permanent scar. My lips have drawn more blood than the demon could ever manage. I have destroyed entire nations with my voice alone. And every shattered mind is here to remind me that I cannot be whole. It is the entire purpose of my study, and yet its conclusion has eluded me for centuries. Why was healing such a horrid thing to search for?

"You are selfish," she answers with ease.

She draws up the next image. A beautiful, young girl with blood-red hair whipping in the wind as she twirls in battle. Watching her fight is akin to viewing a precious dance. Small grey eyes scan the battlefield as the last enemy falls. White light spills from her armor, and her back straightens when the fatigue is eaten away.

"You are toxic."

The warrior turns to find my sister's voice, but when she sees me, her face lights up. She calls my name, and I close my eyes. How long has it been since I have heard her voice? My arms open to receive her in an automatic response to her drawing near to me.

She is the one who brought us all together: me, Kivas, and Abdaziel. The common denominator that had once turned us into a team for the better part of a few hundred years. She is my first love. And the first one that I ruined.

As if my acknowledgement of that fact brings it to life, something warm drips down my back when her arms wrap around me. I know without having to look what it is. How many scars have I traced into my own skin? At that time, I tried to be angry with her for doing such a foolish thing. It stole her away from my grasp. Turned Abdaziel against me. He was alive for the sole purpose of protecting her, and yet the Immortal Trickster was her most trusted guardian. And because of that, she took her life.

It made him sick.

It broke my heart.

I shouldn't have gotten involved.

"I tried to leave," I protest, as if her memory needs protection. "I tried to get out before I broke her. She knew what kind of monster she was choosing to befriend. She took that risk even when I begged her not to."

Her blood soaks my shirt, and I hear a deep rolling laugh to my right. I recognize it. He has found me in here. My skin starts to boil beneath her blood, but I can't release her, or he will have her torn apart.

"Is this better?" Castle inquires, sounding genuinely curious.

I almost laugh. This is like an experiment for her, and I am a test subject. *So, this is how it feels.*

I breathe heavily and look down at the jewel of a woman in my arms. *Let her go.* They pull back in the same stiff, jerking motions as my last tormentors. If we survive each other, I will have to teach her the art of the mind game. A smile creeps across my lips.

"If you could have kept your mouth shut, it would have been," I declare, tossing the woman to the ground and placing my hands on my hips. "Now try it again!"

She fades into the black floor.

Kiro Baroch is still standing there, and he laughs again.

Right. He isn't just a memory. My heart sinks a little.

"Don't kill him," Castle instructs, earning a snort from me.

"As if you can control him!" I yell, doubling over with sudden uncontrollable laughter.

Kiro seems amused as well, though he is quiet as he appraises the manifestation of his physical prison. He isn't the appalling monster that Sable's gift showed her. In here, he is a man with voids for eyes and an attractive face.

"We have never had an opportunity like this," he points out, sounding intrigued. He smiles. "I wonder if it is possible for you to die inside your mind."

Ah, there it is.

My humor gives me confidence as I face the deity. "Remind me again, how were you defeated by a human?"

He frowns. It is pleasing to see, but I cannot dwell on it, because something inside me is growing agitated. The air is thickening, my blood singing in response. I realize we are becoming surrounded by billows of black smoke, and I almost let my grin split my face. My final uninvited companion slithers into the party, hissing and drawing my attention.

It drips ink as it moves, slinking toward us with its head poised. Its tongue slips out with its next hiss, and smoke rolls off the oil dripping out of its mouth. All this time, my illusions have been a by-product of its poison. It is one more moment when I could laugh, but I am halted by all the memories of my rage when you tried to tell me this.

You have always been right. About everything.

My heart aches.

As if responding to your memory, the place I am trapped in begins to unbury your voice.

"Gabe," you whisper, tearing me apart with my own name. "Gabe . . . Gabe . . . Gabe . . .."

It becomes a chant.

"She was a worthy opponent," the demon admits, his arms crossed over his chest.

"If you're going to destroy me, then do it," I demand wearily. "Leave my final victim in peace though."

He smirks, bringing his hand before his eyes as if examining it. "I don't know what you're talking about. We're here out of curiosity alone."

I lock my jaw, but when I curl my hands into fists, he winks at me. "Tsk, tsk."

The serpent lunges, snatching me into its jaws with graceful ease. My bones are heavy, even inside this projection of a body, and I don't bother to fight the attack. I am more than ready to fade away.

I am so tired.

I close my eyes. The poison cools on my skin, but I realize something bizarre. It has not pierced me with its jagged fangs. Instead, I fit behind their curve, caged and yet not dying.

"Do you want to know what happened when the forge and I parted ways?" she inquires in a malicious whisper. "Do you want to know what happened with *the well*?"

I watch the black goo that oozes from the snake's fangs near my hip.

"Not really," I murmur, mesmerized.

It takes a full thirty seconds of silence before I realize that isn't the right answer. My mind is attacked by a phantasmagoria that flashes behind my eyes with such force that it sears them. I clench my teeth until it shoots lightning up into my cheeks.

The images settle into a rhythm that follows someone's heavy breathing.

Castle.

She drags a body through the underbrush of a forest that has gone to sleep for the fall. The leaves crunch beneath her feet. A crimson river spills from her cheek and shoulder, staining the pale blue wrap that covers her abdomen. She falls still, raising her head and closing her eyes as if she will soak up the sun to heal the wound torn into her face.

"Be glad I didn't kill you," she murmurs, turning to the unconscious woman whose ankle is in her hand. "If I see you again though, I will. This should be enough to deter your foolishness."

She lifts the woman with ease. I will not admit to recognizing her.

The thud of the impact is muffled, and Castle allows me to see the bottom for a moment: death. Dried carcases broke the fall. I can't recognize what they are, only that they were animals of some kind. No water is at the bottom, and I don't see how she could have ever climbed out.

It must have been a miracle.

I am returned to my projected body in the serpent's patient jaws before I can utter a snort at my ridiculous thought.

"Did you honestly think anything you did would put her off from trying to save your sorry ass?" I grumble, finding the words hard to push out for their hypocrisy.

She doesn't respond right away, intriguing me. I look at Kiro, whose eyes are filled with a question. He too finds the silence to be strange.

"I couldn't kill her," Castle says, so quietly that I have to strain just to hear her.

"And why not?" the demon asks.

Something twists inside my guts, and somehow, I know the answer, though I have no indication what allows me to predict her next tear-filled statement.

"She reminded me of our mother."

I close my eyes at the words. It is the first time since this torment began that she has hurt me in a way that catches me off guard.

"Do you remember when we were taken?" Castle asks, sounding tired as well, like she is pushing out the words.

"No."

And it's true: I don't.

It was buried by the blood of our captivity. Stained and washed away through my echoing screams as they tore the flesh of my throat.

Something drums like a heartbeat around me, and I wonder if it's hers.

"What about our mother?" she asks, her throat catching just enough for me to notice. "Do you remember her?"

I don't.

I pushed her out to keep Castle there in my mind. That was my lifeline to sanity during those red years. I couldn't keep them both. I had to make a choice. But mother was safe with her broken heart and confusion at her lost children. Castle needed me. Didn't she? Her big brother. We were just kids.

"I'm assuming that our brown eyes come from Anzillu creating us," she says, her voice stronger now.

Two crystal orbs appear before me, as blue as the ocean's surface on a cloudless day.

"Your blue eye comes from her though." The words don't hold the malice that I expect.

I watch the orbs twist and shudder, a black pupil forming in the middle of each. They are her eyes. The eyelids form with a suctioning sound, and she looks at me with a soft, loving twinkle.

"She never yelled at us. Not as far as I can remember. I have memories of time spent with her, but all I know of her distinctly is the color of her eyes and the smell of her perfume. Sometimes, if I try hard enough, I can recall the sound of her laughter."

It is more than my own memory, but I don't have to say this.

"Do you want to know how she died?"

I don't. I close my eyes as the hole in my chest is tugged at the edges.

"They burned her as a witch."

The admission is a steel sword biting into me.

"Who? Who were 'they'?" I inquire with numb lips.

My chin quivers, but I won't weep for her. I don't deserve to.

"Our precious kidnappers turned the town against her when she searched for us. Our own village, who once watched us grow, betrayed her."

It appears that is the theme of this adventure. Betrayal and snakes. It almost makes me laugh, but I refrain.

A flash of light presses against my eyelids, and when I open them, I am sitting down. The serpent and Kiro are gone. Castle is climbing up the branches of the dead tree in which I am already perched.

I am ten years old and innocent, reaching down to help

my sister join me. Her smile is contagious, spreading to my lips as well. The sun is warm on my skin, and it glows in her wide eyes. Her brown curls are pulled back into a loose, messy bun that fails to keep strands out of her face.

Her hand rises, her fingertips brushing my palm.

She yelps as she is dragged down to thud against the chest of a cloaked figure. I cry out as arms wrap around my waist, yanking me down. I thrash in their hold, screaming for my sister, begging for them to leave her alone, to not hurt her. I strike them with my pathetic little elbows, as if it can free me from an adult.

Dark laughter pulsates through my bones, snapping my mouth shut as tears fall. White-hot threads of fear coil inside my belly. I feel it churn and wonder if they will release me if I vomit.

She screeches and bawls and chokes on her sobs. I hear the flesh tear when they slap her into silence. I can't breathe.

She's just a kid!

"We were just kids!"

Her adult voice laughs at me as I cry out. We return to the empty space of her torment in my mind. I am standing on shaking legs. My audience is still gone.

"You forgot that day," she observes, coming toward me and pressing her palm to my cheek. I realize tears are dripping down, her palm wet. "You could handle the pain of all those years, but the memory of being taken had to be the point where you stopped the record."

Her smile is twisted. She jerks her other hand, and it is suddenly adorned with thick, black claws that dig into my belly. Scarlet splashes across her arm as I gurgle on blood. Maybe I *can* die here inside my mind.

"I remember every second," she growls.

Behind her, the serpent returns. Faster than before. A coil of death racing toward us. I watch it with clouded eyes, its hissing filling my head until it pounds and threatens to crack open.

She continues, as if she can't hear the blasted thing behind her. "I kept that day like a sacred object, so that when death finally presented itself, I would welcome it with grace."

It rears its head, towering above her, its eyes no more

than empty holes that show a recognition of weakness.

"You stole that release, you *bastard*!"

It lunges. For one long second, I think it will strike her. I should know better though.

She was never there.

I hear the crunch more than I feel it when those fangs snap through my spine with unforgiving ease.

I close my eyes again.

Black ink races through me. It hisses as it spreads through my body. What once was agitation when I used my power becomes rolling waves of magma melting into me. This is it. My power has finally caught up to me.

And all I can think of is how you tried to warn me all those times.

"*I fear for you . . ..*"

Yeah, and I killed you.

I guess we're even now.

I almost swear that I can hear you whispering though. *No, we were never keeping score.*

But that is only wishful thinking.

And then Castle screams.

CHAPTER 30

Part of me is aware that I have returned to the real world. The other part is still recovering from the poisoned fangs that sank into the mental projection of me.

"Cas—" I cough, spattering blood onto the grass and trying not to recognize the ink tainting it. "Castle?"

My eyes flutter; they won't stay open. They have been weighed down by lead.

Flickering amber eyes gaze down at me. I am still not ready for this.

"You're dead," I say, choking on the words.

Your laugh brushes my face with warm air. You are real. I lift my hand to touch your cheek but halt before I can reach you. It drops to my side, and I look away, coughing again.

"I am not meant to go home yet," you whisper as your slender fingers grip the hand that thought itself worthy to touch you.

You bring my palm up to your cheek, pressing it against your soft *living* skin. I ache with the memory crashing down on my shoulders.

"You need to get away from me," I warn.

"I will not leave you here."

Of course you would say such a ridiculous thing.

A desperate surge rips at my chest. I sit up, forgetting Castle tore me open before she attacked my mind. Fire crackles across the wounds, pulling a gasp from me.

"It's alright," you assure me, pressing your hand against my shoulder. "It's over, Gabe."

The silence begs an answer, and you take a deep breath. I know what you will say, but it doesn't seem real. "Castle didn't make it. When we killed the pseudo-immortal, he took her life with him. I didn't know it would happen; I'm so sorry."

Your chin wobbles, and I am certain you are fighting back a torrent of tears. I frown at the sight.

"She said she wasn't creating them," I find myself explaining. "We can share our power though. It moves through a connection from us to the other, and if they die before the power returns, it kills us."

The memory of a little girl screaming for help jars me out of focus. Fog fills my head until it is a muggy day in there. She has cracked the foundations of all my mental walls. Every shred of my past over the centuries crowds into the forefront and pounds against my skull. The poison of my illusions pulsates beneath the chaos.

That terrified little girl I fought for through a decade of agony . . . she is gone. Whisked away by the hands of hatred and righteousness. A strange duet for a broken child who had waited so patiently through all these years for death's release.

I do not make a sound.

Tears drip from my chin, but I don't give them the luxury of acknowledgement.

"You need to leave me, Sable," I repeat, your name tasting like iron on my tongue.

"Why?"

I laugh. Why is all of this so amusing? I shake my head, hearing the splintering stones inside it beginning to crumble.

"I am toxin," I say with a gentle smile.

My hand is still on your cheek, and I pull you down, pressing my lips against your forehead. Then I push you away.

"I know where the black magic comes from now, and I can't control it any longer. It . . . it got me, Sable. While I was trapped in my mind with Castle . . . the snake was there. It bit me."

Your eyes widen when recognition sets in. I twitch my lips up higher.

You don't get a chance to reply. With the last of my strength, I yank the wind into submission. It gathers beneath you while the serpent's poison drips out of my wrist. Black goo pools in my palm. *Hey look, Edge. We're brothers!* I jest to no one. The hissing in my head rumbles like crashes of thunder.

"I will never hurt you again," I promise as the cyclone pulls you away.

"Gabe!"

You are tucked safely in the arms of the gale, and the smile on my lips turns into a full grin. *Finally . . .* I think half-heartedly.

I sink into the nightmare, welcoming it. Lucifer will laugh when he sees me soon.

~~~

The clouds twist all around me, the same as the cyclone I just sent away. *Come along then, let me die already. Etch the torment of my existence into this wretched soul.* It churns in me until I can't tell if I am lying on my back, my side, or if I've curled up into a ball.

My eyes still won't open all the way. They flutter at the darkness swirling in angry gusts around me. I am paralyzed, my flesh frozen into marble even while my insides boil. The haze in my mind thrums with the wild beating of my heart. My lungs are so tight that I can't even cough anymore. The blood and taint catch and choke me.

All I have left is this shuddering vision of black and black and . . .

But what is that?
~~~

A thread of light dances in the distance like a seam where the darkness meets at either side, yet it cannot overcome. I see a faint shape of someone within. I tell myself that I am imagining it. Only a trick of the mind; it can't be anyone. I will not be saved. My eyes slip shut when a violent shudder takes hold.

A hostile weight settles over the gaping hole punched through my collarbone. It threatens to shatter what is left of the bones and crush me into dust. I smirk despite the pressure. This is a companion that I have shared my life with for as long as I can remember. Why deny its demand for my heart if that very organ has given up on me too?

Part of me isn't ready. It's terrified by this acceptance of the moment for which I have waited my entire life. It thrashes and begs. *Get up, end the nightmare, I'm not ready*!

How strange it is to desire and fear death.

My eyes struggle to open, surrendering to that piece begging for life. They search for the thread inside my twisting shadows. I know I imagined it, and I will prove it. Then I can find my peace. I can give in without fighting myself. Once I prove only darkness is left for us.

The pressure atop me increases impatiently, and I welcome it as it splinters the bone until I feel the cracks spider out toward each arm. *Just hurry up and destroy me already.* How many times today have I demanded this? *Get on with it. I'm tired of this existence . . . of the endless ache that has suffocated me for centuries.* How have I managed to survive all this time when I've been barely able to breathe around the ball of sadness that made its home in my throat? It must be some sick joke of immortality.

Maybe the prolonged torment is some kind of punishment. How many people have I destroyed in my life? My mind games are deadly enough; I don't need to lay hands on people. I loathe violence, though at times it is hard to tell.

Yet, as irony would have it, I am the most violent predator I have ever known. If I weren't choking, I would be chuckling right now as this spinning blackness presses in like a lover responding to my thoughts. It slices into my skin, drawing blood into the storm.

Yes, take it. Have it all. Bleed me dry, if only you would let me die.

Ah, but there it is. Right on time. That light in the seam where the darkness meets yet can't overcome. It tries though, swelling and bulging as if flexing its muscles. My lips twitch like they might smile again.

Inside the light, the shadow is walking. It is not the same shade of the evil spilling around it. It appears as if the light is shining from within them, pushing back on the darkness. I think I might know this person. Tears sting the corners of my eyes as my heart sinks.

She is wearing the smile that I recognize from miles away. The one that sets my heart ablaze as it terrifies me with its overwhelmingly pure *love.* Not for me . . . no, it is not a personalized, romantic sort. Rather, it is innocent and unconditional, raw *acceptance.* Something entirely different that is so much more than just *feelings.* It seeps out of the pores in her skin and thrums in the air around her like an angel's hymn. How can a single person be so filled with such a powerful, infectious love that it pours out and touches every soul nearby?

She comes to stain me with this strange peace, whether I am ready for it or not. But the darkness is going to tear her apart. Why can't she just listen to me for once?

~Because she obeys only one.

Oh, shut up!

My mind screams, buffeting against this paralyzed body as if I can protect her from my self-designed hell. Deep inside, I recognize that I am helpless, and I will watch her die at any moment. Again.

~Trust me.

If I could roll my eyes, I would, but I can't remove them from her. She seems oblivious to the gale twisting about me, but I know she can see it. She thinks it can be reasoned with. Just like when she walked through the wind after what Kiro did to her.

Even as I remember, the difference between this power and that one grates against my flesh. I can't watch her die.

I have to warn her! How can I leave this world if I bring harm to the only person on earth who can bleed golden peace with each smile? She is beautiful and strong, and I destroyed her once already. I can't do it again.

She is too close, her arms stretching out at her sides as

if she will embrace me on arrival. But the illusions will have her first!

~Such little faith . . ..

Stop . . . Please don't let her come any closer.

I shove with my mind, trying to force out a strength I don't have anymore. She must be warned though, even if my psychic power must tear my brain apart to release this spell under the illusions. I will save her.

But oh, how still my body is. Despite the sticky blood and the sweat and the periodic convulsions of my chest. Inside, I am screaming. My ears ring, and the earth vibrates with the rumbling ache. A wretched howl rips free from deep in my belly.

"Sssss . . .."

Her name is on the tip of my tongue, so close to coming out, but my mouth won't move. Doesn't it know the urgency? Or perhaps it does, and it is laughing at me, mocking my efforts. Daring me to fight.

That is one thing I am good at you realize, I muse. I try again to call out to her. To stop her.

"Sssss . . .."

Just say her name. Stop her. Don't let her be a bloody hero.

White flashes of electric terror shake through my core, cooling my blood until it turns to ice. She can't die on me again.

"Sssss . . .."

So close to saying it, to saving her. Yet there she is, near enough I can see the orange fire of her blazing eyes piercing through the thick blackness as if she is staring right at me.

No. Impossible. The cyclone is too wild. Too thick. Yet my own mismatched eyes lock with hers, and the truth crashes down on me like a mirror shattering.

She would die for me.

But . . . why . . .?

Hot tears stream down onto the red earth as my struggling buckles down to the point that my head feels as if it is being squeezed.

I am not worth this! Not for me! Don't do it for me!

She is so near, her dark curls whip across her face. That serene face so full of such a love that it cannot be understood by any being in this world. Why? Why is she not afraid?

I can't watch this. My eyes slip shut.

Please, don't take her life again. Release me instead before she gets here.

The storm pauses. Its silence slows my racing heart. Perhaps it is deliberating my request. I could almost laugh again. Then it rages to life again, roaring louder in my ears until I am certain they are bleeding.

No. Oh no . . ..

Hands press against my shoulders, pulling me up and securing long arms about my back. Soft, silky locks tickle my face. The spell on my body is lifted, and I move.

A strangled cry escapes me like a dying animal as I cling to Sable. It is as if the world has fallen away beneath me, and if I let go, I will fall into that abyss too.

"Make it stop," I plead, my mouth thick with anguish. "I can't take this hissing snake in my mind. I can't stand this pain anymore. Strangle it, Sable. I know you can. I can't live like this anymore!"

Her fingertips trace my spine downward, guiding my lungs to inhale. The air follows her hand coming up again, letting me exhale slowly.

"I can't," she whispers.

My heart stops.

"Only my master has that kind of power."

Of course. It still comes back to that.

"He loves you, Gabe. Just ask him. He will set you free from all of this darkness."

I let out an ugly laugh that is distorted by the rawness of my throat. My head falls back, and I look to the heavens. No blue sky greets me. It is blotted out by the stain of my erupting soul.

"Lord, find compassion for me," I beg, my whisper barely audible. "I can't continue like this. Please . . . save me!"

CHAPTER 31

The storm falls still. Its silence pulls a wool blanket over me, settling on my shoulders like a peaceful cloak. I take in a long breath before I plead with Sable's father.

"I have watched this woman do things no human should be capable of. I watched her make my strongest power null and void with this light that she's found and unearthed from deep inside her. And I know it was you. I don't understand it, and it seems crazy. She doesn't even flinch half the time that she should, and when she does, she continues on when you tell her to do something." I couldn't help the scoff that left my lips. "Who does that? Who would just stare their doom in the face on a regular basis and still not run from it just because the voice in their head says they can handle it? That's insane!"

One more long breath, and her hand traces my spine again. I swear it is the only reason I am not falling into the gaping hole inside me.

"But it is undeniably real. I know this. I watched her die." My throat fills with glass. "I thought I killed her. Yet, here she is . . . because of you. I don't even want to know how. I don't deserve to."

I choke and splutter on those words, incapable of turning down to look at her even as she continues to unflinchingly calm her murderer.

"I have watched her change when you move something to awaken inside her. I know it's you. You . . . you complete her when your spirit rises. She is no longer my Clo-Caillea but rather . . . she is light. She is love.

"Change me like that, lord. I can't stand this ink inside me anymore. I don't care if it removes all my power. I don't want a strength that constantly threatens to tear me apart. Make me clean again. I am so tired of this stain."

I bury my face into Sable's shoulder. The seconds tick away into minutes. Her shirt grows wet beneath my eyes. I can still feel my shadows churning around us, but they are no more than a tiny ring at our feet.

The first thing that I notice is all my tensed muscles are relaxing. The second is my energy draining. I slump against the silent woman, unable to hold myself up any longer.

She understands what is happening though, as she eases me down into the grass, remaining bent over me with her palm covering my cheek.

"He's ready, my lord," she prays. "Come and awaken the gift of your helper within him. Cleanse the pain and the darkness, just as he asked. Bring my friend a new life with you."

My chest tightens as it anticipates an attack from the pressure easing into my veins while she speaks. The snake is wide awake, ready to fight and curling itself into the cavity behind my chest wall. It is slimy and chilled, growing, bulking up until I can't breathe. No longer just a metaphor for subjective emotions, it is real.

The pressure enclosing on the angry serpent remains gentle in its advance, though I feel a ferocity within it. *Go ahead,* I encourage the strange thing. *Destroy the snake.*

It hisses again.

"Free me," I beg, surprised I can still form the words.

Sable's hand comes to my forehead, and her soft hair brushes against my face. I feel her lips at my ear as she begins to speak in an unfamiliar language. It gives a tangible weight to her voice, dripping syrup into me. It is like warm honey rushing in to ease the pressure. *The helper.* It and her voice encircle the coiled serpent at the base of my throat. Black venom drips off sharp, curved fangs, and I know that is what has been racing through my veins, soaking deep into my bones over the years.

Sable's voice grows into a chant, tears catching in her throat.

Why would you care so much still? I killed you.

I am nothing compared to your light. All my years of anguish and all those minds I have shattered, the tally reaching numbers higher than I can fathom, all for the sake of morbid studies to fix my own mind. Yet, it pales in comparison to what I did to you. Even if you were saved, it doesn't change what I have done.

Something snaps inside me, drawing my attention back to the snake retreating into my throat. I bring my hands up to claw at the blockage, coughing and wheezing as my airway is closed off.

Weak, soft fingers wrap around my wrist and pull my nails away with a gentle and familiar fierceness. I look up at her in awe. The entire episode is strangely beautiful, even as this moment terrifies me.

The next thing I know, I am gagging, dry heaving. My bones are drumming with the thick oil, and the snake is making its wild, desperate escape. Sliding up into my throat, stretching it too wide, tearing the skin from the inside. My neck will snap open like a popped balloon.

~*Fight it, Gabe,* says the voice I finally admit to recognizing all this time.

He has always been here, guiding me since I stepped away from his precious child. Since I tore her apart. And yet here they both are.

~*This is your choice: either swallow it back down or release it.*

I roll onto my stomach with no hesitation, holding myself up on my hands and knees, welcoming the warmth of Sable's hand, which moves between my shoulder blades.

"I don't care if losing you takes all my powers away too. Get out! And take your poison with you," I grumble around the obstruction slithering about in my esophagus.

On cue, I convulse and retch, black sludge striking the earth in thick globs of mucus. Thick strands of grey webbing decorate the surface of the mess evacuating me. It burns in my throat, leaving a rancid taste on my tongue.

When I fall still, a new wash of lightning crackles down my spine. A cord coming out of the slime is still connected to something waiting at the base of my throat. I don't move. I don't give myself the ability to panic. The tube is already making me gag.

I simply push.

With one great shove from my mind, I *will* the mass to move. It budges only a few centimetres.

"Get . . . *out*!"

Another psychic strike joins with Sable's strange words and the gentle pressure of the helper. Together, our power forces it out.

Retching again, the cord snaps into the goo like an elastic band. On the other end a beating coal-black heart tumbles to the earth.

"What the f—"

"Gabe, don't look at it. You have to replace what has come out. None of that is yours." Sable's stern instructions pull my attention back up to her face.

She kneels beside me, her lips moving. Her instructions don't affect the rhythm of her prayers.

The organ thumping in the grass draws my gaze back. All the heart's tubes are connected to the cord by branches as if it were a baby attached to a mother's womb.

Badump.

Badump.

Badump.

Each time the heart beats, it sends a lump through the cord until it reaches the goo, which trembles when it receives its treat.

Badump.

Badump.

Badump.

This. Just. Came. Out. Of. Me.

Badump.

This isn't the snake. It is no more than oiled gel and spider webs that reek of death.

Badump.

How—

"Gabe!"

A hand yanks my chin, connecting me once more with bright orange eyes lit by a familiar glow.

"Focus on my master. Let him take over. Let him spill in and refill the empty spaces. We're not done," she commands with gentle sternness.

"What do I do? Guide me, Sable." I nearly stumble over my own words.

"Just allow him to move. Talk with him. You have to allow everything he wants to do. He will never force anything on you."

She is dripping with such gentle love that it thrums in the air with every word. I see them rippling around her.

I nod, gulping down a thick breath.

"I'm not worth this," I grumble, surprised by the *attentive* audience I feel almost immediately. A little laugh escapes me. "Your greatness cannot compare to anything I have ever known . . . and I was on a first-name basis with most of these false gods." Another chuckle almost comes out, but I catch it. "You must know the blood that is on my hands . . . and drawn by my lips. I am not worth saving. You must know this."

Sable's mouth draws into a tight line as she wraps her arms around me again. She does not speak. She realizes I am not addressing her.

~Do you know the joy that swelled within me when you finally cried out?

Gentle warmth floats into my chest. The voice vibrates behind my eyes, but it is the embodiment of that love that I cannot fathom.

"Joy?"

I mustn't have heard it correctly.

~Yes, joy. What was it which you had asked when you read my Word?

"What was the joy that was set before your son?" The words tumble over each other, but now, I don't need him to respond. I understand with a squeeze of my heart. "I'm the joy."

~Yes. Gabe, I love you. I have seen this day coming and have waited patiently for you. Do you realize how it hurt to watch that grow inside of you, knowing the pain that you were in?

"Why would it hurt you, lord? I'm not even your creation. I'm an abomination made by demonic hands. And I lived up to that darkness." My voice cracks on the final word.

~What if I told you that no living thing can come to life without my breath? Even when others think they have the power, it is I who gives life and I alone.

No . . ..

~Yes. If you accept that my son died to make you clean, you are my son as well. Just as Sable is my daughter. Let his sacrifice make you whole again, my child. Allow me to love you.

I am weeping all over again. The words resonate inside me so strongly that I feel as if I can touch their truth with my bare hands.

"I would love to know what it is like to have a real father—and to have all of these wounds in my heart healed. This pain is all I have ever known for far too long."

~I know, child. I know. I will make you like new. I love you.

Many things happen all at once when I finally accept the sacrifice made to allow me this strange kinship to this god. My chest explodes with warmth as the pressure finally uncurls, reaching out through my body. The warmth touches every piece of me, and when it finds my beating heart, it soaks into every crevice until I laugh at the sensation of tickling flower petals blooming inside it.

Outside, my skin grows warm as well. A light from beneath begins to glow, the same as I have seen so often that I begin to rejoice.

The final change starts with a strange gurgling sound across my body. Brown oil seeps from my pores and coats me in a layer of muddy sludge. I turn frightened eyes up to the human girl watching. More irony lies in this action alone, though I don't have the time to care. She doesn't say a word, but her fierce gaze eases the tension in me. She was prepared for whatever this is. She is not worried.

With a suctioning release, the substance falls to the

earth, leaving me clean and with a hollow silence in my mind that I never thought I would know.

"He . . . he's gone," I mutter, struck by the awe of clarity. "How was he released? And with such ease. And I'm not dead."

Sable's brilliant smile radiates again. "Our big guy is bigger than the big guy in you."

As I recall that conversation, a laugh tumbles out. It all feels like too much. It's too intense. Yet, it is not overwhelming. I am drowning in a love that I never imagined could exist. Not in a world like this, and certainly not for someone like me.

I hear footfalls, and I am abruptly aware of the others that had joined this battle. I lift my eyes to watch the figures racing toward us.

"I don't know if I'm ready for this," I croak.

It isn't that I'm afraid; I don't want to rush this feeling along. I am certain this change cannot be explained.

"Sable," I beg under my breath.

"Leave it to me," she replies, standing and brushing dirt off her legs. "Don't deny them for too long though," she says before she leaves. "They were scared for you and risked their lives to help. Let them rejoice with you."

I cannot reply; she is already jogging over to stop them. She holds out her arms as if she could barricade their advance if they didn't want to stop. My short dark-skinned friend meets my gaze still, though he obeys the girl. Beside him is the red-haired half-angel who brought her back to me just in time to be the hero. All these years he's harbored the grudge of what I did to our charge, following my every movement and protecting others from my lethal tongue. Yet here he is, in the aftermath of the ultimate battle with my past. How strange to think that perhaps Abdaziel never truly despised me. What if he merely wanted this ending all along but didn't know how to achieve it?

How naïve I have been . . ..

The assassin stares at Sable, but there is no malice in his face. In fact, he is smiling at her. I don't have to worry about his contract on her head. The look on his face is enough to know he will not touch her. Whether by avoiding my wrath or by the awe of what she just did despite all of them having marks of trying the same thing and failing, I do not know.

The way the divine beings all look at her with something like appreciation and awe is worth the entire ordeal. She deserves the strength her father has given her. She wears weakness well.

~ *Would you like to have the honor of telling your sister that I have found she is ready to see Kazious released*?

He slips in, and I close my eyes.

I breathe in a long, slow breath. I don't want her near that monster ever again. I exhale even slower. But I trust her in his hands.

"Sable," I call out, my voice hoarse. She turns back to me, her eyes appraising my smile as I take another long breath. "It's time. You're ready to got to the one you truly wanted to save all along."

The words sting inside my chest. Her confusion lasts but a moment.

Then her legs collapse beneath her, and I kneel in front of her, watching my warrior of light weep.

THE END . . . FOR NOW.

ABOUT THE AUTHOR

Del Rey Jean is a small bundle of too many emotions, sarcasm, and sass, wrapped up in the heart of a warrior. She is both fighter and empath, caring deeply for the lost and broken while also declaring "I'll fight you," on a semi regular basis. The majority of her time is spent with her head and heart buried under mountains of words; her driving force being the insistence on spreading messages of strength and hope after trauma which she conveys through her characters. When she does resurface to the face of the earth and reality, she's found with her Windword family in church and taking things slow with building new playlists, playing RPG games, and reaching out to her friends - especially those she gets to take long drives to see.

Learn more about the little bundle of love and sass by visiting her den: www.delreyswritingden.wordpress.com

CPSIA information can be obtained
at www.ICGtesting.com
Printed in the USA
BVHW042250210621
609961BV00001B/1